THERAPY FOR MURDER

THERAPY FOR MURDER

Laura Munder

ST. MARTIN'S PRESS / New York

Design by Janet Tingey

Library of Congress Cataloging in Publication Data

Munder, Laura.
    Therapy for murder.

    I. Title
PS3563.U453T46   1984   813'.54   84-13330
ISBN 0-312-79920-9

First Edition

10 9 8 7 6 5 4 3 2 1

To my parents

Acknowledgments

Thanks to Jeffrey Kelman, Robert Mann, Cynthia Potesta, Dan Sweeney, Gloria White, and my husband, Charlie, for their enthusiasm and helpful criticism.

THERAPY FOR MURDER

I

She had been walking back to her dorm, alone. Cutting through the student parking lot, she happened to pass a gray Buick with its headlights on. She must have hesitated, wondering whether she should switch off the lights. I have done the same thing myself many times. First you think you ought to switch them off: your civic duty. Then you think that maybe you're better off not getting involved: It's safer, easier, and the car doors are probably locked anyway. She most likely played over such thoughts in her mind. She walked back to the car. She must have thought: "What can I lose? I'll try the door. If it's open, I'll switch off the lights and be on my way." She walked around to the driver's side and tried the door. It opened. But the light switch was hard to find. She fumbled around in an awkward position, bending over and peering in. Growing frustrated, she slid into the driver's seat behind the wheel. She must not have glanced in the rear-view mirror, or something would have attracted her attention, some shadow or movement from the man in the back seat. She switched off the car lights; he sat up and silently leaned forward behind her. Did she sense his approach? Did she experience a moment of crystallized terror? His hands stole forward over the seat back and closed around her collarbone. Was he after her throat? Did he want her to die? Did she even have time for these thoughts to flash through her mind? His encircling arms thrust her back into the seat with such force that when he released his grip, her body rebounded forward, her head striking the steering wheel, hitting the horn. She passed out.

The horn blared an alarm. He let her lie there, the mechanical scream unchecked. Somebody noticed her lying limp over the steering wheel, then saw the man leaning forward in the backseat, looking vacant and dazed. Cries went out for help. The campus police arrived.

The girl was rushed to the hospital and regained consciousness. She suffered a broken collarbone but no other physical damage. The emotional scars, the fear, I could only guess at.

The young man offered no resistance. In his bizarrely vacant state, he seemed unaware of the harm he had caused. He knew only that someone had been trying to break into his car. The girl had recovered and he had been defending his property. No formal charges were pressed. But he was registered as a freshman and the school administration called the young man's parents and told them to take their son for psychiatric treatment to the Northern Virginia Day Treatment Clinic, where I had just started to work. I tried to put the victim out of my mind and concentrate on what I knew about the young man's family. His parents had given some additional information over the phone. Harry Hopper was an eighteen-year-old white male. He had just moved into a dorm but drove home to have dinner with his mother and fourteen-year-old sister every night. Harry's father ran a restaurant, the Caliban Café, and his mother did not work. He had had no previous psychiatric treatment.

Violence gives me the creeps, and I was extremely nervous as I waited for the Hopper family to arrive for their first appointment. I had other reasons, too, for my anxiety. It was only the second week of my first job, and I was feeling inexperienced and lonely. On top of that, my interview with Harry's family was to be a demonstration to help Frank Thomas, the new psychology intern, learn the ropes. Frank was twenty-four and just starting his year of practical internship training. He might view me as a seasoned staff member, but I knew I had difficulty presenting an air of authority. With the ink still wet on my Ph.D. certificate, I felt like something of an impostor introducing myself as Doctor Sara Marks.

On the other hand, although Frank's presence increased the pressure I felt to do a creditable job, it was also very reassuring to have an able-bodied man in the room. If Harry were to lunge at me during the interview, at least Frank seemed physically equipped to deal with him. I forced my thoughts away from Frank and onto the task at hand.

Frank and I were to do the intake interview, which included getting background data, assessing Harry's mental condition, and formulating a tentative view of how his family functioned and of his role within the family. I was explaining all this to Frank when my intercom buzzed: The secretary told me the family had arrived. I greeted them with as forceful a look of confidence as I could muster.

"I'm Dr. Sara Marks and this is Mr. Frank Thomas. I'm glad you could all come in with Harry today. Please sit down," I instructed the four members of the family. Mother led the way in with Harry, followed by his sister, walking with her head down, and father, slowly bringing up the rear. I turned to mother first, probably because I tend to find mothers reassuring. Mrs. Hopper, who looked to be in her late fifties, was of medium height and slightly plump. Her face was broad, with wide-set blue eyes and small features; an attractive face, but the corners of her mouth were pulled down as if in chronic suffering, and she breathed loudly and with difficulty. Her clothes had a worn and pragmatic look. On her left hand she wore a thin gold wedding band and minute diamond ring. Either Mr. Hopper's restaurant was not as successful as we had been told by the other staff members, or Mrs. Hopper was not one to display the fruits of success. I turned to Mrs. Hopper and asked her to introduce Frank and myself to her family.

"I'm Elizabeth Hopper, Harry's mother, and this is his father, Lawrence Hopper, and Harry, and his younger sister, Judy."

The only sound was Mrs. Hopper's breathing, which had become heavier with the effort of the introductions. Out of the corner of my eye I could see Frank looking at me expectantly. I decided to address Mr. Hopper, since he appeared to be the least involved member of the family and I wanted to draw him in. He was sitting slightly out of the circle and looked like a court stenographer who had but a remote interest in the case at hand. "Mr. Hopper," I said, fighting my reluctance to intrude on him, "I wonder if you could explain to us what brought you here today with Harry."

"I thought you already knew," he said, eyeing me suspiciously.

"I'd like to hear it from you."

"They say Harry knocked a girl unconscious. The girl was breaking into his car. The school told us to bring him here. He's never been in trouble in his life. I think it's a case of the pot calling the kettle black."

"I'm not sure I understand, Mr. Hopper. You think the girl was going to steal the car and instead put the blame on Harry?"

"Now you've said it clear as a bell," was his reply.

I turned to Mrs. Hopper. "Do you also see it that way?" I asked.

"I don't see anything," she responded. I thought she was talking more about her life than this incident. "When everyone's out of the house I don't know what goes on. I was home all day until the man from the college called. It's been a terrible week for me. My allergies are acting up and I can barely breathe. I woke up with a sinus headache fit to kill. The antihistamines the doctor gave me helped somewhat. My headache eased up. But then my mouth got dry. I've been parched all morning, and it's all I can do to keep my eyelids open. Harry's never been in any trouble before, but if he's in trouble now, so be it; I have to leave home and go outside. He's my son. You know the pollution count is up today and expected to climb all week. People say he did something strange and I'm more than willing to come out and do what must be done, but I don't know if it's a mistake or not."

I turned back to Mr. Hopper. "Do you tend to know more about Harry's whereabouts than your wife does?" I asked. "Are you and Harry close?" I was jumping about without a coherent plan, basically hoping to get some conversation and interaction going. I was met with silence, although Mr. Hopper did put his hand to his chin and purse his lips in what I took to be an indication of thought with the promise of a response. Waiting for Mr. Hopper's reply gave me a chance to look at him. He was a tall, thin man, probably also in his late fifties. He was immaculately groomed, in contrast to his wife and to Harry, who was grimy, unshaven, and disheveled. Mr. Hopper's clothes were of an expensive fabric and finely cut. His face was more angular and narrow than that of his wife or son. His hair was thick and sandy colored. Worry lines had started to make inroads down his cheeks. He seemed serious, intent, and introspective. Then he suppressed a yawn, and I began to doubt he would respond to my question.

"Are you and Harry close?" I prompted.

"About the usual," was his response.

I was going to ask what the usual was, but I checked myself. I didn't want to get into a struggle. Instead, I turned to Harry and smiled a greeting. Harry stared straight ahead. "Harry," I said in a friendly tone, "here we are talking *about* you and not *to* you. Can you tell me what happened?" I waited expectantly.

Without turning his head, without even moving a muscle, Harry responded in a tightly controlled shout: "I was protecting our property." I was about to encourage Harry to explain what he meant when he sprang from his chair, his body tensed, his veins pulsing and his eyes boring down on me: "And you are trespassing," he thundered. With his eyes unblinking, he continued to stare at me as he stiffly backed into his chair and sat down. My heart was thumping wildly. Without shifting his laser-beam eyes, Harry soundlessly raised his arm in the air and slowly extended his forefinger from his clenched fist. He pointed his finger directly at me in a gesture of accusation. His rigid body held this bizarre posture. I stared back at him, terrified and immobile.

It was Frank who finally broke the spell. He turned to Judy and said, "Hello." Freed by the normality of his voice, I also looked at Judy. She turned her eyes up at Frank, although she kept her head down, her chin jutting into her chest. "This must be pretty confusing for you," Frank said.

"Yes," Judy whispered. "It is." She was a thin girl, knobby-looking, all elbows and pointy chin.

"What do you make of all this?" Frank asked. "Has Harry been acting kind of funny at home? Have things seemed different to you?"

Judy looked at her mother. "Not really, if you know what I mean," she said.

I didn't want Judy to be put on the spot if she needed her mother's permission to talk, so I again addressed Mr. and Mrs. Hopper. I conversationally mentioned that Harry's moving out of

5

their home and living on campus was a big change for everyone. I got no acknowledgment. I asked if there had been other changes in their family. I was met with silence.

"As I'm sure you all know," I proceeded, not yet daring to look at Harry for fear I would lose control and start shaking, "when a family member has a problem, everyone in the family is affected to some extent."

"No one in our family has a problem. What are you driving at?" Mr. Hopper said. His tone was becoming irritated. "Our son gets sent here for unproven charges and you want to know all about our family. I want to know what you're going to do to help our son. Not that I'm convinced that he needs help or that he can get it here."

"Amen," chimed in Mrs. Hopper with a grim look on her face.

"Why don't I explain how our center works?" I offered in a conciliatory tone. "Then if any of you have questions, please feel free to ask, and Mr. Thomas and I will answer them to the best of our ability. First of all, as you know, this is a day treatment center for adults who need a structured all-day program but who are able to live in the community. The fact that Harry's enrolled in a school program is all to the good. We'll try to work his treatment program here around his classes. He'll be assigned a case administrator, who will coordinate his activities and meet with him regularly. Although most of the therapy takes place in groups, we also like to meet regularly with the families, usually in weekly sessions." I looked at both Mr. and Mrs. Hopper, but could read no response in their faces. I continued: "Now my understanding is that Harry is not under court order to be here. There were no charges filed against him. The college administrators recommended that he enroll here, but there is no order stating that he must do so. His registration would be voluntary, although he'll still be expected to conform to the requirements of our program."

Conform was perhaps a poor choice of words. I was about to continue my explanation when Harry catapulted from his chair. "Conform!" he bellowed. "Never! A man lives his own life by his own rules." Harry began pacing the room, becoming more and

6

more agitated, his eyes darting from side to side. "I will never conform!" He stalked out of the room and out of doors where, I could see through the window, he paced back and forth until his family emerged. After Harry's exit, Mr. Hopper took Judy by the arm and steered her out. Mrs. Hopper shrugged her shoulders at Frank and me, wheezed several times, pulled herself up and followed them out. Through the window, I saw them all walk off together.

"What a family," Frank said nervously.

I nodded, still petrified. It took several minutes for my pulse and breathing to slow down. Fear was replaced by dejection. I had not exactly dazzled Frank with my competence. But I tried to salvage a sense of professionalism. "Maybe we can learn something from what went wrong. What do you think I should have done differently?"

Before Frank could evaluate the session, several staff members walked in to find out what had happened. They'd seen Harry pacing out front and then seen the whole family walk off together. I filled them in. Their only comments, to my relief, were to the effect that the crucial factor in the family's leaving was probably the information that Harry was not legally required to register. His parents had probably misassumed that he was. They told me this kind of thing happened a lot and not to take it personally. Anyway, they were sure the Hoppers would return. They did not view the family or the interview as atypical. But, of course, none of us then anticipated the murder.

2

My experience with Harry's family left me shaken, and it was with trepidation that I approached my next family interview. The referred patient was a woman named Helena Morgan who had almost starved herself to death. She had returned to her parent's home in northern Virginia in July, a few months before I saw her for the first time. She was twenty-two years old, and in July had been an attractive woman of medium height—five-feet-six— with a little extra padding. By September, she had dieted down to ninety pounds and was brought to Robert E. Lee General Hospital in an ambulance after collapsing during a several-mile run along the towpath of the canal. She spent two days in Intensive Care and then was declared out of mortal danger. On discharge, she was referred to Day Treatment.

Helena's parents, who seemed to want to do whatever was right for their daughter, promptly made an appointment for an intake interview. What caught my attention the moment they entered my office was Helena's waiflike beauty. She was still extremely thin, which revealed the elegant bone structure of her face and emphasized her large, almond-shaped, blue-green eyes. Her blond hair was thick and wavy. Helena sat primly between her parents, with her bony knees held tightly together, her legs crossed chastely at the ankles, and her hands folded in her lap. She looked as if she were sitting in the front row of a Sunday school class. She had on a carefully ironed white cotton blouse with a Peter Pan collar and a blue linen pleated skirt. Her mother, Margaret Morgan, was pretty and carefully groomed. She smiled somewhat nervously, with her lips closed, and waited for me to begin. Her father, Dr. Steven Morgan, a dentist, had a militaristic look, highlighted by a crew cut.

I started in by introducing myself and asking the family how they viewed the problems Helena had been having.

Mrs. Morgan jumped in first to answer. "We've a very close family and a very loving family. Helena's always had everything she needed. She's always been a very attractive girl, although somewhat plump. But she never went out with boys when she was growing up. I think when she decided to leave her boyfriend, Matthew, is that his name?"—Helena gave a just perceptible nod— "and come home, she wanted to get herself together and that meant taking off a lot of excess baggage she'd accumulated. She weighed a hundred and forty when she came home in July. She wanted to slim down and look fit before starting to date again. Cleanse her system and start afresh. I think it's pretty natural. She kept busy. She jogged and swam at the neighborhood pool. She and Jeb got a chance to spend some time together—the kids never seem to see each other anymore. You liked having time to spend with your brother, didn't you, honey?"

"Yes, Mother."

"Really. It was delightful to have our little girl back with us this summer. It's her first summer home since she went away to college. I think, as is so common with children her age, she does things to excess. She got too carried away with her diet. I don't think that she really has, you know, mental problems."

I didn't want to lose another family. I chose my words carefully. "She's right at an age where she needs to come to some decisions about what to do with her life, which, as you say, is common in someone her age. These decisions are very important and it might be a good time to spend some time talking about how and when she'll leave home and how she'll support herself. Things like this."

Mrs. Morgan continued, "Helena's really very intelligent. She was an English major at Cornell. Then she went with this Matthew character to New York and worked as a waitress. Heavens above. Working as a waitress when she's a college graduate."

"It's good, honest work, Margaret. She's young. She doesn't have to be Professor Morgan just yet," Dr. Morgan interjected, before Mrs. Morgan continued.

"She had a lovely summer here with us. I think this Matthew was not a very wholesome influence and our Helena's very suggestible. Now she just needs to find a respectable job and I think she'll be okay."

"How about you, Helena?" I asked. "Where do you stand in all of this?"

"Matthew's an exquisitely sensitive man."

Dr. Morgan turned to his daughter. "I don't understand, Helena. I thought your romance with Matthew was over. When you returned home you said that you'd left him in New York and it was finished. You haven't mentioned him since. Have you been writing to him or talking to him?"

"I've been communicating with him by spirit. I think I'm ready to go back to him now."

9

"Maybe we could back up a little," I suggested, feeling confused. "Has Matthew ever met your parents, Helena?"

"No."

"Can you tell me a little about where you met him and what your relationship was?"

Helena looked sullen and sat immobile. "Why don't Helena and I talk alone for a few minutes," I said.

Helena looked visibly relieved.

"You can sit in the waiting room and I'll come back and get you when we're done," I said to Dr. and Mrs. Morgan.

"I like your earrings, Dr. Marks. They're very handsome," Helena said to me as soon as her parents had left.

"Thank you, Helena. Is it easier to talk with your parents out of the room?"

"Much easier. Thank you ever so much. You see, my parents are very strict and formal and religious. They're Christian Scientists. No liquor. No friends. They don't believe in fun. I don't think they have sex together. Other than for Jeb and me, of course. So I can't talk about Matthew. Is what we say strictly confidential, you won't tell them anything?"

"Not if you don't want me to."

"Jeb and I slept together. It was my first time. It was the summer after freshman year. I left and spent the rest of the summer with friends in Boston—friends from school—that's why I never went back home for a summer. We had both been drinking. We didn't know what we were doing."

"You slept with your brother?" I inquired, striving to keep my voice casual and my eyebrows in neutral. "Jeb *is* your brother?"

"Yes. Incest."

"Incest. Yes," I agreed, as if we'd just remembered the name of a flower or bird. Unflappably, I continued, "Did you see Jeb again this summer?"

"This time I seduced him. He's very handsome. Just once, the night before he left for school. He's up at Williams College now. I've slept with fifty-two men. Not one a week. That's spread over about three years. After the first time with Jeb. Do you like sex?"

To regain control of the interview as well as of my eyebrows, I gave Helena an authoritative, no-nonsense look.

"Now I've embarrassed you," Helena apologized. My authoritative looks rarely did produce the desired effect. "Don't answer. Unless you want to. I've been in therapy before. At college. My parents don't know. I went to the counseling center. My friends told me I should go. I had wonderful friends in college. It was the first time in my life that I ever had any friends. I was a glumpy, frumpy kid growing up. No friends. I stayed home and read all the time. I never talked to anybody. I was always clumsy."

"You don't look clumsy."

Helena's whole face shone with the compliment. "I really don't look clumsy? You know what Matthew called me?" Helena blushed crimson and buried her head in her hands.

"You don't have to tell me, if you'd . . ."

"He called me an *F-A-T S-L-O-B.*"

"A fat slob?"

Helena nodded, deeply ashamed. "That's why I had to get in shape. I think he wants me back now. My brother couldn't resist me."

"Helena, what happened between you and Matthew? Were you living together or what?"

"We met in college. We had a very romantic affair. I'd get so excited about seeing him that I sometimes threw up right before he came over. It was truly exciting."

"How long did you go out?"

Helena's face transposed from ecstasy to distress in seconds. "We only actually went out three times. I think the greater part of our relationship remains in the future. I met him the start of my senior year, but I didn't really see him much between February and graduation. He was in Labor Relations, but he moved to New York to be an actor. He's brimming with talent. I found out he was going to share a big apartment and they were looking for two other roommates to share the rent. My friend Bonnie and I asked if we could move in. That was in June. I worked as a waitress and studied Tarot and palm reading. I'll read the cards for you if you'd like. Matthew worked as a bartender and went on auditions. It was working out beautifully until he called me a—you know—and told me either I should leave or he would leave. Things between us are very intense. Don't you think love and hate are two sides of the same coin? It's kind of Lawrencean. I left. It seemed the dignified thing to do. I think I'm ready to go back now."

"Why did he tell you to move out? Did you have a fight?"

"He didn't like my body. He thought I was too *f-a-t*."

"He asked you to leave because he didn't like your body?"

"He used to tell me to cover up my body. He'd tell me to stop walking around naked. Nobody wanted to see my fat body." Helena looked as if she was going to cry, but her facial expression evolved suddenly into the look of a naughty girl. "Sometimes I used to stand in front of the windows without any clothes on, and people would give me these shocked looks." Helena giggled. "Matthew thought it was dangerous. The others didn't like it either. Or so they said. Once I brought a poor innocent named Arnold up to our apartment and I seduced him and everyone came home right in the middle and poor Arnold was so embarrassed. He was a busboy at the restaurant."

I gave Helena a warm smile. It was such a relief to be interviewing a nonviolent flake after Harry Hopper. I called Helena's parents back in and then registered her. As soon as they left, I went to make an appointment with Richard Meyer to get some family therapy supervision on the case. Working with him was a real opportunity for someone like me, whose background in family work was skimpy.

I had never met with Richard before, but I felt immediately at ease in his presence. In keeping with my previous training, I started right in giving him my diagnostic impressions of Helena: "She seems like a real hysteric. Her family is very repressed and Victorian. She comes on like a shrinking violet and then goes and acts out sexually all over the place. But her sexuality isn't at all integrated into her personality." I was warming to my subject when Richard interrupted me.

"I know your training was psychodynamic," he said to me. "Mine was too. You were taught to think in terms of individuals and their internal conflicts. But when you work with families, I want you to think in terms of the entire family system, not the separate people. Watch the interactions, see what transactions take place: Who's involved and what are the sequences? When a family stops being able to find creative solutions to its problems, you can infer that its transactional patterns have become stereotyped. They're repetitive and restrictive. Watch for them and test them. You want to restructure the way the family members interact. Open up new possibilities. You have to try not to get sidetracked by trying to understand the internal workings of each family member. Focus on the whole system. Crazy behavior is purposeful within the context that created it."

Before our next family meeting, Helena and I worked together for a week at the center. She followed her schedule of group meetings and activities without complaint. The combination of her youth and beauty were causing quite a stir, which she seemed to be enjoying. I had a half-hour individual meeting with her every day to discuss any issues, in or out of the center, that might crop up. During these meetings I learned that her maternal grandmother lived in the house with them and had lived there ever since Helena was two and Jeb was an infant. Accordingly, I asked that she, too, attend the family meeting.

The family meetings were on Wednesday evenings, when all the staff members stayed late to meet with families that could not come during the day. At the family meeting, Helena, who veered toward the loose and irreverent in her daily interactions at the clinic, was again the prim and constricted child she had been with her parents at the first meeting. She walked in holding her mother's hand like a five-year-old. Grandma and Dr. Morgan came in behind them. Mrs. Morgan took off Helena's jacket for her and slipped her arm around Helena's shoulders as she sat down. Father took Grandma's wrap and sat himself on the other side of Helena. Grandma, disconcertingly, pulled her chair over next to mine and seemed ready to run the session.

"This is my mother, Mrs. Allen," Mrs. Morgan volunteered. "Dear me. She's been a part of our household since Daddy died, at least twenty years ago. Helena and Jeb always had two mothers."

"It's nice to meet you, Mrs. Allen. I'm glad you could come."

"You can call me Grandma. Everybody does." I smiled weakly but withheld assent. She spoke with barely any lip movement. "Helena's a good girl. Just goes overboard sometimes. I've tried to teach her moderation in all things, but you know what kids are like these days. Sex, drugs, that loud music. Hippies roaming around, never doing a day's work. You look like a nice girl."

"Thank you," I responded. "I wonder if we could start by talking about how the household changes when Helena is there. I'd like to hear from all of you about how you got along and spent your time when the children had left home, and how that's changed now that Helena's back with you. It will help me to understand the family better." I wanted to know what role Helena played within the family structure.

"We all love it when the children come home," Grandma responded. "I don't think the household changes much, though. We follow the Lord's way in our house. See no evil, hear no evil, speak no evil. That's how I brought up my daughter and that's how we're bringing up Helena. And that remains the same, whether Helena's home or away. Helena's always curled up with a book somewhere or sitting by herself contemplating. The house stays quiet." Helena had given me some idea of what those contemplations consisted of. In fact, she now began to show her tension by smacking her knees together in little movements. Her father put his hands on her knees and stopped her. She sat, again, immobile. "She's a serious girl. Not like these painted hippies you see these days."

"Punks, I believe they're called," Mrs. Morgan interrupted. "Helena's a great help around the house when she's home," Mrs. Morgan continued. "She makes these exquisite shortbread cookies and always sets the table for us. She's back to eating again; she's even getting a little more than her figure back." Mrs. Morgan playfully pinched together a minute bulge around Helena's waist. Helena looked crestfallen but remained silent.

Dr. Morgan appeared to notice and said, "She looks just fine. You're a fine-looking girl, honey."

"Thanks, Daddy, but Mother doesn't seem to think so."

Dr. Morgan continued his assertion, "Your mother thinks you're lovely, sweetie. She said to me yesterday, 'Helena's a real beauty. She's going to have to watch herself with the boys.' Didn't you, Margaret?" Mrs. Morgan inclined her head down in an ambiguous gesture, maybe assent.

"Do you worry as a family about Helena's dating men?" I asked, and Helena shot me a warning look.

"No more than your parents worry about you, I'm sure," responded Grandma. "Any single woman—and I notice you don't wear a wedding ring—who isn't living with her family is asking for trouble in today's world. Margaret was with me until she married. And grateful for it to this day. Isn't that so?"

"Yes, Mother." Mrs. Morgan's face hardly reflected gratitude. I turned to Helena's father.

"Dr. Morgan, you've been awfully quiet. How do you see what's been going on with Helena? Her coming back to live at home after being away. Her dieting and exercising to exhaustion?"

"The women all talk together, I don't get to see too much of my little girl. Unless she has a cavity that needs filling."

"You take care of her teeth?"

"Whole family's. I'll bet you couldn't tell that Grandma's teeth aren't her own."

"No. I'd never have known. Have you and your wife discussed Helena's collapse? Have you talked about it together?"

"Oh, yes," Mrs. Morgan replied. "We were terribly frightened. We were so pleased at first when she started dieting, because she's always had a weight problem. But I must say, we had very divided feelings about this jogging business. The kids wear these little shorts and you don't know who you might encounter on these trails. I'm glad she's given it up, if you want to know the truth. So is Steven."

"Is that right, Dr. Morgan? You also disapprove of jogging?"

"I never liked the idea. But Helena's getting to be a big girl. I didn't think we should stop her."

"How would you have stopped her?"

"She's a good girl. She wouldn't have disobeyed," Grandma offered. I had a sneaking suspicion she was right. She would have obeyed and then, one day, gone jogging naked.

Although I had felt out of my depth, Richard was pleased with my session with the Morgans. He told me to address Grandma as Mrs. Allen and urged me to insist that all family members speak for themselves and not make global pronouncements. He lent me *Psychosomatic Families*, by Salvador Minuchin, and told me to use all the techniques for dealing with an enmeshed family. I was stimulated by the ideas and by Richard's interest in the case.

3

She had been eating lunch with her girlfriend in the school cafeteria, seated at one of the long tables. A handsome but sloppy-looking young man sat down next to them. She glanced up and caught his eye. A mistake. She knew it instantly. But a glance is a hard thing to retract. She and her friend continued their conversation, the girl feigning more interest than she felt, to show she was unavailable to outsiders. Her friend said something funny and they both laughed together. Nervousness made it hard for her to stop. She was still convulsed with laughter as she got up to leave with her girlfriend. The young man put down his sandwich and followed her out. Across the lawn he kept pace behind her, as she parted from her girlfriend and entered the mathematics building. His footsteps echoed in the corridor behind her lighter, quicker steps. She pivoted abruptly and turned into a classroom. She released her breath as she heard his steps continue down the hall.

But when she emerged from her class, the young man was waiting outside. He fell into step beside her as she walked, turning his head so as to stare right at her, but without uttering a word. The girl was spooked. She stopped walking and demanded that he tell her what he wanted. The man jumped as if startled. Slowly he bent his head down to her level and put his lips to her ear. *"Pssst, pssst, pssst,"* he hissed. "I've got secrets, too." He jerked back up and darted off. The girl was shaken and scared.

For the next few days the girl was careful not to walk unaccompanied. But one night her girlfriend was ready to leave the library before she had finished her work, and she felt silly asking her friend to wait. She had easily an hour's more work to do, and her friend was anxious to get back to the dorm. They convinced themselves they were going overboard with precautions. The friend left. The girl hurried through her work and walked cautiously out of the library, alone, into the dark September night. Not twenty paces from the library, he swooped down behind her. He didn't give her time to run. His arms surrounded her shoulders, pinioning her arms flat against her body. "I could tell secrets, too," he hissed at her. "If I had someone to share them with. Who are you to laugh at me? We could laugh together." With those words, he released her and started to laugh—a high-pitched, shrieking laugh. "You laugh, too!" he commanded the terrified girl. The girl screamed for help. The man cupped his hand over her mouth. "Don't scream. It's a secret." But she had already given the secret away. The security police arrived and subdued the man.

Frank dramatized the story as if he'd been there. He related the incident to me, full of excitement at Harry Hopper's return. This time the girl had pressed charges. Harry's parents had had no choice but to register him. Frank was assigned the case with the backup of the team and with Richard's supervision of the family work. I was easily as pleased as Frank that the case was given to him and not to me. Violence definitely made me shudder, which did nothing for my clinical skills.

Frank grabbed me for lunch the day of Harry's registration, spilling over with news of his interview with the Hopper family. "I wish you'd been there, Sara. Mrs. Hopper started wheezing—I was afraid she'd go into a decline in the office. Luckily, she had one of those hand breathing things. She revived herself. Actually, I like her. She kept asking what had happened to Harry. She seemed genuinely concerned and bewildered. You know they own the

Caliban Café. It's a terrific place, I've heard. Not that I get to go on my student stipend. There's something to be said for being kept."

Frank, as he had confided in me, was gay.

"They started the restaurant together, Mr. and Mrs. Hopper. He has another partner with whom he runs it now, though. Maury Roden. When I asked Harry who he felt he could talk to in his family, he said, 'Maury.' So he must be like a family member. Harry's mother seemed disappointed at that. I think she was jealous. Harry doesn't say much to either of his parents, but he watches them like a hawk. There's incredible tension in the family. Harry's moved back home, by the way. He's under his parents' supervision. Judy, the sister, seems withdrawn. I did get her to talk a little. She's in tenth grade, does well in school, and hinted that her mother is a worrier and sort of picky. She seemed angry at Harry for getting into trouble and upsetting everyone. She said she wished everyone was happier. Mr. Hopper has to be one of the saddest men I've seen. Tired, drawn, haggard. No one seems to know what's troubling him, although Harry's clearly part of it. Do you mind my jabbering away like this, Sara? I'm just so keyed up. I can't wait to talk with Richard." I didn't mind at all. Better Frank than me.

4

All of these events happened by the third week of my job and the fourth week of my living down south in Washington, D.C. To be honest, it was, at age twenty-six, my first real move away from home. Although I had lived in Hartford, Connecticut, for college and graduate school, my parents were only forty-five minutes away. I was still doing my laundry at their house. I hardly felt like an adult. Before I left for Washington, my parents bought me six months' worth of cotton balls and other toilet articles and reluctantly released me to go and live in the "crime capital of the world," which apparently did not have any drugstores. They were reassured by the fact that I was living in an apartment on Connecticut Avenue (Massachusetts, Vermont, New Hampshire, or Maine would also have been acceptable) and reassured by my having an excellent job as a staff psychologist.

The Adult Day Treatment Center was run by Melvin Harley, M.D., who had a reputation as a leader in the field of deinstitutionalizing mental hospital patients. Except for Dr. Harley, all staff members and patients were assigned to one of the three treatment teams. The teams really functioned as cohesive units so that, as was explained to each patient, the staff within each team openly shared information on all their patients. Our team consisted of the team leader, Joyce Elkind, a warm, maternal woman who had trained as a psychiatric nurse in the sixties; a very part-time psychiatrist; a social worker; and our psychology intern, Frank Thomas.

The clinic, located in a tree-shaded suburban neighborhood, consisted of two single-story beige brick buildings with large windows facing the street. The effect was inviting. Each building was very deep, with a long corridor lined on either side with offices. One building housed our day-treatment center and the other housed the outpatient clinic. The only official contact between the two clinics came once a month at the centerwide meeting. Some of the staff members at the outpatient clinic, however, were supervised by our most experienced staff workers.

My best friend from Hartford, Mike Sweeney, worked at the outpatient clinic. While still finishing our dissertations, we had decided to apply for jobs at the same center. I, for one, don't know if I would have moved to Washington without the backup of a friend I could count on. Mike and I were platonic friends and had been since graduate school. Neither of us had a great track record with love relationships: He was your basic extremely handsome don't-tie-me-down, noncommittal male who ended most of his relationships around the three-month point. I was your basic pleasant-looking, dark-haired, average-height, average-weight (not distributed completely to my liking) female, who of course had a fatal attraction to noncommital males and went through agony trying to assess their level of involvement, which never matched my fantasies. Consequently, as Mike Sweeney and I got to know each other in graduate school, we swore to remain just friends and not ruin our relationship.

I was delighted to find that Mike's family therapy was also being supervised by Richard Meyer. I was already developing a crush on Richard. On the day Harry Hopper returned, I ran into Mike in the clinic waiting room. "Sara, Sara, Sara," was his greeting. "I am about to be delivered from a physical pressure that seeks release. I'm psyching up already. With hate in my heart and no mercy in my soul."

"Oh," I responded. "Racquetball or tennis?"

"Racquetball. I'm ready to give 110 percent out there and bring him to his knees. Interested in the name of my worthy opponent?"

"Who?"

"Richard Meyer. He has a court reserved every Tuesday at nine and his regular partner canceled out this week. I haven't played racquetball since Hartford. What a pleasure."

"Why did he or she cancel out?" I asked casually.

"Sara," Mike said, eyeing me suspiciously. "Richard's living with someone. A woman named Dorothy."

"So he's not married."

"Divorced."

"Good work, Mike. You're good to have in the field. I want hard information on Richard. After racquetball, if it's your place or his, make it his and please make the most of it. You'll be rewarded. Come to dinner Friday night."

"I'm not sure that qualifies as a reward, but if you promise not to experiment, I'll come." Mike was ungallantly referring to a somewhat inedible dinner I'd once cooked him. "If you can settle down to listen, I've got more for you. Richard Meyer is thirty-nine. He was married at twenty-six and divorced at thirty-one. He has a ten-year-old son being raised by his ex-wife. He would like to spend more time with him. I even mentioned your name in the conversation by telling him we were old friends from Hartford. Publicity never hurts."

"You are a sweetheart, Mike."

"And apparently you're not the only one who thinks so. I had a date last Saturday night."

"Brought her to her knees, did you?"

"How indelicate of you, Sara. Now I'm not giving out any information. Anyway, I didn't quite finish what I started to say. I told Richard that I kept meeting women I found exciting and interesting, but they always wanted more involvement than I did. He said that he'd been like that for years after his divorce, until he'd met Dorothy. He sounded pretty committed to her, Sara."

"Yeah. Well. I'll be realistic. I have a date, too. Sidney Markowitz, the psychiatrist on Mimi's team."

"I don't know him, but I do know Mimi. She has the beautiful long red hair. In her mid-thirties. She sat with Dr. Harley at the centerwide meeting."

"Sidney seems nice, but I can't get excited. On the other hand, a date is a date. Who's this woman you went out with?"

"As it happens, you know her. Marcy Blather. She works in your clinic. The Team One social worker. She lives in my building and I met her at the pool. We started talking, realized we worked in adjoining agencies. I played my ace by mentioning that I knew you. Your name had the desired effect, and she went out with me."

"Cute, Sweeney. I've never even spoken to her. She seems nice."

"She is nice. I'm going to see her again next Saturday."

"Someone who lives in your building. Is that wise?"

"Lower your eyebrows. No. It's not wise. I like her."

"You liked Loretta, too, if you recall and you practically had to put on a disguise to sneak in and out of your own building after desire went the way of all flesh."

"This is a bigger building with two entrances."

"Weak, Mike. Very weak."

"Come on. Who knows? Maybe she won't even like me."

"Not likely. Where do you do laundry?"

"Where do I do laundry?"

"Yes. Laundry. Is there one room for the whole building?"

"Oh. I see your point."

"When it's over you'll need a Groucho Marx mask to wear to the laundry room. Loretta was not too pleased, as I recall, when she had shared your beige sheets with you Friday night and saw you washing purple ones Sunday morning. It rather left Saturday night unaccounted for."

"You've made your point, Sara. You will have the privilege of saying I-told-you-so."

With a firm promise to Mike that I'd stick to tuna salad, he agreed to come for dinner Friday night.

When my apartment buzzer went off on Friday, I was putting the final touches on dinner. I buzzed open the door and then unlocked my own door and headed back into the kitchen. Consequently, as I heard Mike come in, I had no idea that he was not alone.

"Frank thinks you have an exquisite ass, Mike," I called from the kitchen. "Positively two standard deviations above the norm. There is less than a .05 percent possibility that an ass like yours could be created by chance. There must have been a purpose . . ." I chattered on before I saw Mimi Shear actually standing in my living room with Mike.

Mike quickly explained. "I ran into Mimi on the elevator. We recognized each other and I told her I was visiting you. She asked which apartment you were in and I said, 'Come on and see.' I knew you'd be pleased."

"I live here, too," Mimi quickly interjected. "In 208. The back of the building, where you go out to the parking lot." Mimi used both hands to pull her abundant, brilliantly colored red hair back from her face before releasing it to fall in luxuriant waves down her back. I caught a glint in Mike's eyes as he watched her, but he kept himself under control.

"I'm surprised I haven't run into you," I said. "I moved here in August before starting work at Day Treatment. Have you lived here long?"

"Three years, actually. I really don't want to intrude. I just ran into Mike and thought I'd come along and see where you lived and let you know I was around. Are you free tomorrow? Come by for lunch. Number 208. Just come down around noon."

"That would be very nice. Thank you." I was pleased by the invitation.

The next day I took Mimi up on her offer. I was a little nervous and excited about going to her apartment. She was a team leader, which was a position of considerable authority. She was older than I and gave the appearance of being aloof and self-contained, yet full of energy.

"Hi. Make yourself at home, Sara. I'm on the phone. I'll be right there."

Mimi's apartment was similar to mine, but it seemed more spacious. I was impressed with the graciousness of the effect, and as it turned out, I had plenty of time to be impressed as the phone call dragged on past the point of courtesy and into the half-hour stretch. Finally, Mimi returned.

"I'm awfully sorry, Sara. That wasn't a phone call I could just hang up on. I'm going through some unnerving changes right now. Let me get us some food."

As we ate lunch, Mimi asked me about myself. I started out answering politely, but by my second dish of Breyer's mint chocolate-chip ice cream, I was ready to throw discretion to the winds. I confessed my crush on Richard. Mimi's advice was succinct: "Stay away."

Although I was also curious about Mimi's life, something in her manner made me hesitate to ask her about herself. Not that she gave me a chance. As soon as she was certain I was really finished with my ice cream (I think she'd been a little surprised by my refills), she jumped up from the table.

"It's a glorious day, Sara. Let's not waste it sitting indoors. What haven't you seen yet in Washington?"

"All I've seen is the National Gallery and the Air and Space Museum. And, you know," I added, sensing that my list was meager, "I've driven by the White House and the Capitol and all the monuments. And I've been up to the Lincoln Memorial."

"Let's go to the Phillips Collection. It's a wonderful turn-of-the-century home filled with Impressionists. You'll like it. Even if you're not into museums, you'll like it."

"Sounds great," I agreed, catching her enthusiasm and eager to be out and about. It was an early fall day: The leaves were just starting to turn and the air held the slightest hint of a chill.

"I'm a frustrated museum curator," Mimi told me as we trotted to the Metro stop. "I had a wonderful time as an undergraduate majoring in art history. I couldn't understand how anyone could find college boring. I was having such a ball. I was always hanging out in museums and it counted as work. What could be better? It wasn't until I graduated and looked at the employment opportunities that I realized I'd have to marry rich or change fields." Mimi laughed. "I changed fields. On to psychiatric social work! Ta-dah! But my true passion erupts on the weekends. It's like an addiction."

"Well, you can try to hook me," I said, feeling open to anything. The prospect of a new friend and a new interest filled me with pleasure: It hadn't been easy leaving my friends in Hartford.

We explored the Phillips inside and out. "Van Gogh can really make that canvas sizzle!" Mimi exclaimed, her eyes brilliant with appreciation, as they devoured the seething yellows and reds. "God. Look at this, Sara. Over here. Did you ever see such spectacular light!" Mimi was like a butterfly, alighting first in front of one then another of the pictures. And like a butterfly with her own brilliant coloring and graceful movements, she attracted a bit of a following. People watched her as she moved around and then, like filings to a magnet, they gathered in when she stood communing with a picture and responded to her comments as if she'd been talking to them directly. In the end, we turned down two invitations for coffee and one for dinner. I was tempted by one of the invitations, put forth by two young men; but since my previous forays to museums had never before yielded any such invitations, I could only conclude that it was Mimi who had inspired them and who had the right of refusal. Nevertheless, it was a wonderful afternoon, and when I returned home for my solo dinner, I felt pleasantly weary and peaceful. The fact that we made plans to start carpooling together regularly cinched in my mind that I'd made a new friend.

5

October rushed by. The weather turned chilly, and I loved the crisp, exhilarating fall air. Every morning I felt anticipation of the day to come. Hot, steamy coffee, the *Washington Post* in the morning, a quick shower, bulky sweaters, my suede jacket, the bracing air, the sting on my cheeks. I loved it. The Potomac waves were turbulent in the fall breezes beneath Chain Bridge as Mimi and I rode into work. The cliffs were full of color, the vista breathtaking. Trees filled with reds, greens, yellows, browns, bright with sunshine or subdued with rain. More coffee at the clinic, smiles and hellos to staff and patients, a sense of community, a sense of belonging. The working days sped by. I felt busy and productive. I relished the evenings, too. No dissertation. No work hanging over me. Nothing I had to do. I could watch TV, talk on the phone, read novels, go to museums, visit friends, see movies, walk through Georgetown, eat out, eat in. I was rid of the nagging guilt of schoolwork. Freedom. I was earning a real salary, not a student stipend. I was an independent woman. Launched at last. Free to make my own mistakes.

I continued working with Helena and her family and was starting to feel like a family member myself. The combination of Richard's supervision and my enthusiasm had salutary effects. The family began to loosen up and allow more individual freedom to its members. Helena became an active participant in the community. She revealed more and shocked less.

"I feel so stymied, Dr. Marks. How can I give vent to my need for self-expression? It's like I've been thwarted since childhood. I want to be creative. Slender and creative, but with large breasts."

We'd have these conversations several times a week. I found her goofiness appealing, and our attachment grew. Helena did not readily reveal how painfully isolated she often felt, but as our work progressed, I caught glimpses of her suffering. I felt for her in a way I never could have felt for Harry Hopper. Our cases had been well assigned.

My friendship with Mimi also blossomed. She had just ended a five-year "exhausting" relationship around the time I met her and was once again living in her own apartment. We both had no one to please but ourselves; or, to put it another way, plenty of time on our hands. Mimi gave me a respectable background in art history, and I talked her into getting a five-play subscription to Arena Stage with me.

Although I talked easily about family and friends, Mimi was not one for self-disclosure. I knew that she was distressed about her mother only because I was in her apartment one time when her mother called, and I overheard Mimi's part of the conversation. I guess she thought she owed me an explanation: "Mother's current crisis," she explained with disdain, "is that she has to move. She's totally incapable of fending for herself, and my father hasn't been around for years. Jesus, it's been twenty years since he died. Mother can't manage money and now she has to sell our house in New Hampshire. It's the house where I grew up. Her sister's arranged for her to move into a small condominium in Florida. It's a good move for her. I think she knows it. But she's depressed and doing her helpless routine. She's never moved by herself before and she wants me to make all the moving arrangements and help her pack. I know I shouldn't resent it, but I do."

"That's difficult," I said, sympathetically, but Mimi only shrugged and changed the subject. Basically, I knew little of Mimi's personal life, but one day she finally decided to confide in me.

"Sara, you must promise me you won't tell anyone what I tell you." She was breathy and excited; her eyes gleamed and her fingers repetitiously combed through her sumptuous red mane. I'd never seen her so impassioned. Need I say that I promised?

"Melvin. Dr. Harley. He loves me. We're lovers. You can't tell anyone."

"What about his wife?" I asked, trying to sound merely interested.

"He left her. Last week. Before we slept together. He made it clear his decision to leave her was in no way related to me. He had a lousy marriage, and he wanted out. But you know what he said to me, Sara? He said he realized how barren his marriage was when he thought about me. He felt so much more for me than he'd ever felt for his wife. More than he ever knew he could feel. He's loved me for years, he said. It just took him this long to do something about it. It's hard. He's got two kids."

"What about you, Mimi? Do you love him? I mean, he's your boss."

"God, Sara. I've loved him for years. I came to Day Treatment six years ago and I've loved him since day one. Day one!"

"But weren't you practically living with that other guy for five years?" I asked, hopeful of getting more details.

"Don't be stupid, Sara," Mimi responded. "I've always loved Melvin, but he's always been unavailable. I never dreamed he was unhappy with his wife."

"Never dreamed he was unhappy with his wife!" I mocked her gleefully. "Never had even a quick, passing fantasy." We both burst out laughing. "Never allowed one teensy thought . . ." I went on despite the fact that I'd totally lost my audience. Mimi was off in her own musings. But I was caught up in the drama of her life and was having trouble toning down my response.

As Dr. Harley swiftly and surely moved himself into Mimi's apartment, she had less time available to spend with me. But I was also becoming close friends with Frank, and together we started poking around the city. One chilly Saturday we wound up in a café bookstore, standing at a table of gay literature and rating the men in a glossy picture book on their looks.

"Here's your problem, Sara," Frank was saying. "You seem unable to separate aesthetic judgments from moral ones." The problem was that if I thought someone looked sullen, mean, or degenerate, I didn't find him very appealing. Frank, on the other hand, felt that he completely separated his aesthetic visual sense from any other consideration. Knowing him better now, I think he actually rated them higher when they looked sullen or depraved.

"Now this one I think we can both agree on." I leaned over to show Frank my find. When I looked up, Frank had a stricken look on his face.

As I registered Frank's expression, a large, bulky man, dressed formally and smiling graciously, squeezed by and surprised me by saying, "What a pleasure, Mr. Thomas." He had an armful of books.

"It's nice to see you, Mr. Roden." Frank actually seemed to hold his breath until Mr. Roden paid for his books and left the store. "Let's get a cappuccino, Sara. I know he saw what I was looking at. Oh, Sara. Oh, my God." We walked to the café section and sat down.

"Let's order, Frank." We got cappuccinos and ham-and-cheese melts on croissants.

"Sara, you don't understand. That was Maury Roden, who runs the Caliban Café with Mr. Hopper, Harry's father. He came to our last session. He was very helpful. Richard thought it might help to get input from a friend. Actually, what we really wanted was someone in the session to talk. The Hoppers aren't exactly loquacious, except Mrs. Hopper when it comes to her allergies. God, Sara. He saw me lasciviously eyeing gay pictures. I'll lose all credibility. I know he noticed. He glanced down at the table as he squeezed by."

"He was thinking about the books he'd just bought. He noticed you, not the table."

"I thought I saw him glance down at the table. Did you specifically notice?"

"I don't think he even looked at the table. He's rather large, you know. I think he had trouble squeezing through. He was probably trying to hold in his stomach so he didn't knock over a display. You're acting silly. I wouldn't worry about it. Anyway, it has nothing to do with your work. Now he's a man who looks charming and has a warm smile, but he's not handsome. You see I can discriminate between the two: appealing, yes; aesthetically alluring, no. Tell me about the case, Frank. Harry seems so much better lately."

"I know. He's doing real well. We've never even had him on medication. Richard thinks that when Harry started college and moved away from home, he upset the delicate balance that kept his parents together. He thinks that prior to Harry's episodes there was a lot of tension in the family and that Mrs. Hopper was thinking of leaving. In the last session, she actually came out and said she had been. Her threats to leave had raised everybody's anxiety level and right away brought out all kinds of conflicts between Mr. and Mrs. Hopper. Then Harry went nuts and moved back home, and everyone relaxed somewhat and started to take care of him. Mrs. Hopper hasn't mentioned leaving since, and her anger at Mr. Hopper has been submerged. I think some of the conflict has to do with the café. I get the sense that Mrs. Hopper feels she was pushed out; she didn't really want to stop working. I think she's jealous of Mr. Hopper's relationship with Maury. No, I don't think they're gay, so lower your eyebrows, Sara. But she and her husband started it together, and now she has no part in it and her husband works long hours. Mrs. Hopper's never found much else to do with her time. I don't really know why she left the café. None of them exactly invite questions. They don't like revealing their business. That's why it was so nice to have Mr. Roden there. He actually talks and answers questions. He has a sense of humor, too, which Mr. and Mrs. Hopper decidedly do not have. Mr. Hopper has a pathetic way of gently touching his kids, like he's trying to reassure himself that they're still there. It's weird. He's very awkward with his wife. They don't seem to talk directly to each other. Oh, yes, I just remembered. A tidbit. I hear your little bag of bones, Helena, finally deflowered Harry. They've become quite an item."

"It makes me uneasy—he's not exactly Mr. Stability. But she was certainly pleased with herself. She's doing really well, too. She's due to start meeting with Cynthia Potter, the vocational rehab counselor next week. They'll start talking abouts jobs and training programs."

"That's great. I know what else I meant to tell you. Harry's taken a strong dislike to your friend Mimi. She and Dr. Harley also seem to be quite an item. How you people say, heterosexually involved."

"My lips are sealed." I felt bound by my promise of discretion. "What's for dessert?"

"Carrot cake for me. I've always thought that sex was a sublimation of my food drive, and time keeps proving me right."

"Carrot cake or ice cream. I can't decide. Unless you think I owe it to myself to get both."

"It's your waistline, or should I say, was your waistline. I've got to get you out for some exercise, Sara. You're developing pockets of heavy resistance. Let's go for a long walk tomorrow. Unless you'd prefer to jog."

"Let me ask Sweeney. About the walk, that is. He and I are supposed to spend the day together."

"He'd be a welcome and decorative addition. Sara! That's a lot of ice cream you put away."

"Hey, Frank. I gotta be me."

"And more me and more me."

6

The trees kept their leaves as Thanksgiving approached. Although I talked to my parents weekly by phone, I missed their presence and their familiar, comfortable home; and I was eagerly anticipating the holiday. My brother, Jeffrey, and his pregnant wife, Nancy, were due to drive down from Massachusetts. Mike was also going to visit his family in Hartford, and we planned on making the drive together. He was glad of the break and relieved, I think, to be free of the responsibility of having to divide a four-day weekend between Marcy and a second woman he'd started dating.

But my plans changed suddenly when Jeffrey called, on the Sunday night before Thanksgiving.

"You're an aunt!" he yelled into the phone. "Nancy had a little girl. We were up all night."

"Jeff, that's wonderful. Congratulations! I'm thrilled for you. How is everyone? What's her name?"

"Rebecca. After Grandma. We're all doing fine. Nancy's asleep or I'd put her on."

"It's a beautiful name. I'm so excited. But wasn't Nancy due in January? For some reason I thought it wasn't supposed to happen yet."

"She's six weeks premature. But they're both doing great. Rebecca's in an incubator, but she's real healthy and the doctor doesn't think there'll be any problems. Nancy's sort of out of it, but yes, we were pretty surprised. It all happened so suddenly. Nancy worked on Friday. She hadn't even started her preparations for maternity leave. It's been pretty exciting around here. But everyone seems fine now. Mom and Dad are driving up on Tuesday and I think they'll stay a week or two, at least. Mom will, anyway. We're canceling Thanksgiving this year, Sara. I hope you don't mind. But we're going to need all the help we can get. I'm up to my eyeballs in work. I'd planned to do a ton of work by Christmas so I could take it easy and be available when the baby was due. But who ever thought Rebecca would put in such an early appearance? We're just overwhelmed. I've got things I've got to get out—I don't know how I'm going to get them done—and Nancy should be home from the hospital Tuesday or Wednesday, but they'll probably keep the baby a little while longer. I don't know. Anyway, we need Mom and Dad."

"You've got them," I said. "They'll be great. Mom will be in her element. Should I come up, too, Jeff? I'd love to see the baby and help out. I wouldn't get in until late Thursday and I'd have to leave early Sunday morning."

"I think it would be better if you waited and came another time. It's going to be very crowded and hectic and mostly Nancy will need to sleep and I'll be trying desperately to get all this work out of the way. Mom and Dad will be cooking and shopping and driving Nancy to the hospital while the baby's still there. We won't get to visit and there really won't be anything left for you to do."

"Okay." I was disappointed. I'd never been away from my family for such an extended period and I yearned to see everyone. A flood of maternal longing swept over me as I held the phone. I wanted to cradle a fragile, snuggly infant. And I wanted my mother there to cradle me, if need be. I envied Nancy, the pivotal woman, being mothered, mothering. "I'm really happy for you, Jeff," I said. "And I'd love to come see my niece. Let me know when's a good time."

"I will. We're just too overwhelmed right now. We'll call you in a few days when the folks are here. Sorry we won't get to see you. How are you doing?"

"I'm fine, Jeff. What can I send for the baby? Is there anything in particular you need?"

"Anything. Anything. I can't really think what we need. Sleep is what we need. Send a full night's worth." Jeff was usually precise and organized, not to mention on the laconic side.

"Okay. I'll find something. Hang up and get some sleep. Give my love to Nancy and thanks for calling."

"Bye, Sara."

"Bye."

I called my parents immediately. My dad got on the extension as soon as my mother said, "Hi, Sara."

"Hi," I said. "Jeff just called. "I heard the good news. Isn't it thrilling?"

"Yes, sweetie, it sure is. We've been calling everyone we know, but Jeff made us promise not to call you so he could tell you himself."

"I'm excited at being an aunt," I said. "You must be delirious at being grandparents."

"I think that's an accurate description," my dad said with a chuckle.

"Sweetie, I'm sorry about Thanksgiving," my mother said. "We'll miss you. We never expected the baby to arrive so suddenly. But thank God, everyone seems to be doing okay."

"Well, don't worry about me, please," I said. "Although I really was looking forward to seeing you guys."

"We'll miss seeing you, Sara dear," my dad put in. "It would be so much easier if you lived closer."

"I know," I agreed, for the first time realizing that I had moved out of the family orbit. "I wish I were there now," I said honestly.

We were all so stirred up by the news of the baby that it was impossible to talk about anything else. Immediately on hanging up, I called Mike to tell him about Rebecca and to cancel out on the ride. Then I called an old college friend, Susan, whose Thanksgiving invitation I had previously turned down. Susan and I had been close in college but had kept in touch mainly through holiday greetings as our lives diverged. She lived in a rural part of Virginia, although it was actually only a fifty-minute drive from where I lived in the District. We'd gotten together several times since I'd moved to Washington. When I called back to tell her about Rebecca and my new availability, she urged me to pack my bags and stay Thursday through Sunday.

Susan lived in a spectacular showcase of a house designed by her architect husband. They had a three-year-old boy named Lee and a baby on the way. Her days were filled with creating and nurturing, not just children but also magnificent gardens covering large sections of their five-acre lot. Although I enjoyed Susan's company, I don't think I would have agreed to spend four days there if I hadn't just become an aunt. Rebecca's birth had irrevocably changed my status in life and boosted me back a generation. I suddenly had an intense urge to find out all Susan would tell me about being pregnant and to get to know her son, Lee.

Susan was gratified by my interest in her pregnancy and motherhood, and our visit was relaxed and pleasurable. Lee took some getting used to since I had never been a babysitter or spent much time around kids. But he had beguiling ways. My last night there he requested that I put him to bed. We read a Berenstain Bears book, and then I waited patiently while he gathered together his stuffed animal clan in preparation for the tucking-in ceremony. I had been coached on the correct responses, and I performed my role perfectly. When the whole gang was covered up and in place, Lee looked up at me out of his serious brown eyes and asked in his lispy voice, "Do you like me, Sara?"

"Like you? I like you this much and this much." I made my arms stretch wider and wider apart. "I like you so much, you could say I love you." It was true.

"I love you, Sara."

"Get comfy and I'll give you three super-duper kisses."

"I am comfy."

I gave Lee his super-dupers and tiptoed out of the room. How could I bring myself to part from him in the morning?

Mimi called me as soon as I got back Sunday night. As I picked up the phone, I noticed her favorite coffee mug, with her name printed in gold leaf, sitting on my bookcase. She must have used my apartment as a refuge while I was away. We had exchanged spare apartment keys several weeks earlier, and I was pleased she had felt free to let herself in during my absence. Mimi was desperate to talk. Melvin's kids had just spent two days and two nights with them. The girls, ages ten and seven, were rude to her and refused to obey even the most basic of her requests. All weekend she heard, "You're not my mother." The worst thing, though, was that Melvin was out there seeing private patients half the time and when he was there he didn't back her up.

"He'd try to charm them out of it. 'Do it for Daddy.' He'd tease them, call them funny names, entertain them; but he never told them to obey me. They're ill-mannered brats. I don't know what I'm going to do."

"I wouldn't give up, Mimi. I mean, think what it must be like for them. Their father moved out. They're probably furious with him, but they don't want to lose him altogether. They feel loyal to their mother, they . . ."

"Don't you think I know all that," Mimi said with a sharpness I'd never heard before. "I'm sorry, Sara. I didn't mean to snap at you. It was just so awful. I have to talk to Melvin. He feels so damn guilty about the whole thing, he seems incapable of saying no to his children. I've got a week to recover before I have to see them again. They're coming next Saturday."

"How did your mother get through Thanksgiving? This is her last one in New Hampshire, right?"

"Oh, Mother bitched and moaned her way through another Thanksgiving. I shouldn't say that. She's been a good mother to me. She'll be moving in February. She wants me to drive up to New Hampshire and help her pack. I'm trying to talk Melvin into coming with me and we can ski and make a vacation out of it. And he can help pack and give me some moral support. Lord knows, I'll need it."

"That sounds like a great way to do it." Skiing, hot baths, a fireplace and hot cider after a day on the slopes with a man you loved: It sounded pretty good to me. I hadn't had a date since Sidney Markowitz, whom I'd discouraged early on.

7

Helena started right in on me the next day. "Dr. Marks, I have a smashing idea, and Harry and I couldn't wait for you to get back to discuss it. You know how you've been pestering me—well, not really pestering me, encouraging me—to start thinking about a career and all. Well, Cynthia Potter finally thinks I'm ready to start in part-time employment. I really don't want to go to graduate school, at least not yet. You know how you always tell my parents to treat me like a twenty-two-year-old—'Helena's twenty-two, she can make up her own mind about that'—and stuff, well, I'm starting to feel twenty-two and I'll be twenty-three next week so I think I'm ready to plan for my future. I think it'll be fun to work a cash register or something. Then I could pay my parents some money and save some. Harry and I are thinking of getting an apartment together."

"Helena, I'm delighted at all the thought you've given this. I think you're certainly ready to start part-time work and continue with half-days here. And keep up the family sessions. But let's wait and see how you do working, and how things do in general before making plans to move in with Harry. Okay?"

"Okay," she acquiesced, but she looked down as she said it and wouldn't meet my eyes. I didn't like the idea of her living with Harry.

"I'll give Cynthia Potter a call this afternoon to see what employment possibilities she has."

"That's what I want to talk to you about. I have a job. Harry says I can work at the Caliban."

"Is Harry in charge of personnel there?"

Helena's face colored red.

"Helena, I only mean, I hate to see you get your hopes up for a particular job when it isn't definite. Did Harry's father agree?"

"Harry told me that he was 100 percent absolute that I could get a job there. He said he'd arrange it for me. It was his idea, I didn't ask him, you know. He wants me to work there. And then he can go back to college and I can support us until he's done. He's a wonderful lover, Dr. Marks. You do like Harry, don't you?"

"Do you know what sort of job Harry had in mind?" I asked gently.

"Working the cash register. You don't believe me, but I have a real appetite, I mean aptitude, for numbers. Ask me a math problem, you'll see."

"Helena, I do believe you. If I have any reservations, they are not because I think you incapable. I'm just a little concerned that Harry got carried away, because he's so fond of you, and that he promised more than he could deliver. I don't want you getting too disappointed. There are other jobs if this one doesn't work out."

"Harry loves me and I love him. He's the most sensitive man I know. I don't think you understand." Helena was right. I didn't understand.

On Wednesday night, after our family sessions, I got to talk to Frank about Harry's job offer. As usual, we both needed to unwind, and we went to the American Café. Frank began to talk about Harry, who had of late taken to washing himself and his clothes. "That child gets more handsome every day. You'd think he was gay, he's started to look so good."

"That reminds me. Did Mr. Roden ever say, 'Hi, Fruit, I mean Frank,' or anything after that day in the bookstore?"

"No, Sara dear. He hasn't acted at all strange around me. I feel much better. Well, cheers. Listen, Sweet-tooth, do you want me to tell you about the family session or not?"

"Tell away."

"First off, something is rotten in the Hopper family."

36

"Derivative, Frank. Speak in your own voice."

"They were all there, and Mr. Roden. First I asked how things were going, and everyone agreed they had nothing to complain about. I commented on how good Harry was looking and they all acknowledged that he was back to taking care of himself and pulling his weight in the family. Doing chores. Stuff like that. Everyone agreed that he was in contact and making sense. No one had any issues to bring up, not that they ever do, it's like pulling teeth. I wanted to find out why Mrs. Hopper gave up working."

"She would do better if she had a job, don't you think, Frank? At least part time. It seems like she has nothing to occupy her—just her asthma and her aches and pains. She must be so oppressed in the house."

"That's what Richard thinks, too. He wanted me to find out what she did all day. It's weird. When I ask her real concretely how she spends her time, she seems unable to account for it. It's like the day floats by. I can't pin her down. She tidies up the house and takes care of 'little errands' all day long. I can't conceive of it. Anyway, I asked her why she stopped working and she said to ask Mr. Hopper. That was all she'd say. I turned to Mr. Hopper and he shrugged as if to say, 'You know women.' Harry asked her if it was before or after he was born that she stopped. She said, 'Before.' I was surprised. I think the children were, too. I commented on how mysterious they were making it sound. I made a general interpretation about this being a family with a lot of secrets. Mr. Hopper gave me the most pathetic look. Maury took over and said it might be hard for my generation to understand, but that back when they were younger, especially having grown up in the Depression, supporting your wife was a manly thing to do. Women were proud to be taken care of. Maury said that his own wife had never worked. Business was not seen as a place for women in those days."

"I didn't know that Maury was married."

"His wife died five years ago. Cancer. He has two grown kids, but they live in California. I get the impression that they're kind of dropouts and he's disappointed in them. Just an impression. Anyway, Mr. Hopper agreed with him and said that after his wife had worked in the restaurant for three or four years, he thought she should have some leisure. About a year later, she became pregnant anyway, so that was that."

"But why doesn't she go back now?"

"Exactly what I asked. See how quickly I learn. For one thing, she's depressed. She's worried about her health. Too much cigarette smoke in the café. Also, she used to bake, and the restaurant's expanded from fifteen tables to sixty tables and a separate bar. That's intimidating. I think they were having a rough time until Maury bought into it and they had enough capital to hire more cooks and spruce it up. It's really thriving now. It was hard to get a clear idea. The Hoppers seem confused when they talk about it."

"How does Mr. Hopper know Maury? They seem like a strange pair. Mr. Hopper's so withdrawn and Maury seems so outgoing and full of vitality."

"I don't know. I think they're real old friends. Maybe grew up together. I'll ask if I get a chance, although Maury won't be back for several weeks. Not until after the New Year. They do enormous business now because all the Christmas shoppers stop in to eat. It's right at Dupont Circle."

"Do Harry and Judy ever work there? As busboys or waiting tables? It seems as if they would with a family business."

"I don't think so, although Maury always makes a big point of the kids being welcome. This time, when he said the kids were welcome, Harry asked if Helena could work there. The Hoppers were thrown off balance. I don't think they realized he had a girlfriend. Lord only knows what they thought the poor child went in for. Lord only knows what my parents think; they refer to me as a young bachelor. Anyway, Maury said that he thought it a wonderful opportunity for a young lady and he didn't see why not. Then Mr. Hopper agreed. Mrs. Hopper looked sullen but didn't object."

"She may feel that they put her out to pasture and now they're taking a young woman in."

"Maybe," Frank said. "Anyway, it turns out they have two cash registers going all the time, one at the bar and one for the

38

dining room. Everyone's been in and out with colds and the flu, so they're actually shorthanded. Maury said to have Helena call him and say that she's Harry's friend. He'll arrange for her to start. No problem."

"Well," I said, bowing to the inevitable. "Here's to Helena's new career."

I was pleased and not a little relieved to hear from Helena that her first week on the job went well. She started to attend the clinic only in the mornings, and we cut our individual meetings down to twice weekly. Helena either brought a sandwich to the clinic for lunch, or left at noon and ate on her own. She reported to the Caliban at three, Sundays through Thursdays, and worked until eleven P.M. Friday afternoons she had to herself. Because Frank met with the Hopper family at the same time Wednesday evenings that I met with the Morgans, Mr. Hopper graciously offered to drive Helena back and forth with him to the clinic for their appointments. He arranged for Helena's cash register to be covered during that time period.

Helena was ecstatic when she spoke to me of her new-found sense of competency and independence. All week she had stories about this customer or that waiter. I teased her about staying away from the busboys. She reported that Mr. Hopper and Maury treated her well. And Harry stopped by several times to see her. Helena manned the dining room register and seemed to get an endless kick out of ringing up checks. Although it was an expensive restaurant with high quality food, customers paid on their way out so as to speed things up a bit. They served a lot of people and served them efficiently.

On Saturday, after her first week of work, Helena went out and splurged on new clothes. No more Peter Pan collars. She showed up Monday in a red knit dress with a scoop neckline. She was still slender enough to have the knit cling provocatively around her thighs. As the weeks went by, the Morgans' repertoire expanded. They allowed not only Helena more personal freedom but themselves as well. At our Wednesday night meeting, several weeks before Christmas, Dr. Morgan announced that he had made reservations for himself and his wife to fly to San Francisco the following Tuesday night to attend a dental convention. They had never traveled together alone before. We decided to cancel our next Wednesday night meeting, since Helena's parents would be away. I was both pleased and proud of the family's progress.

It was the very next day that Helena decided to end her relationship with Harry. "He is, after all, a child," Helena said. "He's been ever so sweet to me. But Harry's just a boy and the world is full of men. You know, he is four years younger than me. I don't think we're right for each other. I've never broken up with anyone before. What should I do, Dr. Marks?"

"I think you have to talk to him and tell him. It won't be easy. He's sure to be hurt. But he'll get over it."

"Everyone will blame me. It's not my fault."

"Everyone's gone through it themselves, Helena. No one will blame you. Tell Harry as gently as you can and before anyone else tells him."

To say that Harry was hurt does not begin to describe the enormity involved. Harry went on a rampage of denunciation. When he wasn't ranting about the "whores and ingrates," he was mute and withdrawn. Helena had told him Thursday after our talk. Friday, for the first time since registering, Harry did not come to the clinic. When Frank called his home, Mrs. Hopper said he'd skipped his supper the night before and gone straight to his room. He had left the house in the morning before she got up, and she had assumed he'd come to the clinic. Her breathing grew labored over the phone, and Frank begged her not to worry. He then called the Caliban and got Maury on the phone. Mr. Hopper was busy. Maury hadn't seen Harry there and had not known anything was amiss. He promised to tell Mr. Hopper and have him call back if he heard from Harry. No call came. Dr. Harley was informed of the situation and seemed to think that Frank was overreacting. It was not unusual for patients to take an occasional unauthorized day off.

Harry never did show up that day. Frank gave Mrs. Hopper his home number and asked her to call if she heard any word from Harry. She finally called Frank around four A.M., when Harry dragged into his home. Harry stayed in all weekend. On Monday, looking gaunt and ravaged, he showed up at the clinic. Frank grabbed me for lunch after meeting with Harry. Although Frank was upset by Harry's deteriorated grooming, he was relieved to have him back at the clinic.

"The eerie thing is," Frank explained, "he has no memory of any of the time between talking to Helena and arriving home Saturday morning. Isn't that spooky? A fugue state. Nothing. He remembers his mother being awake when he came home. He remembers her crying and saying, 'Thank God, you're safe. Thank God. You had us so worried.' He'd never seen her like that and it made an impression on him. He didn't see his father all weekend. He was out at the restaurant early the next morning and home late. Sunday, too. I guess they're swamped with business right now. Still, you'd expect his father at least to stop in to see how Harry was. Or to call from the restaurant to touch base. Give him some support. Harry spent the whole weekend in his room. He wouldn't talk to his mother. But she was relieved just to know where he was. I don't think I've ever been so scared in my life. I would have been devastated if he'd killed himself."

"I know," I said gently.

"Thank God he's okay. He's still upset, but at least he can talk about it. He was planning on marrying Helena. She's the first woman he's ever really talked to, let alone slept with."

"This sounds callous, but it is a part of growing up."

"I know. I know. But that doesn't make it easy. It gives me some idea what parents feel like. You can't prevent the pain."

8

Tuesday ushered in the first snowfall of the season. When I woke up I was aware of a stillness that was both familiar and comforting. Mimi called as I was drinking my coffee and skimming the *Washington Post*, and explained with New England superiority that ten flakes of snow were enough to paralyze Washington and environs. Melvin had called the northern Virginia snow emergency number and, learning that the clinic road was not yet ploughed, had telephoned a ten o'clock opening in to the local radio station. The three of us would drive to work together, because Melvin had canceled his morning private patients. I got to savor a leisurely second cup of coffee. I thought of my parents in Connecticut.

Driving up in the boss's car felt special to me, although I sensed Melvin and Mimi's discomfort as several patients who had arrived early stared at our group. Harry was there, still looking disheveled.

We began the late day with a community meeting at ten A.M. The meeting started pleasantly, with a patient actually volunteering to shovel the walk. Suddenly, without warning, Harry leapt from his chair and squatted on the floor in front of Mimi. "You lying whore!" he bellowed. "You. I'm talking to you. Payment is due." Mimi blanched.

I looked away, scared that if I made eye contact, Harry might turn on me. Time seemed suspended.

Finally, Richard walked over to Harry and took his arm. "Let's talk outside for a minute. Come on." He led Harry out, and they returned together about ten minutes later. Richard sat with his hand on Harry's arm, and Harry sat still.

Dr. Harley broke the silence. "Often in a group, one person expresses anger for the rest of the group. I wonder if anyone else might share in the anger Harry's expressing?" Mimi's face crumpled up. She looked ready to cry and bolted out of the room. No one spoke. The community sat in silence for the rest of the meeting. Dr. Harley kept shaking his head back and forth, wordlessly. Mimi never reappeared. Helena looked small and shrunken. Harry's body looked spent, but his face retained the fierceness of conviction.

When the meeting mercifully ended, we filed out, looking as if we were leaving a funeral. The staff always took a five-minute break and then reassembled to "post" the meeting. I ran to find Mimi. I couldn't believe Melvin had turned on her that way. She opened the door, her face tear stained, her eyes puffy. She began immediately: "How could he! Harry's angry with Helena, not me.

Melvin knows that. He invited the entire community to dump on me. I can't go back in there. Do you know I spent the whole goddamn weekend catering to his family? I took those two brats of his to the Air and Space Museum so he could do some work. It was torture. I wanted to scream. My whole Sunday shot to hell. I see his family more than I see him. Now he humiliates me in front of the whole community. I can't go in there, Sara. I can't do it. He lets his children treat me like shit. I didn't break up his marriage. They blame me and he doesn't stop it. It serves his purpose. If he and I can't work this out, there's nowhere for me to go. Do you understand? Nowhere."

"I know, Mimi. It's terrible. Everyone understands how you felt in there. It was horrible." Reluctantly, Mimi accompanied me back to the meeting.

Melvin looked as if his troops had let him down. He began by criticizing Richard for removing Harry from the meeting. "You did a good job of quieting him down, Richard, but you know how hard we try to keep patients from walking out of meetings when we can. The more they can tolerate and remain in the situation, the better. If you had just calmed Harry down and taken him back to his seat, the meeting would have gone better." I thought Richard had been wonderful.

"I wanted to make sure he was really in better control of himself," Richard countered. "That kind of attack is destructive. People get hurt and the patient only feels guilty afterward. We see it differently."

"Yes, we do," Melvin acknowledged, with a sadness suggesting personal loss. "You know I think patients must be free to express themselves verbally no matter how ugly their thoughts are. Violence won't be tolerated, but they must be able to speak their minds even if their thoughts are repugnant to you or me. We must accept the ugly, vicious side if they are to accept it and integrate it into the whole. It can't be cut off and given a life of its own."

I wanted to put in a word for Mimi. "Don't you think," I said, "don't you think that Harry was really angry with Helena?"

Melvin responded impatiently, "Of course, his rage was meant for Helena. But it's a lot safer, while his rage is so virulent

43

and intense, if he can direct it at a staff member who has the training and strength not to take it personally or be thrown by it. It was a mistake for Mimi to leave the meeting. It gives the patients the sense that their anger can kill her off. One patient gets a little out of control, and two seasoned staff members go haywire. I don't understand it. I'd hate to answer for the consequences if Harry directed his fury at Helena. He needs to direct his anger at Mimi right now as a protective defense. I'm sure he felt Mimi could take it without being destroyed. Her walking out has made things considerably harder for him. The last thing he needs is to feel that he has that kind of destructive power. I tried to take some of the burden of the anger off his shoulders by broadening it to a group issue." Melvin shifted his eyes to Mimi. "Evidently you took that to mean that I was endorsing his point of view, Mimi. That was hardly the case. You're becoming too sensitive. It's hurting your work."

"But there's another issue here," Richard persisted. "Something is obviously going on between you and Mimi. Although I personally don't think, given your position here, that it's a good idea for you to have an affair or romance with Mimi, you're consenting adults. You do what you want. But you ought to realize that it affects the whole system here, particularly the patients. They see you wearing a wedding ring. Don't you suppose that means something to them? Don't you suppose they think about it? Some of the oldtimers have met your wife and kids. Then you join Mimi in her office for lunch. Or arrive with her, like this morning. I heard Stanley telling Harold he'd seen the two of you together at a movie Saturday night. What kind of message does that give them?"

Melvin nodded sadly. "It's not a good position to be in."

Richard pressed on. "I think Harry is angry with Mimi, as well as Helena. The force, the intensity of his anger may be meant for Helena, but as far as he knows, you're married and Mimi's an adulteress. From what Frank tells me, there's a big issue in Harry's family about whether his mother's going to leave his father. He's been willing to go crazy to keep that family together, and then he comes here and there are unacknowledged, secret affairs. He doesn't know what his father does all day. I'm sure he wonders. He sees his mother abandoned and suffering at home. But that's beside the point. It's not good for any of the patients to have this kept a secret. Their fantasies and resentments will just grow. You need to announce that you're legally separated from your wife. They think you're getting a little on the side, they think Mimi's a home wrecker, and here we are trying to teach them intimacy and trust. It's crazy. Jesus, Melvin, part of why these people went crazy in the first place is because they weren't allowed to talk about what they saw going on before their very eyes. By not acknowledging it, we're conspiring to deny it and that's crazy-making."

I had never seen Richard so adamant. I had no idea he thought that way, but I completely agreed. I also began to think that Harley was keeping Mimi in the position of mistress. He still wore a wedding ring. It *was* crazy.

"Maybe you're right." It was the first time I'd ever heard Harley admit defeat.

"Look," Richard said, softened by Harley's agreement, "maybe it would be easier if we brought it up in our team meetings this afternoon. They're smaller groups and everyone knows each other better. It won't be as intimidating for the patients to speak up as in the large group."

The meeting broke up. I felt considerable relief. Something productive had been salvaged. I ran immediately to find Helena. Her half-day ended at noon, but she usually hung around during lunch. I wanted to offer her some reassurance and support: She had looked as though she needed it. But one of the patients told me that Helena had gone for the day. At least she and I had a scheduled meeting set for the next day. I could give her some support then and it would also give me a chance to clear up the Mimi–Dr. Harley affair with her. She would miss this afternoon's discussion in the team meeting.

Next, I went to hunt down Mimi. I found her by herself, in her office, contemplating her roast beef sandwich.

"You look better," I said. "You know, it really didn't sound like Melvin was trying to hurt you. He just was so insensitive to what it was like for you. Do you agree?"

"Sara. I feel so much better. God, I hit a low. It scared me. Melvin's under so much strain. You don't know the half of it. His family is so dependent on him and his wife's trying to turn the children against him. He hasn't been sleeping well. I don't think he realizes his impact on me sometimes. His evening patient canceled, and he's going to take me out to dinner. We desperately need some time together to talk. Will you be able to find a ride home?"

"No problem. I'm having dinner with Mike. I have to run and get a sandwich." But I was hesitant to leave. I wanted to offer something to Mimi, but I didn't know what. I couldn't quite go yet. "And good luck in your team meeting today. I hope it goes okay. You know. It won't be easy, but I think Richard's right. It'll be better when it's out in the open. More legitimate, don't you think?" I felt unsure of myself. I wasn't sure why.

"I don't know what you mean by legitimate," Mimi said sharply. "Richard is such a self-righteous asshole. I know how much you like him, but he's always got to compete with Melvin. He never misses a chance to try to show that he knows more or could run the center better. Melvin thinks he wants his job. Not that he'll ever get it. He'd be out of his depth. You don't know what Melvin goes through with the staff. Richard always thinks he knows best. Melvin is his boss. But Richard sets his own rules. As if he has any right to disapprove of Melvin and me. It's outrageous."

"Mimi," I implored. "He was trying to be helpful. To you and Melvin as well as the patients. He didn't want you to be a target."

"Richard is such an expert at legitimizing women."

"Mimi, really. I've got to go. It's not Richard's fault. You've had a terrible morning. And I know this afternoon's going to be difficult for you." I left feeling forlorn and inadequate. I hadn't been very helpful to Mimi. And I hadn't been very helpful to Richard. I was churned up inside. Was Richard really just a middle-aged man, a failure at marriage, who was disappointed with his job? I hated to think of him in those terms. He seemed so much more than that to me. It was hard to fit all the pieces together.

46

I had no time left to go out for a sandwich, and when our two o'clock team meeting rolled around I had a fullblown headache. I was dimly aware that Joyce announced Melvin's separation and invited reactions from the patients. No one responded until five minutes before the meeting was due to end, then the comments poured forth. By then, of course, there wasn't enough time to talk about it, which is one way to avoid painful subjects.

I remember Frank asking if anyone had seen Harry, and only then did I realize that he was not in the meeting. I felt a faint tingle of alarm, but was concentrating most of my energy on getting through the day despite my headache. I went through the motions until five, when Mike showed up right on time. I was so distraught by the events of the day that when we finally got to Sweeney's apartment, I surprised him by bursting into tears. Luckily, I knew Mike well enough not to be too embarrassed. Mike tended to me kindly. I think he was relieved to be with a woman whose crying was unrelated to anything he had done. With my tears spent, I realized I was hungry and we sat down to talk and eat. I tried to explain to Mike about Helena and Harry, and Harry yelling at Mimi in the meeting, and Melvin and Mimi, and Richard and Melvin, and finally, Mimi and Richard. I wasn't very articulate.

Mike was interested. Our "community" intrigued him. He had always respected Dr. Harley and admired Richard. I calmed down. Mike said he felt I was old enough to hold two opposing thoughts in my mind at the same time. Of course, the hard part was the opposing emotions, not the thoughts. But Mike's friendliness and care helped, and by the time I got home, I thought only of crawling into bed and starting afresh Wednesday.

But as I opened my apartment door and switched on the light, I noticed a piece of paper that had been pushed under the door. I read, *Please call no matter how late you get home. Important. Mimi.* I dashed to the phone and dialed her number. It was only ten-fifteen. She answered immediately and said, "I'm glad it's you. Can you come right down?"

Mimi was a sight. Her face, pale to begin with, was dead white. Her eyes seemed stuck in a wide, frightened stare. I thought that Melvin had gone back to his wife. I was wrong.

47

Mimi told me the following story. She and Melvin had left the clinic together around ten after five. They went to the back lot and walked up to Melvin's car. They were deep in conversation as Melvin headed around to the driver's side, while Mimi went to wait at the passenger side. Then she looked down. The passenger window was completely shattered. Inside, amid the broken glass fragments, were porcelain pieces from her cherished coffee mug. Someone had thrown her mug, which had her name printed in gold leaf and, more importantly, had been a Christmas gift from her mother back when her mother used to buy her Christmas gifts, into the passenger side of Melvin's car. Someone had aimed at Mimi's heart and scored a hit.

Melvin had gone back to the clinic to call the police and the body shop while Mimi waited at the car. As she was standing there, Melvin's oldest daughter, Lucy, came running up. Melvin's wife and children lived only three blocks from the clinic, which used to be a convenience. Lucy had a smirk on her face, and Mimi had an eerie feeling that she had come to view her own work. When Lucy got up close to the car, she began laughing hysterically. Mimi ran inside to get Melvin. She and Lucy had not exchanged a word. She ran into Melvin's office and fired her words at him: "Your little Lucy is outside laughing at the damage. She's very pleased with herself." When they had first discovered the vandalism, she and Melvin had both assumed it had been done by Harry, who had not returned to the clinic at all that afternoon. The thought of Harry doing it was upsetting enough. But when Mimi saw Lucy standing there laughing, she became convinced of her guilt.

Melvin was furious when he heard Mimi's accusation. "What the hell do you mean by that?" he'd yelled at her.

"Come and see," she'd screamed back, on the verge of hysterics herself. "I'm not going back out there alone."

He had marched out ahead of her. "What are you doing here, Lucy? What do you have to do with this?" he had demanded. Lucy had sobered up immediately.

"Mother sent me over. She tried to call. She wants you to watch us tonight. She said to tell you something very important came up and she has to go out. She wants you to come at seven and stay till eleven. What happened to your car?"

"Why don't you tell us?" Mimi had challenged.

"Shut up, Mimi," Melvin had responded with icy coldness. He had never told her to shut up before.

"Then," Mimi continued, "he asked her very gently if she knew anything about the car. Of course, she denied it. He practically pleaded with her not to admit to it."

"How would she have gotten your mug?" I asked.

"I spent the whole weekend playing the evil stepmother. I'm pretty sure I had the mug at home." It was hard to know where the mug had been. Mimi was a habitual tea drinker. She had numerous mugs and often took a half-filled one in the car with her in the morning. Her mugs were always going back and forth between her home and office. Once in the office, they rotated around different meeting rooms or offices where she might stop to chat.

"How awful, Mimi." I couldn't think of anything else to say.

"And for his wife to demand for him to sit like that. First of all, he usually has patients. He can't just break his appointments. She still gets whatever she wants from him. He took me to the goddamn Hot Shoppes and raced me home so he could get over there by seven. She probably had an important, unexpected big date."

I felt terrible for Mimi. Someone was out to wound her. That was painful enough. If it was someone in Melvin's family, she was convinced she was sunk. Everything, for her, was riding on Melvin. I stayed with Mimi, trying to reassure her. Melvin came in at eleven-thirty, and I left gratefully. I just wanted to go to sleep.

9

As I drove into work with Mimi the next morning, I was heartened to see Helena also arriving at the clinic. Here was someone that I had helped to improve. But now, in the dead of winter, she raced up to me wearing a light spring jacket over her dress. Clearly, there was still work to be done with her. Helena was anxious to talk to me immediately, but I had to put her off until our scheduled meeting time from nine-thirty to ten. By nine-thirty she had observed Harry, who had shown up that morning around nine, acting completely psychotic. He had walked right by her as if he hadn't seen her, she told me. By nine-thirty she had also had time to hear the scuttlebutt about Mimi and Melvin, the news that she had missed the previous day and was on everyone's tongue by Wednesday morning. And then whatever it was that had made Helena so anxious to talk with me had been pushed to the back of her mind by these new events. Harry's withdrawal upset and saddened her. But she received the news of Melvin's separation and relationship with Mimi as a tasty morsel to chew over with delight. In fact, her response was, "How delectable." Fantasies derived from books in which the lord of the manor gained biblical knowledge of the parlormaid while her ladyship was having a clothes fitting had accompanied Helena throughout her adolescence, lifting her up and out of the grim reality of her own life. No surprise then, that with all that was on Helena's mind, she latched onto this bit of gossip as onto a lifeboat and sailed away with it. She savored every angle and let her own concerns drift away unmentioned to me. I should have pressed her. But she'd been through such a bad time breaking off with Harry that I felt she could use a respite. Probably, and unconscionably, I also encouraged her to play around with this piece of gossip because her silly way of dealing with it made me feel more light-hearted. Helena turned a somber melodrama into a frolicking farce.

At five minutes to ten, I told Helena our time was almost up and she reminded me that her parents were in San Francisco and she would not be attending the family meeting that night. "I'm glad I don't have to come," she confessed. "How could I ever ride in with Mr. Hopper after what I've done to Harry? He must hate me. I feel like a pariah. It's really terrible, Dr. Marks. I'm considering quitting my job."

"These things have a way of settling down, Helena. I wouldn't do anything until we have a chance to discuss it." I ushered Helena out of my office and into the community room.

The community meeting was tense and uneasy. Harry would not sit down but stood stiffly, like a zombie, in the corner. He was mute. Neither patients nor staff seemed able to thaw him. Helena was a study in contrasts. She alternated looks of extreme pain and sadness with looks that can only be described as insinuating leers. She had seated herself next to Dr. Harley, or Lord Harem, as she called him during the meeting, and treated him to some of the most brazenly suggestive looks I have ever witnessed.

The topic for the day, which Dr. Harley immediately introduced, was his vandalized car. "Something very serious occurred on clinic property yesterday." Looking straight at Harry, he continued, "As those of you who were present yesterday know from the team meetings, I have separated from my wife. Since the separation, Mimi Shear and I have developed a social relationship and sometimes see each other away from the clinic. That is between Mimi and myself, but we thought it necessary to announce it here because we didn't want to cause any confusion or bad feelings. Yesterday, Mimi and I left work together and discovered that the passenger seat of my car had been vandalized. I don't know if it was the angry and, I think, confused act of someone in our community or if it was done by some neighborhood youngsters. I notified the police, because vandalism is a serious crime. It very much concerns us as a community. I don't want people whispering about each other and filled with suspicion. I want us to have an open discussion about what has happened. If anyone was involved or saw anything suspicious, I want you to speak up in this meeting. If someone in our community is responsible, we can work with that person to try and understand what occurred and why, and to help that person find other ways of venting his or her anger. There would be no need to press charges if we could work together as a community." Dr. Harley spoke very slowly and thoughtfully. I'd never seen him choose his words so carefully. It was a delicate situation.

The community members responded well. There was a discus-

51

sion about whether the act had been random or directed specifically against Mimi or against the two of them. Finally, I think it
was Stanley, the oldtimer, who said, "Beg pardon, sir" (his form
of address for Dr. Harley), "but young Harry was quite put out
over Miss Shear yesterday. The gentleman seemed perturbed over
what he deemed was Miss Shear's dubiety and promiscuity."

"What the hell are you trying to say, Stanley? Use English,"
yelled another oldtimer. The topic of Harry's involvement had
been raised, although Harry himself remained stiff and immobile
and mute. We couldn't tell whether or not he even heard what
was being said. And no one had seen anything suspicious.

We labeled the meeting a success in the postsession, probably
because, after yesterday's meeting, the staff wanted to be supportive of each other. I was reassured that we were, after all, a well-
functioning staff. I attributed my feelings of gloom and confusion
to premenstrual stress. I usually had one day of anxiety and depression, and I had just gotten my period that morning. I was about a
week early, so I hadn't anticipated my mood change. I was grateful
that Helena's family wouldn't be in that night. I'd be able to go
home early and tend to my cramps with ritualistic pampering.

I left the clinic at five P.M. and was home by five-thirty. By
seven-thirty, I'd read the newspaper, eaten my dinner and desserts, and taken my cramps medication, which had a generally
mellowing effect. I stepped into the shower for a long, hot and
steamy soaking. I must have stayed in for forty-five minutes. The
beating water soothed me into a trancelike state and I totally forgot myself. When I emerged, I blow-dried my hair and put on
knee socks, a flannel nightgown, and a wraparound robe. I read in
bed for about half an hour and then started to doze off. Around
nine-thirty I was awakened by my telephone, which rang twice
and then stopped. I noticed the red light flashing on the phone
machine and realized that I had left it on and hadn't listened to
my messages. I picked up the phone and sat through my awkward
recording about what to say at the sound of the beep. Then I
heard Frank starting to swear into the machine and interrupted
him. "I'm here, Frank. I forgot to turn the machine off."

"Are you sick? Why'd you leave the clinic?"

"No. I left early because Helena's parents are away so we canceled the family session. How was your meeting with Harry's family?"

"Thought you'd never ask. Let me come over and tell you. I'm still at the clinic. I detained Richard as long as I could, but he has this creepy way of liking to go home after work. Oh, to have a honey."

"Come right over."

"I'm on my way. Cream and two sugars. It's bitter cold out."

I pulled myself out of bed and put on a pair of jeans and a sweater. Then I headed for the kitchen. When Frank came shivering and bustling in, I had a coffee with brandy and Ready Whip waiting for him. For some reason, I had a craving for Ovaltine, which I kept in stock.

"What a session. I can't believe it."

"Tell me, already."

"You know Harry was rigid and in a catatonic stupor all day."

"I know," I said. "Very spooky. Do you think he might need to be hospitalized?"

"Joyce and I talked about it at dinner. You weren't at dinner either, you creep." (Staff and patients cooked Wednesday night dinner together.) "We asked Dr. Harley what he thought, and he was very disapproving of the idea. I didn't realize he had such a strong antihospitalization bias. He doesn't see hospitalizing a patient for treatment, only for drug detox or in an emergency, like danger to self or others. He didn't think Harry's behavior warranted either of those classifications. Not even after the car vandalism."

"That might not have been Harry. Melvin's family isn't exactly overjoyed about their affair, either."

"That's true. It's just that he's my patient so I'm extra sensitive to what he might do. Anyway, when Harry's family arrived at seven, he followed them into my office with that stiff-legged walk of his. They all sat down, and Harry remained standing in the corner. At least he came into the room. It was spooky. I had no idea what to do. I felt terrible. His parents had been so pleased with how good he was looking last week. And Mrs. Hopper had seemed piqued by Helena's work at the café. I got the impression that she might be opening up to the possibility of resuming work. Then they had to come back this week with Harry in a stupor and the vandalism and that awful day Harry didn't show up. Harry's been practically mute the entire week. Richard tried to help me relax before the session. You know how reassuring he can be. He told me that if I just got Harry into the room for the meeting I would have accomplished a lot. He told me not to worry about trying to get him to respond. Just to include him, but not to push him. He told me to find out from the family members how they viewed what was happening and also if they'd ever been through anything similar themselves. Thank God for Richard. I really had no idea what to do."

"He is a wonderful supervisor," I agreed.

"Sara, it was like taking your finger out of the dike and unleashing the floods. I mean they had been so withholding. Usually it took ten questions from me to elicit a monosyllable. Except if I asked about something of vital interest, like Mrs. Hopper's asthma. But all I did was ask if anyone in the family had ever experienced anything like what they saw Harry going through and I didn't have to say another word. Mr. Hopper started to cry. Mr., not Mrs. *She* opened her mouth and forgot to close it, she was so surprised. Mr. Hopper must have sobbed for about a minute. When he looked up, I was looking at him quizzically, and he said that Harry reminded him of himself. Seeing Harry that way brought back memories he had hoped to keep buried forever. He served in the South Pacific in World War II. I think he said he was in New Guinea and the Philippines. Harry's withdrawal brought back his memories of fear and sickness and cold and rain and heat and confusion and starvation and loss and fatigue. Especially fatigue, he said. He said there was a time when his waking and sleeping were indistinguishable. People who had been killed reappeared before him as if alive, while people alive soon died and were resurrected again. He couldn't distinguish. Can you imagine? He said the fatigue, the malaria, and the continuous loss sapped him of reality. He experienced a blur filled with young faces and faces withered with disease and faces splattered apart. He was there for three years. Three years. Thank God I was too young for Vietnam. Anyway, something weird happened to Mr. Hopper. The faces, the fighting, the noise, heat, and fatigue all oozed out of his body, leaving it stiff and rigid. They retreated further in the distance, leaving him alone and still. He was transported to an aid station in that condition and shipped back to a stateside hospital. It was like he had spilled his life juices and the empty, dry, crusty shell got sent home. He spent a year in a West Coast V.A. hospital before he began to notice his surroundings. Like he'd been suspended on ice for a year. I can't conceive of it. His recovery was slow. He talked to the nurses and other patients, but he never talked about himself or about all the faces of the dead he kept seeing. He talked only in the present. He said he couldn't tell which nightmares had been real and which unreal. He didn't know who was dead and who had survived. He could visualize his three closest buddies both dead and alive and he didn't know. Can you imagine what that would be like, Sara?"

I shook my head. "No."

Frank continued, "Maury Roden was one of his close friends. He saw him one day in the hospital canteen and thought at first that it was an illusion. He'd thought he'd seen him and the others a couple of times before, but they always turned into strangers at closer inspection. He walked up to Maury real slowly, trying not to stare. Maury said, 'Larry Hopper, you son of a bitch. I thought you were dead and gone.' They embraced. They were the only two survivors in their company. Maury's head was bandaged when he'd seen him. Maury had actually been at the V.A. for five months already. He had one more operation to go and then release, if all went well. 'Grace under pressure,' that's how Mr. Hopper described Maury. He said he remembers what Maury said to him that day; he said, 'An occasional headache, I got off easy.' Seeing Maury gave Mr. Hopper something back. He hadn't survived alone. It gave me goosebumps, Sara.

"It was clear that no one one else in the family had ever heard Mr. Hopper talk like that. He's very closed usually. I don't think his children had really even known that he'd been in the war. Harry was listening intently. I kept looking at him to see his reaction. His body posture had relaxed, so I invited him to sit down and he did. It was like his father's story melted him. I couldn't believe it. He and Judy began plying Mr. Hopper with questions, like I remember doing when I was a kid. He told them that he had gone to West Virginia to see his family after the hospital discharged him. His father and brothers were all coal miners. It was so interesting. Mr. Hopper always felt like odd man out in his family, and after the visit, he left to be out on his own. He moved to D.C. for no particular reason that he was aware of. He had no real purpose and didn't know anyone. But he did go to church and that's where he met Mrs. Hopper. He said she was the prettiest darn lady in the church that day, and, Sara, she blushed crimson. I bet he's never told her that. The kids started giggling. He really complimented her. He said the restaurant was her idea and she was the driving force behind it. They didn't even know about wholesalers when they started. They bought all their goods at the PX, the commissary, which was pretty cheap. She did the baking and they ran the place together. It was like a coffeeshop with sandwiches, drinks, and her baked goods. One friend of hers helped with the waitressing. Otherwise, it was just the two of them. They were married by that time. Harry pinned him down on exactly when he married her. It sounded like one decision to both get married and open a café. They'd been running it together for about four years when, one day, Maury walked into the café unexpectedly. Evidently, he and Mr. Hopper had sent each other Christmas cards and such. They'd kept in touch. It was strange. Mr. Hopper said he had to continue to know that Maury existed. He had to kind of keep tabs on him and know he was still around. Plus, of course, they'd been very close. The four of them who had been so close in the war had used to talk about forming a partnership when they got home. He said they always said *when*, never *if*, they'd return home. But the other two never came back. So when Maury walked in, they became partners. Maury got a loan and they built on and added tables and enlarged the menu. 'That's when it started to swing,' he said. Mr. Hopper started to cry again, and on an impulse I got up and took Harry's arm and whispered to him to comfort his father. I steered him to his father, and he crouched down and took his hand. I was so moved, I almost started to cry. Mrs. Hopper turned to me and said, 'He's never talked like this, so much of himself.' She began to weep softly, and Judy started to cry. I looked at my watch and realized our time was up. I gave them a couple of minutes, then said we'd have to stop. I told Mr. Hopper that he'd really shared a lot of himself with his family, and I could see that it meant a lot to them and had really helped Harry. What a session! Mr. Hopper had his arm around Harry as they walked out. It was the most poignant meeting I've ever had. Richard saw them all walk out together and came up to me in wonder. He looked very pleased and proud."

"I don't think I've ever had a session like that," I said. "Harry just walked away like a regular person?"

"That's right. Oh, and guess what, Sara? Richard said we're getting the videotape equipment. We should have it after the first of the year. I wish I had this session on tape."

Frank gradually wound down, and we gossiped for about half an hour and then he zipped back into the cold. It was supposed to start sleeting by eleven and he wanted to be home before then. I went right to bed and slept soundly. I didn't hear of the tragedy until I arrived at work the next morning.

10

"We've had a fatality" were the first words to greet Mimi and me as we entered the building. They were spoken by Joyce. "Helena was found dead this morning. She must have jumped off Key Bridge. Her body was fished out of the Potomac."

Helena dead. Suicide. It didn't really register. My first thought was how I would face her family. I felt more guilt and failure than loss. The thought of Helena actually being gone, never to return, set in only later. It was beyond my comprehension.

Joyce had gotten details from the police and filled me in.

"Construction men found her body along the waterfront in Georgetown. She'd been washed ashore. Drowned."

"What time did she do it? She was doing so well, Joyce. What could have happened?"

"The medical examiner has the body and they're going to do an autopsy. They're going to call Dr. Harley with the results later today. Then they'll want to meet with you, me and Dr. Harley. I hate to give you paperwork to do at a time like this—I know what you must be feeling—but her chart has to be totally up to date and ready for review and discharge today. There's a special "Death Summary" form to fill out. I'll get you one."

I nodded. "Does her family know?"

"The police notified them. Helena's wallet with her identification was zipped into her jacket pocket. They found her phone number and got her grandmother. They told her and she called Dr. and Mrs. Morgan in San Francisco. They're due back late this morning. They're going to identify the body before the autopsy. The grandmother refused to do it. Who can blame her?"

I nodded again.

"Do you want to talk to me about it?"

"Thanks, Joyce. Let me do the charting now before it really hits me. I might need you later." The charting provided an immediate escape. Nevertheless, it was mid-afternoon by the time I finished, because my mind kept drifting. Images of Helena and her family would intrude on my thoughts, and I would look down to find that I'd stopped writing mid-sentence, the ink running with my tears. I skipped lunch, and by the time Joyce came to fetch me for the meeting with Dr. Harley, the charting was at least complete.

Dr. Harley looked visibly upset. "Let's get Richard in here, too," he commanded. "He's been supervising the family work with Helena. Is that right, Sara?"

I nodded. "Yes."

Joyce called Richard on the intercom, and he came in immediately.

Dr. Harley rubbed his hand over his eyes and addressed the three of us. "I just had a call from the District police. A man-named Detective Harrison. He's on his way over. He has the medical examiner's report, and I think he wants to interview those of us involved in the case to try and determine Helena's state of mind. He said on the phone that it looked like a suicide. Did you bring the chart, Sara? Good. I'll look through it while we're waiting. It's got to be handed into Medical Records Review by close of business today."

Dr. Harley began leafing through the chart. Richard turned to me and said how sorry he was. "I had no idea, Sara. Not even a clue. I wasn't much help to you, I'm afraid."

"You only knew what I told you. I must have missed something important."

"Try to keep your self-pity under control when the police get here." Dr. Harley said. "There's not one mention in the chart of any suicidal ideation. This is the girl who collapsed jogging, right? She came close to dying that time. Between the intake and now, there's no mention of any suicidal attempt or ideas. Is that right?"

"That's right, Dr. Harley," I replied. I felt as if I was on the witness stand. "Honestly, she never said anything. She was doing beautifully until she broke off with Harry. His reaction really upset her. She felt enormously guilty. She did say to me yesterday that she was scared to face Harry's father. She felt like a pariah at the Caliban. Here, too, I think. She thought people would hate her for being so mean to Harry. And she did have something on her mind yesterday, because she particularly wanted to talk to me and was impatient to see me. But by the time we sat down together, she ended up talking about Harry. And you and Mimi," I added softly.

"I talked to her right before she left the clinic yesterday," Richard said. "She looked a little under the weather and seemed nervous, but I never would have thought she'd go jump off a bridge. Her judgment was pretty poor, though. It's the middle of winter and she had on this light spring jacket and her skirt was up to her knees. At least she had on boots."

"That's because she took her winter jacket into the dry cleaners," I put in. "Its grunginess had become a family joke, and she wanted to have it cleaned while her parents were away, you know, to surprise them."

"But there was more to her lack of judgment," Richard continued. "I said something to her about going out dressed like that, especially since the weather report for last night was so cold. She said to me, 'Someone always offers me a ride home, so I won't be standing out in the cold.' Then she walked right at me so I had to keep moving back or we'd have been pressed up against each other. She said something like, 'Some people like to do favors for me,' in her seductive way. I felt a little concerned for her as she left. She could pick up any jerk for a ride home. She certainly wasn't planning on walking around outside last night. It doesn't make sense to me that she'd kill herself. Unless something happened that we don't know about."

"Let's see what the police have to say," Dr. Harley said. "I don't think there was any irresponsibility on our part. Maybe poor judgment. We might have been more cautious. The highest risk of suicide is when a patient starts to improve. They have the energy to make decisions and act on them. Maybe we got swept away with her progress and didn't proceed cautiously enough." Dr. Harley was interrupted by the arrival of Detective Harrison.

The detective asked his questions first, before giving us any information. I suppose he did not want to prejudice our answers. We said to him pretty much what we had already said to each other. We were surprised by the suicide; there had been no warning signs. It must have been an impulsive decision. We did not view Helena as someone who would make secret plans to do away with herself. We knew her to be immature and to show poor judgment. She could have easily allowed herself to be picked up by a relative stranger. Key Bridge was on her way home from the café. She might have found someone to give her a ride who for his own crazy reasons threw her over the bridge. She was incredibly light, not hard to pick up and carry. She usually kept her keys and wallet in her pockets; she rarely carried a purse. With heavy boots on, once she hit the water she'd go down pretty quickly.

Detective Harrison encouraged us to theorize, without offering much himself. Another possibility, one that I thought of, was that someone was to drive her home and they had a quarrel. Maybe Helena tried to seduce him and he was uninterested. Who knew? But anyway, maybe they fought and she stubbornly got out on the bridge to walk the rest of the way herself. Or maybe he stopped the car and told her to get out. Either way, she would have felt angry, rejected, upset. And it had been a miserable night out. Bitter cold, windy, sleet mixed with rain: She might have despaired of ever getting home in that weather, especially if she had been upset. The loneliness of her walking alone, probably chilled to the bone, and then just giving up filled me with grief.

Richard took over for me. "That's the only way I could see her killing herself," he said. "She was so sensitive to rejection and to what people thought. If she had had an argument or felt rejected, especially if someone had kicked her out of their car and left her to walk home, I could see her just wanting to end her misery, and impulsively jumping. I don't think she'd have thought of it as final, though. Do you know what I mean? My sense of Helena is that it would be like losing consciousness so she could wake up from a nightmare. Even if she jumped last night, I don't think she was trying to kill herself. Her thinking was magical sometimes. I can see her wanting to get out of the cold and home to her own bed and wanting to get rid of her thoughts about whatever it was that was troubling her. She was the type to do something dramatic. She probably had a fantasy of waking up in the hospital safe and warm. Like when she practically starved and jogged herself to death.

"I just can't believe that she wanted to die. She didn't have a very high frustration tolerance, at least not from what I've observed. It was foggy last night, too. Walking in the fog, she probably couldn't see much in front of her or behind her. She probably couldn't really see well enough to hail a cab. What a stupid thing to do. She must have felt so alone and scared. Sorry I keep rambling. Do you have specific questions for us?" he asked the detective.

"Nope." The detective continued. "Let me tell you some of what we know, and see if your thinking changes in any way. First off, she was two months pregnant. Is that news to you?"

"I had no idea," I admitted. The others also expressed surprise. "She was so impatient to talk to me yesterday. But she didn't say anything about being pregnant. Maybe she didn't know. But maybe she suspected. Her parents would have really been upset. They would have hit the roof. She must have been thinking about an abortion, if she knew."

"You know, she'd been looking under the weather lately. I wonder if her pregnancy, the hormonal changes, didn't heighten her mood swings," Joyce suggested. "The first trimester can be rough. She might have been overcome with despair."

"Let me throw out some more info," Detective Harrison said. "Given the tides and where and when the body washed ashore, the most likely point of entry to the Potomac was off Key Bridge. Death was due to asphyxiation due to drowning. There was no sign of struggle. She had had only a sandwich for dinner but had consumed a fair amount of alcohol for her size. She was probably intoxicated when she went over. She died around midnight, give or take thirty minutes. Any comments?" Detective Harrison looked at each of us in turn.

"I don't think she'd have been drinking alone," I said. "She must have gone out with someone. You know where she worked, don't you?" I asked the detective.

He nodded and remained silent.

"Have you asked them who she left with?" I asked.

He nodded again.

"They could tell you better than I," I continued, "but I think Helena said the registers closed at ten-thirty weeknights. She would add up her money and hand it in to the other register worker who always collected it to give to Mr. Hopper or Mr. Roden. She usually left by eleven. Most of their weekday business was lunch." Why didn't the detective say something? "The restaurant owners could tell you more than I could."

"But I'm asking you, lady," the detective said.

I must have blushed. I felt compelled to continue talking. "She might have had a drink at the café, I imagine. She'd never mentioned doing that, but it's possible. Actually, I suppose she might have gone drinking alone. I mean, if no one at the café offered her a ride home. I wonder if she had a crush on someone. She didn't read her relationships with men very clearly. She might have expected some man to ask to take her home, and he might have left without her. I could see her wandering into a bar if that had happened."

"Did she have a boyfriend?" the detective asked. "Someone got her pregnant. Was it someone special?"

Did we look guilty, as if we had colluded not to mention Harry? I thought it more than possible, although we had not discussed him among ourselves. Dr. Harley took over. "She became involved with another of the patients at the clinic here. Because of the confidentiality of his records, we cannot reveal his name to you. They both came to the clinic around the same time and struck up a close friendship. They became lovers and made plans to live together. After Helena started work at the café, she met a number of other men and broke off her relationship with the man here. He was hurt and angry and vented his anger against one of our staff members. Helena's rejection also sent him into a severe withdrawal."

"He emerged from that withdrawal last night," Richard interjected.

"If she was two months pregnant, this patient probably was the father. I doubt that he had been informed of that fact."

"Frank might know," I volunteered.

"That's all right, lady," the detective said. He flipped open a notebook and took a deep yawn. "I talked to the people at the café. There was an incident there last night that involved the owner's son, Harry Hopper. His father said he's a registered patient here. He also said that Helena had been his girlfriend, and Harry had gotten her the job at the café. Harry had gone crazy over Helena's rejection. Mr. Hopper reported that he had met his wife and children here at your clinic Wednesday night for a family therapy session. From seven to eight-thirty, is that correct?"

Dr. Harley said yes.

We were all waiting nervously. The detective continued. "Mr. Hopper reported that the session had moved him very deeply and had brought him closer to his son than they had been in years. Mr. Hopper was headed back to the café afterward and Harry was going home with his mother and sister, as was usual.

However, Harry asked his father if he might go back to the café with him. He was glad to have his son along. But when they got to the café, Harry saw Helena at the cash register and started harassing her. He called her a 'lying whore.' He kept asking her if she had meant anything she'd ever said to him. He accused her of never loving him. He said she'd used him to get the job. Mr. Hopper led him out and drove him back home. He left him at home around nine-thirty."

"My God," I said. "That would have upset her terribly. She already felt hated and despised for what she had done to him. Plus carrying his baby."

"It sounds as if Harry was lucid in his anger last night." Richard observed. "He said what any rejected lover might say. To have her wind up dead the next morning. God."

Our group had sunk into a despondent mood. By that time we were all convinced that a set of tragic circumstances, ill-fated to coincide, had thrown Helena into a despair and confusion that she had ended by jumping off a bridge. I blamed myself bitterly. Richard also seemed to feel responsible.

Dr. Harley broke the silence. He addressed Detective Harrison, who had stood up and was putting his notebook away. "Could you tell us the rest of the information from the café? We have so many questions to answer for ourselves, the more information we have, I think, the more it will help us to deal with this loss."

"Okay, Doc. Nobody that I questioned remembers seeing her leave that night. That was unusual. Usually the deceased would say a lot of good-byes. She was very friendly. There was a waitress there who usually dropped her off. The waitress passes within a block of the deceased's home. She looked for Helena around eleven to offer her a ride, but didn't see her. Since Helena hadn't asked for a ride, she assumed Helena had made other plans, and so she left. Mr. Roden, the co-owner, said he remembered seeing Helena empty her register and give the take to the other girl around ten forty-five but doesn't recall seeing her after that. Other employees had the same impression—that Helena was there until about ten forty-five, but had left by eleven. But no one actually remembers seeing her go out. The weather was nasty. People left as quickly as they could and the place was more cleared out than usual by eleven. Mr. Roden locked up an empty café by eleven-fifteen."

We all looked puzzled. "What about Mr. Hopper?" Joyce asked.

The detective eyed her intently. It was his first show of interest. "He never returned," he said. "He took his son out a little after nine and never came back."

"Where did he go? Did you ask him?" Joyce persisted.

"Mr. Hopper made a statement that he dropped Harry off at home and got back in his car to return to the café, but instead he drove to an old rundown area of the city and sat in his car. He said there used to be a women's hotel on the site, and his wife had lived there when he first met her. He claimed to have driven there automatically; he hadn't planned it out. When he looked down at his watch it was almost one A.M. He had a sense of unreality and thought his watch might be off, so he drove to the café to see if it was still open. He didn't get out of his car. When he didn't see any light through the fog, he assumed it was closed. Also, his car radio announced the time as one in the morning just as he pulled up, so he figured Mr. Roden had closed up. He went home and to bed. Harry was home when he got in around one-twenty. Mr. Hopper said he'd been very fond of Helena. He expressed concern over his son."

"Did he check to see that Harry was in bed?" Joyce asked, and Dr. Harley sent her what looked like a warning look.

"That's an interesting question," the detective commented. "As it happened, he didn't have to. Harry was asleep on the couch in the living room when he got in. He said it reminded him of when Harry was a little boy and would try to wait up for him when he got in late. Mr. Hopper seems like a very emotional man. He cried when he talked about his sleeping son. He said," —the detective started to read from his notebook—"'The need to protect a sleeping child is one of the tenderest feelings a parent can have. I'd forgotten.' Now, would any of you know what he meant by that?"

"He probably meant what he said," Dr. Harley said. "You evidently don't have children."

"Let me ask you another question then. Has Harry ever made any threats or shown any violence against Helena? Is he a violent man?"

"Look," Dr. Harley retorted with a fierce edge to his voice, "you have access to his police record. He was in love with Helena and has undergone considerable stress and grief. He's fragile to begin with, and I do not want him being harrassed. If you have any evidence that he has committed a crime, then charge him with it. If not, I don't want you badgering him or floating rumors about him. Suspicion is a terrible thing and Helena was very popular here. Harry needs treatment more than ever now, and I won't have the atmosphere at the center turned against him. Is that clear?"

The detective looked nonplussed. He shrugged. "Sure, Doc. Here are cards with my number," he said to us as he distributed them, one per person. "Call me if you think of anything important. You never know with a suicide."

As soon as he left, Dr. Harley addressed the three of us. "I know this is a difficult time for all of you. The tendency is for the staff to cluster and comfort each other. There's nothing wrong with that on occasion, but I want us all to keep in focus that our primary responsibility is to the other patients. You must make yourselves more available than usual, not less. Have you spoken to her parents, Sara?"

"Not yet. I guess I'll call them now. I thought I'd offer to come over and pay my respects, if they want to see me. They probably won't."

"That's a good idea," Joyce said. "And I'll make an announcement at the community meeting and see if anyone wants to contribute to send the family flowers or whatever they request."

"Okay," Dr. Harley said. He turned to me. "Find out when the funeral is. As soon as you know announce it in the community meeting and we'll make arrangements for whoever wants to go." Dr. Harley stood up. Since it was his office, we took that as a signal and left.

66

My head was splitting as I dialed Helena's number. Her father answered. I blurted out how sorry I was and how I'd had no idea. I offered to do anything if I could. Dr. Morgan was crying. He couldn't pull himself together enough to talk. We hung up. It was after five when I got off the phone, but Mimi had waited patiently for me. She gave me a sympathetic look but seemed at a loss for what to say.

"It's my worst fear come true, Mimi. I keep thinking I should have known. The worst part is that Helena had something important she wanted to discuss with me yesterday and I let her ramble on about you and Melvin. I could kick myself. She was pregnant, Mimi. Two months. I hope to God her parents don't find out. It would make it a million times worse for them." We were silent for the rest of the ride.

It wasn't until we were entering our building that Mimi spoke. "Do you want me to keep you company for a while?" she asked gently.

"I appreciate the offer, Mimi, but I'll be all right. Thanks."

With a desolation I had never before experienced, I walked into my apartment, crossed to the bedroom, and plopped face-down on the bed. When I finally raised my head to look for some tissues, I noticed that the red light on my telephone answering machine was still blinking. It had been blinking since before Frank had called the previous night. But I hadn't bothered to play it back. Although I had no intention of returning any call right then, I needed a diversion from my tears. I pushed the playback button. My stomach leapt into my throat as I heard Helena's voice. She spoke hurriedly: "Dr. Marks, this is Helena. I know I shouldn't call you at home, but I found out something and I have to talk to you. I need your help. You can reach me at the Caliban till nine. It's 485-0300. Or else make time for me tomorrow, please." That was it.

I didn't know if she had spoken so quickly because she was in a hurry or in order to get it all on the tape after the beep. I must have been in the shower when she called. What had been so important to tell me about? Her pregnancy? Had she had it confirmed? Had she been to a doctor yesterday? If only I'd played back my messages I would have called her immediately. But I'd been tired, careless: I didn't think there was anything that couldn't wait.

I was pacing around, having these thoughts, knowing I'd never be able to forgive myself for ignoring Helena's signal, when I noticed the detective's card and thought I'd better call him with this information. I left a message, and he called me back within fifteen minutes. He took down the information I gave him and was ready to hang up, but I couldn't let him go. "Were Helena's parents informed about her pregnancy?" I asked. "I think it might be better for them not to know, although I know I have no business interfering. It'll help me when I talk to them if I know whether or not they know."

"Okay, lady. Let—"

"Dr. Marks," I interjected.

"Okay, Doc. Here's how we work it. After the autopsy, the body is released to the next of kin. They have the right to request a copy of the coroner's report. I don't think the Morgans have done so. If they don't request it, they don't get it. The coroner's report will show cause of death. Maybe suicide? Maybe accidental death? I don't know."

"You don't suspect Harry, then?" I asked.

"Look, lady. Nobody knows where Harry was. You say he's a goddamned mental case anyway and it looks like it was his baby. So you tell me, Doctor. I'm just trying to do my job."

"What do you mean, 'Nobody knows where Harry was.' Mr. Hopper brought him home at nine-thirty, didn't he? Isn't that what he said?"

"Yeah, that's right. He brought him home. But he left again. Mrs. Hopper was already asleep and the sister was awake when he brought him home, but went to sleep within an hour. So Harry could have been anywhere. He could have gone out again. He slept the night *downstairs*, Doc. Not in his room. No one need have heard him go in or out. Look. I'm just being openminded. Like they tell us in court: You're innocent until proven guilty. Relax. I'll let you know if I need that tape. Don't record over it. Take it out of the machine just in case we need it."

"Okay. Thanks, officer."

I took out the tape, labeled it carefully, and put it in a drawer. Detective Harrison never did ask for it. Helena's death was officially called a suicide and forgotten by the police.

I I

Helena's funeral, held on Saturday, was a somber affair. The Morgans conducted themselves with dignity and were courteous to me. Some of the patients and staff on our team attended, and we all clung together. Harry didn't come. I offered my condolences to the family and again pleaded with them to let me know if there was anything I could do. I couldn't help feeling that they blamed me for Helena's death, although I realized that they mostly blamed themselves. I returned home with a sickening sense of failure.

The following week I heard from the Morgans. They thanked me for the flowers and requested a meeting to talk about Helena. I offered to go to their home, but they insisted on coming to the clinic on Wednesday night. They were scared of what would happen if they began avoiding all the places they'd gone with her. It was an act of will. As I had expected but was powerless to prevent, they blamed themselves for going to San Francisco. I told them about my unanswered phone message, so as to alleviate their guilt. It's hard to say whether it was a helpful meeting or not. It certainly was a sad one. It was also our last.

Frank insisted that I allow him to treat me to a drink afterward. He had an ulterior motive, because he again wanted to talk about Harry. Richard had told him that it would have been better in their last session if he had had Mrs. Hopper comfort her husband and not have Harry comfort him. The kids were caught between the parents, who did not communicate directly. Frank was to concentrate on opening up communication between the parents, and if possible, getting them to comfort each other. The children were to be moved out of that role.

At the session Frank had just finished. Mr. Hopper had looked very sad and drawn. Frank had positioned Mrs. Hopper next to her husband and encouraged her to draw him out. By coaching her on how to question him, he had Mrs. Hopper asking her husband about his feelings. Mr. Hopper responded. The more he responded, the more Mrs. Hopper was able to ask questions and to express herself. By the end of the session, she was asking, "Why have we never talked like this, Larry?" And Harry, sitting on the sidelines, had relaxed.

"What *is* making Mr. Hopper so sad, Frank?" I asked.

"He thinks he's a failure as a husband and father. As a man, I guess. He acknowledged pushing his family out of his life. He said he never wanted to do it, but he had really believed that it was for their sake. He wanted them to know that he loved them and was trying to protect them, not reject them."

"That doesn't make sense. I don't understand."

"Details, details. I don't understand either, but the point is, he told them he loved them. He told his wife he loved her and hadn't meant to exclude her from his life. He said he had done it *for* her, not to get away from her. I guess it's probably like Mr. Roden said. I must have told you. He said that's the way it used to be. Men provided for women and protected them. Those were the social mores at the time. She cried and said that she wished she'd known. She'd always thought he didn't want her around. It was wonderful. Do you want to talk about Helena, Sara? I've been kind of avoiding it. I'm sorry."

"No, that's okay. There's not much to say."

"You can't keep beating yourself. You might get to like it," he suggested with a smile. "I'd have to whip you down in the evenings. It'd get old fast for me."

I told Frank about Helena's phone message.

"I'm as much to blame then as you are. I saw your phone machine lit up and I purposely didn't mention it to you because I was enjoying our talk and didn't want to interrupt it. So stop this self-flagellation."

"Okay. No more. Do you have anything planned for New Year's?"

"Something divine. Nothing I'd want to have bandied about at the clinic."

"My lips are sealed."

"Joey's having an 'always a bridesmaid, never a bride' party. We're all to come in bridal attire. I have a lovely white gown with a lace veil and train. What a hoot. Lots of champagne and we've even got an accordion player coming."

"Jesus Christ, Frank. Jesus. You've got to take pictures. And burn the negatives."

"I expect I'll look radiant. That extra glow. What're you doing?"

"Mike and I are going to go to the Folger Theater and then he's cooking dinner. We'll have a nice time together."

"I'd put that one to better use if I were you, Sara."

I was still feeing glum and lethargic as New Year's Eve rolled around. I was grateful to be spending the evening with Mike: I would have been a basket case had I been left to spend it alone. New Year's Eve was a Thursday night and the clinic was closed Friday. The prospect of a three-day weekend also filled my heart with gratitude. I had arranged one other event to look forward to: Mimi was due over for dinner Saturday night and we'd agreed to share a bottle of champagne and make at least ten resolutions each. She was to have Melvin's kids for Friday and Saturday nights, but he agreed to take them out for dinner by himself on Saturday night. Mimi and I would have some time together, which we hadn't had for several weeks. One of my resolutions, which I was determined to fulfill, would be to stop feeling sorry for myself. I'd been dwelling on the fact that I had no husband to come home to or children to take care of. I didn't have the fullness of a family to keep Helena's death from being so important to me. My life seemed unbalanced and empty.

Mike picked me up at seven and we drove to the Folger. We saw A Midsummer Night's Dream, which I could tell was beautifully staged, but I never got involved in it. Afterward, we drove to Mike's apartment. Dinner was already prepared and it just had to be heated up. I took off my boots and curled up on the couch with some wine while Mike put dinner in the oven. He was chatting away about the play and I kept up a show of interest. Then we switched to the clinic. Mike tried to make the conversation upbeat by talking about the videotape equipment due in Monday.

"Richard suggested that you and Frank join us during my supervision time to run through how to use the equipment since we'll all be using it. The man can't seem to see enough of you, Sara. He's pulling you in on my time. I told him I didn't think a woman could learn to work the videotape, but if he just had to see you, I didn't mind."

"Cute, Sweeney. I'll have to think of which family I want to tape. I'd been planning on using Helena's family."

"I know, Sara. Listen, do you want to talk about it? I don't want to intrude if you don't want to. But if you want to talk, it's okay."

"You're sweet to me, Mike. Thanks. I think it's just one of those things that will always be with me. It's hard to accept that she's dead. She was so young and I liked her so much. But what gives me the creeps is that I had no idea. Maybe it could happen with any one of my patients and I wouldn't know how to read the signals."

"But Sara, sometimes the signals aren't clear. Not every suicide is a textbook case. She really didn't sound like the type. She was anything but isolated. It's not impossible that she was pushed. Let's face it. The bridge was fogged in, there wasn't much traffic, and she weighed next to nothing. She was full of alcohol. She would have gone down in no time. We can just hope she didn't know what hit her. Anyone could have thrown her over. There's a lot of crime in Washington. If she was out alone at that time of night, she was asking for trouble. I hate to say this because it's so gruesome, but it could even have been some kids doing it just for the kick. The fact that there was no motive doesn't make it suicide."

"I know. Even Richard missed any sign that this was coming. We'll never know."

We had a leisurely meal and lots of wine. For the first time since Helena's death, I enjoyed myself. We came back to the topic of Helena several times, but when we left it in conversation, I genuinely also left it. We had just finished our dessert and begun wrestling over the almost empty ice cream carton, which was an old routine we went through at every meal, when midnight struck. We poured the champagne, clinked our glasses, and toasted the New Year.

I insisted on doing the dishes, since I'd done nothing else, but Mike kept me company and lent a hand so it went quickly. Neither of us were late-night types, and we were both suppressing yawns. We were also both more than a little tipsy. I could tell that Mike didn't want to go back in the cold to drive me home, while leaving the sanctuary of his warm apartment for my cold, sterile, lonely home was the last thing I wanted as well. It was, however, awkward.

Finally, I spoke: "Not to be too forward, although Lord only knows what you've been exposed to, but can I stay here tonight? On your fold-out sofa in the living room," I added very quickly.

"Thought you'd never ask. That would be a lot simpler. Let me make up the sofa. Are you ready to go to bed now?" That sounded very strange.

"Yes," I giggled. "This feels like a sleep-over date, like when you're a kid. Do you have a bathrobe or pajamas or something?"

"I have just the thing." Mike returned with a pair of cotton pajamas and a terrycloth robe. "Why don't you use the bathroom while I make up the bed? Then I'll tuck you in before I get ready."

"Can I pick out a book for a story? You do make me feel secure and cozy. I have to tell you, Mike, this is better than I've felt in a long time." I trooped into the bathroom.

"The infamous beige sheets," I said as I returned to the living room and saw the made-up couch.

Mike laughed. We were both a little nervous. "Hop in, Sara." I nestled down under the covers. Mike sat down at the side of the bed. He leaned over to kiss me goodnight. On the lips. A taboo was broken. I reached up and stroked his face with my hand. "If you don't say something, I'm going to lie down with you, Sara." He kissed me again. "This could be your last chance."

"You don't make it easy. Mike, you're one of my closest

friends. You know I haven't had any sex life at all since coming to Washington. None," I said, starting to giggle.

"You didn't even score with Sidney?" Mike asked, starting to laugh.

"Hardly," I blurted out, my laughter getting the better of me.

"Get a grip on yourself," Mike said.

"Okay. Okay," I said, as I took several deep breaths and was able to resume speaking. "How can you do this to me? I'm totally drunk, totally horny, and you're totally appealing."

"I'm not exactly sober or satiated myself."

"I know. Here's the thing. You know I wouldn't be able to let you go. You know that. I'd want to spend every night with you. I've been having irrepressible thoughts about marriage and children. It would be awful, Mike. You'd withdraw and I'd become a bag lady roaming the streets in search of you. Really. I know deep down inside that we'd both regret it. Unfortunately, you'd probably regret it first."

"You're right. You're right. I'll retire like a gentleman."

"Do you want to just lie down and cuddle?"

"In some ways, Sara, you don't know me very well. Reveille's at six-thirty. See you then." He gave me another kiss and left.

I didn't wake up Friday morning until about ten A.M., and when I did, it was with a feeling of wellbeing that I'd forgotten existed. The rich aroma of coffee filled the room. Mike was unloading the dishwasher in the kitchen which was connected to the living room, my sleeping quarters. He was dressed and ready for the day.

"I'm awake," I announced. "Cream, no sugar, and leave the paper on the side of the tray. Just kidding."

"I'm going to run out to the gourmet shop. Be back in fifteen minutes." Mike was gone. Maybe he was a little uneasy with me, too. It gave me a chance to get dressed in privacy, and by the time he returned I'd stripped and folded up the couch and it looked like a living room again.

He'd brought back fresh croissants filled with chocolate, and his coffee was delicious. We ate in silence. I suggested the paper and he quickly brought it to the table. He took the sports section

74

and I took "Style," and finally I broke the silence. "There's a double feature of old Sherlock Holmes movies at the Inner Circle. *Hound of the Baskervilles* and *Spider Woman*. With Basil Rathbone and Nigel Bruce. Let's go, Mike. I'll treat. We're still friends, aren't we?"

"Sounds good. Okay. Of course we're still friends. I just realize I have my work cut out for me. Now I won't just worry about whether you're able to score or not when you go out, I have to worry about whether the men are good marriage material. Do you really want to get married and settle down?"

"Yeah," I confessed. That was all I could think of to say about that. "Not to change the subject, but since I'm still single and since we're still friends, and since you've assumed responsibility for my life, I don't want you to forget that my birthday's next week."

"Don't hold back, Sara."

"You know how awful you'd feel if you forgot it."

"As a matter of fact, I didn't forget it and I was planning on taking you out for dinner to celebrate it. It's the Friday after next. You pick the restaurant."

"Thanks, Mike. I'll let you know where I decide. You know I appreciate being nursed like this."

12

Saturday, with some energy finally at my disposal, I set about reclaiming my apartment. I dusted, I polished, I vacuumed. I even washed the bathroom. Cleaned and revived by a shower, I set out for the grocery store and stocked up for the rest of the winter. I would not let my apartment ever become so barren again. What was left of the afternoon, I spent preparing dinner for Mimi and me. My cooking was mediocre, but I was giving it my best shot.

It seemed like months since Mimi and I had had a chance to

sit down together and talk. Her rapid pop-ins were litle more than bitch session about the "monsters." I needed the comfort and lack of ambiguity of time spent with a female friend.

"How are you doing?" Mimi asked as she came in. "You look good. Better than when I last saw you."

"I feel like I just started to heal last night. Mike nursed me through New Year's. He certainly is nice to have around."

"You're not joining his fan club?" Mimi asked, somewhat warily, I thought.

"I'm tempted. But I know him too well. It would be a disaster and our friendship's too good to ruin."

"What's the story with Mike? Why can't he get involved with anyone?"

"I don't really know. At some level he must be scared of women or scared of commitment. He did have several years in a seminary before the strain of celibacy caused him to bolt. Maybe the philosophy of nonexclusive friendship stuck with him." I shrugged. "Tell me how you're doing, Mimi. What've you been up to?"

"I got Melvin into a museum today! Ta-dah! No small accomplishment. I mean as soon as the door closed behind us his knees sagged and he started to shuffle. I plastered myself between him and the exit, hoping he'd buck up when he realized everything there was beautiful and Oriental. I took him to the Freer. His criteria for a work of art is, 'Is it pleasing to look at?' Well, everything in the Freer is exquisite."

"Good choice," I said. Mimi and I had also spent an afternoon in the Freer. "It's such a restful, calm place. I hope he enjoyed it."

"I think he did. Not that he'd come out and say so. But we had a nice afternoon."

"I'm glad. I've got to go back there again sometime soon. I don't know what I do with my time."

"Who does? Did I tell you? My mother's condo's all set in Florida. That's a load off my mind. Although she hasn't gotten off her ass to do anything about packing or selling her furniture. It gives me indigestion just to think about it."

"It might be my cooking."

"It might be," Mimi said, eyeing her food suspiciously. We both laughed. "No, it tastes fine. Anyway, Melvin and I will go up in February and then this whole mess will be over."

"I noticed that Melvin's not wearing a wedding ring anymore. Progress, progress."

"Yeah," Mimi said, her voice suddenly drained of animation. "I suppose it's progress. But he never talks to me about marriage. I know he's not divorced yet, but still, it's not as if he's not getting a divorce. I don't know."

"What, Mimi?"

"Well, I want children of my own and I don't have too much more time if I'm going to have them. It's not even the time thing. There's enough time if he wants to have children with me. But I don't think he does. I don't think he wants any more kids. We haven't really talked about it. He has a way of evading the issue when I try to bring it up. It's discouraging. His two keep us so busy. We had a big fight over them; things really came to a head. I told him I would never again have them in my apartment if he didn't back me up when I tried to discipline them. I told him he didn't have to agree with me, but he'd damn well better back me up anyway and we could argue about it later. I really put my foot down."

"Good for you!" I cheered.

"I was getting desperate. He was continually undercutting me. I really let him have it, Sara. I didn't know I had it in me."

"How did he react?"

"At first, total denial. 'They're good kids. They've had a rough time. You're too sensitive. I told you it wouldn't be easy to be involved with me.' On and on. I don't think anything I said made a difference. What made a difference was that I told him not to bring them over. If he couldn't make them obey my rules, they were unwelcome in my apartment. I meant it, too. It took an out-and-out threat. Things have been a little better since then. I feel like he's trying and the girls are a little more respectful."

"Good for you, Mimi. That took guts. I think I'd be scared to really challenge someone like Melvin."

"What sort of person would someone like Melvin be?"

"Mimi"—her tone had been caustic—"you know what I mean. He's pretty tough. You know. You've said so a million times. That's one of the things you always loved about him. He's strongwilled. He doesn't cave in easily. He knows how he likes to have things done. I would have trouble standing up to someone like that. I meant it as a compliment to you."

"Sorry. I'm a little touchy. It was scary for me to do. I wouldn't have done it if I hadn't been desperate. I literally felt like I could not stand it another day the way it was. I figured if something didn't give, I'd murder both those children of his and then I'd have to kill myself. So I risked it, figuring if he left me, I'd only have to kill myself. That seemed the easier solution. It worked out better than I'd thought."

"Mimi, I had no idea things were so bad. Why didn't you come up to talk to me? Not that I could have done anything, but I could have sympathized."

"You've been pretty wrapped up in your own problems, Sara. I didn't want to trouble you with all this."

"I guess that's true. I'm on the road to recovery now, though, so please come and talk when you need to. Really."

"Things have improved so I shouldn't complain. I'm hanging on till February. After we help Mother move, we're going to try to tack on a week's skiing. That's what I'm living for now. All I want to think about is getting over moguls and avoiding trees. Or maybe I should graze a tree and get myself laid up with a minor yet incapacitating-for-housework injury. Let Melvin wait on me for a week or two."

"We can't let our dependency needs keep us from coping with the everyday realities of life," I said, imitating Melvin in a community meeting. I continued, "If it takes you twice as long and is twice as hard, it's still worth it not to give in to that dependency pull." In my own voice I continued: "I wouldn't do it, Mimi. You'll just have to get up at five A.M. and hobble about on one foot." I laughed. Mimi didn't.

13

I thought about Mimi on and off all day Sunday with a sense of disquiet. My parents called and gave an exhilarated account of Rebecca's eating, sleeping, and diapering schedule. I reported only that I was healthy and my job was going great. I had not told them about Helena. For once in my life, I would get through a rough time without upsetting them.

Mimi and I drove in together Monday morning and talked about the new videotape equipment. Monday afternoon, Frank and I butted in on Mike's supervision time and ran through the videotape procedures. The machine took cassettes and was easy to use. Richard went through his checklist with us and we all passed. Frank claimed the equipment for Wednesday nights and I agreed to help him set up the coming Wednesday. He'd already announced to the Hoppers that he'd be using it and explained that his supervisor would be reviewing the tapes with him, and that the team staff would also have access to the tapes since they all worked with Harry in one or more groups. The Hoppers had voiced no objections. Mike and I planned to schedule the equipment for other families we were seeing at other times. I asked Frank if I could sit in with Richard and him at his next supervision on Friday and see his taped session. I was pretty sure I could clear my schedule. They seemed pleased to have me.

Frank's voice sounded smoother and more resonant than I'd ever heard it as we set up the videotape equipment on Wednesday night. I realized it was stage fright. I was nervous for him. We went to his interview room early to set up, and Frank arranged to be sitting with his best side to the camera as the Hoppers and Mr. Roden came in. I waited only to be sure everyone was on the camera. They all nodded to me and I smiled a greeting and left. I couldn't wait to see the results, especially since I'd heard so much about the family.

Friday morning, Frank, Richard, and I assembled, full of anticipation. Frank had told me nothing of the session, saying he wanted me to see it for myself without his biases imposed. Richard pushed the playback button, and we all sat forward.

The first sight that met our eyes was Frank, holding the microphone like a Vegas crooner, down on one knee, singing the closing lines of "I Gotta Be Me." He stood up, made a hold-the-applause type gesture, swung the mike cord behind him with a theatrical flourish, and asked, "What golden oldie can I sing for the little lady in back?" When no request was forthcoming, he started on "Old Man River."

The first line was interrupted by my voice, a note of urgency clearly present: "Frank, for God's sake, they'll be here any minute. Get a grip." Frank straightened up, and almost immediately the Hoppers and Mr. Roden filed in.

Mr. Roden was the first to speak. "Hi, how are you doing?" The camera caught his eyes widen in surprise at the equipment. "Are we being broadcast on the seven o'clock news?"

Frank was quick to explain. "I'm sorry, Mr. Roden. I cleared it with the Hoppers, but they must have forgotten to mention it to you. Now that we have videotape equipment, I'll be using it routinely. The Hoppers signed a permission form stating that it will not be used outside of this clinic. The tapes will be used to help me in supervision of the work I'm doing here. They'll be taped over every week or so. They won't be on file or anything like that."

Mr. Roden waved a disclaiming hand. "Quite all right."

Mr. and Mrs. Hopper seated themselves next to each other, and the kids flanked Mr. Roden on either side. (Richard was pleased at their seating arrangements.) Harry's body posture was normal, and he looked sad, not crazed. "It's nice to have you back, Mr. Roden," Frank said. "A lot has happened since our last meeting with you here."

"Yes," responded Mr. Roden. His expression was grave. "Terrible about poor Helena. What a charming child. A real tragedy." He gave Harry's arm a squeeze. "A terrible loss for you." Harry looked down. The family group took on a somber air.

"No one ever told me what happened," Judy complained. "I never know anything that goes on." ("Good," Richard said. "She's starting to speak up.") "Why doesn't anyone tell me what's going on?"

"The young girl that Harry was so fond of died, Judy. We thought you knew." Mr. Hopper responded.

Judy rolled her eyes. "I know that, Daddy. But what happened?"

Nobody answered. Frank let the silence stand for about a minute, then spoke: "We never really have discussed Helena's death in here. Judy's curiosity is very understandable and I think it would be useful to talk about what happened. Especially for Harry. His feelings for Helena are so intense and so confused."

Richard stopped the tape. "Why did you focus it on Harry?" he asked.

Frank replied, "The family organizes around doing for Harry. I thought it would get them started."

"I don't think you need it," Richard countered. "And you want to break that organization. Let's go on." He pushed Play.

Mr. Hopper looked around helplessly. Mr. Roden began, "Judy, no one really knows what happened, so it's hard to explain. She came to work at the restaurant Wednesday night and left around eleven, although I don't think an one actually remembered seeing her leave. Her body was found the next morning. She seems to have jumped off a bridge. She had a lot on her mind."

"You mean she killed herself. Why, Uncle Maury?"

Frank stopped the tape. "I didn't know whether to say anything about her pregnancy or not. Harry's never mentioned it. I don't think he knows. I didn't know what to do. I hate to keep it from him, but it might be awful for him to know. Anyway, I didn't say anything. What do you think?"

We discussed the pros and cons. We all felt that Harry would feel more guilty if he knew his unborn child had died, although we couldn't account for why we thought he'd feel guilty, and not just sad. But it was Frank's decision, and he decided that telling him would serve no constructive purpose.

Frank turned the tape back on. "This part," he said, "was very tense. No one's ever talked about Harry's outburst or the thing with Dr. Harley's car. Mrs. Hopper just opened it right up. I think she felt like Judy. She's left out of things."

Mrs. Hopper looked straight at her husband and said, "What happened with Harry that night? He went to the café with you and then you said you had to bring him home almost immediately. He was asleep in the living room in the morning with mud tracked all over the carpet. What went on?"

We all sat forward in our chairs. *Mud.* On the screen Mr. Hopper looked tired. "Harry made a scene," he said. "He yelled at Helena about betraying him and not loving him. I thought I'd better take him home. It was about nine-thirty when I dropped him back home. You were already in bed. When I came in later he was asleep on the sofa like when he was a little boy and used to try to wait up for me. Remember, Lizzie?" She nodded, tears starting to form.

"Where was all the mud from?" she asked in a whisper.

"He went out again," Judy volunteered. "I heard him go back out."

Frank spoke up: "You know, you talk as if Harry wasn't present in the room right now. Why don't you ask him what happened that night?"

I held my breath.

Mrs. Hopper leveled her eyes at Harry. "What happened, son?"

"Wait," Mr. Hopper said. "Is everything we say here confidential? I want your word on it."

Frank looked nervous. "It is confidential," he said, "within the clinic. The tapes are open to the team staff, all of whom work with Harry. And, of course, the director of the clinic has access to them and my supervisor, Dr. Meyer, reviews them with me. That's really the reason for taping, so Dr. Meyer can help me in my work. But everything said here is confidential in that we'd never tell anyone outside of the clinic unless someone was judged to be a danger to himself or others. Then we would warn the police and anyone in danger if a threat was made. Or we'd break confidentiality to protect a person who was suicidal." Frank was looking increasingly uncomfortable. "We don't have to tape this, you know," he said, including all the family members in his glance. "I can shut off the machine. And as long as no one makes a direct threat against anybody or says they're going to kill themselves, I will be more than willing to keep whatever is said confidential, just between you and me." Frank started to walk toward the camera to turn the equipment off.

"No," Mrs. Hopper said. "You can leave it on." No one contradicted her. She looked directly at her son. "Harry, I'm asking you to answer that question, confidential or not. We must know what happened. If you've done something you couldn't control, we must see that it doesn't happen again. It's better to know the truth," she said to her husband.

Harry held his hands palms up. "I don't know," he said. "I remember seeing Helena in the Caliban and I felt like nothing was right. All I know is I wanted to touch her. I remember Dad leading me out. That's all I remember, honest. I'm not trying to hide anything. I don't remember that day with the car, either," he said turning to Frank.

"What's this about a car?" demanded Mrs. Hopper.

Frank explained about the incident with Mimi's mug. The family looked shocked but remained silent.

"Look," Mr. Hopper said. "Harry was sound asleep when I got in Wednesday night. Sound asleep. I swear to you, Lizzie. You make it sound like you thought he'd done something. What's gotten into you?"

"When did you come in, Larry?" she asked.

"What do you mean, when did I come in? I guess it was around one-thirty. I lost track of the time. I drove to your old neighborhood. The ladies-only hotel. It's not there anymore. I lost track of the time."

I felt a chill pass through my body. Harry and his father had been out in the fog that night.

"What made you go there?" Mrs. Hopper asked her husband.

83

"I got to remembering how things were when I first met you. Our meeting last week brought it all back. It was almost like a dream. I found myself there. It's all changed. Adult bookstores, that kind of crap. But I could see the hotel in my mind's eye and you, Lizzie, with your hair long and parted on the side. Remember?"

Mrs. Hopper nodded. "Seems like another world." There was a long silence. "I've been thinking," Mrs. Hopper continued. "Larry, Maury, if it's okay with you two, maybe I could come back to work at the café?"

"Good," Richard said. "She brought it up herself. That's great." Richard turned to me, "Frank and I have been working toward getting her reinvolved outside of the house."

Maury responded, "What did you have in mind?"

"Look!" I exclaimed. "Look at Mr. Hopper's expression." Richard stopped the action, and we stared at the screen. Mr. Hopper had what we all interpreted as a look of frozen panic on his face. "What's that about?" I asked.

"I don't know," was Frank's reply. "I didn't notice it at the time. I wasn't even looking at him. I'm totally confused."

Richard switched the action back on. "I thought maybe I could act as a hostess," Mrs. Hopper continued. "You know. Circulate, make sure everyone is taken care of. Cover the register or clear a table if we're shorthanded. Make myself useful. I'd kind of like to get back in the swing. Try to understand the business. See how to deal with wholesalers and waiters. Really learn about the business. Maybe I could do a little baking now and again. What do you think?"

Mr. Roden turned to Mr. Hopper. "What do you say, Larry? She's your wife. I know how wonderful Lizzie is in your home. Everything always fresh and clean. Excellent meals. You're the one with the most to lose if she comes back to work."

"Let's discuss it a little more," said Mr. Hopper.

"Discuss it in what way?" Frank asked.

"Talk things out," Mr. Hopper said. "In more depth. What do you think, Maury?"

"I think," Mr. Roden replied, "that if I had Lizzie for me at home in my house, I'd probably want to keep her there. I'm a selfish man. But I don't, so I've no objection to her coming to the café. I particularly like the idea of her doing some baking. She might even want to work up some desserts at home and bring them in. How would that suit you, Lizzie?"

"I wouldn't mind doing that once in a while. But I really want to get out of the house. I do enough baking at home as it is. I want out. I want to meet people and find out how things work. How is the business run? I used to have a good mind for that sort of thing. I want to know if I still do. I need to learn something new." Mrs. Hopper turned to her husband. "Is that enough discussion for you?"

"It's a big decision, Lizzie. I guess I don't see why not." He didn't sound convinced.

"What are you concerned about?" Frank asked Mr. Hopper.

"It's not that I"m concerned about anything," Mr. Hopper asserted in a testy voice. "It's a big change. We need to talk about it. The restaurant's a lot different than it was when she and I did it together. She'd have a lot of adjusting to do."

"Don't you want me there? Tell me the truth, Larry. If you don't want me, just say so. There are other jobs. There are other men, too. Just for once in your life tell me where I stand."

"Look. Look at Harry. He's gone all rigid," I pointed out.

"Of course I want you," Mr. Hopper responded. "That's the truth. If Maury thinks it's okay, then I've no objection."

"Look, Larry," Mrs. Hopper continued. "We are joint owners of the restaurant. I have the same decision-making authority as you do. I have as much authority as Maury does. I haven't used it, but I could. I want to come back. There's no way you can buy me out without my consent. I want to come back. I'm too old to start in a new business. And I'm part owner of this one anyway. And I know you and Maury. I don't want to start over from scratch." Mrs. Hopper began to cry. "What's so terrible about that? Why don't you want me? I won't change everything around. I won't interfere. I just want to get out of the goddamned house each day and have something useful to do. How can you deny me that? I could tell you to stay home. I have as much authority."

"Lizzie, I don't want to hurt you. Can't you understand? Come back. If it's okay with Maury, it's okay with me."

Frank broke in. "I guess it's up to you, Mr. Roden. What do you say?"

Mr. Roden smiled. "I say that if there's one thing I've learned after all these years, it's that Lizzie Hopper is one determined lady. When she makes up her mind, look out! I would no more ask a waterfall to travel upstream than I would object to Lizzie's coming back. And," he added graciously, "I would be delighted to have her. I think she'd bring a personal touch to the restaurant that would be very enticing to our patrons. And her baking is unsurpassed."

"Thank you," Mrs. Hopper said to Mr. Roden, but she turned abruptly back to her husband. "Look, Larry. Maury has nothing to do with whether you want me working with you every day or not. What are you scared of?"

Mr. Hopper shrugged. "Lizzie, how many times do I have to say it, yes, come back to work."

"Why do you think he might not want you back?" Frank asked Mrs. Hopper. "You seem to think he doesn't want you there."

"Ask the children. They can tell you."

"Can *you* tell me?" Frank persisted, still addressing Mrs. Hopper.

She stopped and thought. "I think Larry might think I'm a little too fussy. I like things done just so. I think that there's a right way to do things. He's worried that I'll interfere and want things done differently. I guess I can be strongwilled. Maybe *stubborn's* a better word."

"Is that worrying you?" Frank asked Mr. Hopper.

"Nothing's worrying me. I want her back at the restaurant."

"What do you think, Harry? Judy?" Frank asked.

"She can be fussy," Judy said. "She sort of has to know about everything all the time. It's out of love. But she has to know everything that's going on. She likes things to be done a certain way and she always has to know why you're doing them another way and sometimes there's no reason. It's just the way that you do things. Maybe Daddy thinks she'll try to boss him around. Daddy likes to do things quietly without telling anyone. He doesn't like people to know what he does."

"Are you like that, Mr. Hopper? Are you a private person?" Frank asked.

"I suppose you could say so. I like my office to be my office. I don't like anyone coming in and cleaning up my desk for me or straightening up my belongings. I like them to be just where I leave them. I always lock my office at work when I'm not in it. Maury leaves his open. The waiters are in and out using his bathroom, shower, sitting at his desk. I can't function like that. I'm not trying to hide anything from you, Lizzie. I just need privacy. Like Mr. Thomas put it."

"So I was right," Mrs. Hopper pounced. "You think I'll rummage in your drawers and interfere. I recognize that you and Maury have your ways of working, and they've been very successful." Her tone softened. "I want to learn about them, not change them."

"Give a little, Larry." Maury said. "Mr. Thomas will be here to help you keep her in line if she starts snooping around." He gave Mrs. Hopper a wink.

"I've been saying that I have no objection for the past forty-five minutes. Enough. Subject is closed. You can come in with me tomorrow in the morning, Lizzie."

"I don't want to come if you don't really want me there."

"He's given you an invitation, Mrs. Hopper," Frank interrupted. "Why don't you take it and see how things work out. It is a big change. You're both probably a little uneasy about it. Don't make him say he has no reservations, when he does. But he's more than willing to give it a try. Okay?" Frank turned his most appealing, seductive look on Mrs. Hopper and smiled at her.

She softened. "Okay."

"What would you like to do tomorrow?" Maury asked.

"Let me wait until Friday. I've got the dishwasher repairman coming tomorrow and the Salvation Army's picking up a load of stuff. I just want to meet the cooks and waiters and busboys. Get to know everyone. And I'd like to go round to the wholesalers. I'd like to see how the accounts are kept. Learn the business."

"Well," Maury spoke thoughtfully. "Let's see. We do a lot of our ordering by phone. The deliveries come by truck."

"You mean," Judy asked, "Daddy will call the liquor store and say, 'We need thirty bottles of red wine and thirty bottles of white wine this week,' and they'll send them over?"

"That's right, Judy," her father asnwered. Frank's intervention on his behalf seemed to have relaxed him. "Except Maury is very particular about his wines and spirits. That's the one order he makes in person." Maury laughed.

"Mr. Hopper's teasing him, Frank," I said. "You said the Hoppers had no sense of humor. That was a glimmering."

"I swear to God, Sara. That's the first even mildly funny thing I've ever heard him say."

"Quiet," Richard said.

"Could I accompany you, Maury? Just once to see what it's like?"

"Of course. I go every Wednesday. I usually have lunch out, but I'm always at Herb's right at two-thirty. We look over the stock, maybe try a new wine that's in, chew the fat. Herb and I go back a long way. We're done with our business by three-thirty, four. I'm back at the café by four-thirty at the latest. It's a light afternoon for me. I enjoy it. I've already made lunch plans for next Wednesday or I'd take you out, but I can pick you up at the café at two and we'll drive out together. Sound good?"

"Thanks, Maury. That's just the sort of thing I'd like to do. Get out and meet the people. I would like to be home when Judy gets back from school, though. Is there any way to do it a little earlier? No. I shouldn't ask that, I don't want to interfere. That'll be just fine. I can make arrangements for Judy. Can you drop me back home afterward?"

"Certainly, Lizzie."

"Why not take a cab home?" Frank suggested. "Then if you feel uncomfortable about the time, you can leave. It would give you both more freedom of movement. These are some of the things you'll have to start working on when you go back."

"I can go over to Lorraine's house, Mom," Judy pleaded. "You don't have to make arrangements for me. Please."

"Sounds like a reasonable request," Frank interjected. "Do you know her friend Lorraine?"

"Yes," both parents replied.

"Okay," Mrs. Hopper said. "Make your plans with Lorraine but be home for dinner. Get home by five. I don't want you out after dark."

"Let's stop the tape now unless something of note happens later on," Richard remarked, turning to Frank.

"No," Frank said. "There's more of the same. Mrs. Hopper was very concerned about being home each day at three-thirty for Judy, who was not too pleased about it. Except for Wednesday, she was determined to be home so she could supervise Judy. Harry never said much, but he looked pretty good. Not crazy or tight. Judy told her mother a couple times that she was fourteen and didn't need constant supervision. I let that issue go for now. I thought if mother could get interested in the café and out of the house more, that would be the first step. I didn't want to throw too many things in at once. After mother's got more going for her, we can negotiate age-appropriate rules and privileges for the kids."

"I agree." Richard said. "Very good, Frank. I thought your interventions around mother's interference at the café were well done and that's a big enough issue for now. Did you ever get back to the issue of Harry and Helena? That seemed conspicuously avoided after it became apparent that he and father went back out that night. Was there any more on it?"

"No. We were all too nervous, I think. In fact, until I saw the tape again, I'd pretty much forgotten it. It's creepy. It didn't start raining or sleeting until pretty late that night. Where could he have gone? I didn't know how to bring it up or what to say. I was torn because I kept thinking throughout the session that it would be a good time to suggest not bringing the kids next week. You know, Richard, like we talked about. Having just the parents come in and drawing clear boundary lines between the generations. I thought it would be good to do that and include Mr. Roden this once, and the main issue would be easing Mrs. Hopper back into the café. But I never suggested it because I felt uneasy about having them leave Harry home alone. No adults present. They'll all be back next week. Mr. Roden, too, although I think we can stop including him in the future. But I thought since Mrs. Hopper will have just finished her first week at the café, and they're all partners, it would be good to have him one more time. He's so much more supportive of her being there than her husband is. That's kind of weird, too."

"I know," I said. "It's like Mr. Hopper cares for her, but he doesn't want her around too much. She is pretty intrusive, so in a way it's understandable. She seemed very controlling to me." Frank and Richard agreed. "And Mr. Hopper's not exactly the easygoing type like Maury."

Richard spoke. "I agree with you, Frank, that Mr. Roden doesn't need to be included indefinitely. If this café thing goes smoothly, or relatively smoothly, I would have him stop coming. He's been very generous with his time. But you know, I asked you and Sara about this business with Harry and Helena, and you both got off the subject. Is it too horrible to even think about?"

"It *is* horrible," I said. "It gives me the chills to say, but what if he followed her or met her after she left? He could have thrown her over. He could have. It sounds so melodramatic, I'm embarrassed to say it. He could have killed her. It's not as if things like that don't happen. It's just you can't believe it of someone you know. Helena is dead and it's pretty strange. I feel like we should do something to protect the public, but it's not like there's anything to do."

"There's nothing you can do," Richard said. "Her death has been ruled a suicide and there's no proof otherwise. He's made no threats. If Harry was in some way involved with Helena's death . . . God, it is a chilling thought, but it's not as if he hates all women. He hasn't threatened anyone. Although, if it was something he did in a rage, there is one person who might be in danger."

I nodded, goosebumps forming on my arms and legs. "Mimi," I said.

I did not drive home with Mimi that Friday afternoon because she and Melvin had plans and she left with him. I flew to New York that evening to attend the wedding of my closest college friend and did not get back to Washington until Sunday night. Monday morning was my first chance to talk with Mimi about my concern for her safety. I was uneasy about broaching the subject, but I opened it up by asking how Harry'd been treating her at the clinic.

"Fine," Mimii responded. "Why do you ask?"

"I just wanted to make sure. Harry was out, his time unaccounted for the night Helena died. It gives me the creeps. I wanted to make sure he was no longer angry with you. I know how silly it sounds. I was just nervous, that's all."

"You think he murdered her and now he's out to murder me. Well, he hasn't spoken to me one way or the other. Contrary to Richard's theory that Harry hates me, he hasn't been at all hostile since Helena died."

"I just thought if Harry *was* acting weird with you, you ought to be careful and we ought to see that he has more supervision."

"I thought Melvin talked to you about spreading rumors and arousing suspicion. Is Richard subverting him again, or is it you?"

"Mimi, please. I'm sorry. I was only trying to err on the safe side. Please forget it. I wasn't trying to upset you or start rumors."

"All right, Sara. Your intentions were good. I'm under a lot of pressure, and I don't need someone coming to me and telling me I'm in constant danger of being murdered. I've got enough to worry about. The police did rule her death a suicide."

"Mimi, I won't mention it again."

"I didn't mean to jump on you." Mimi gave me a smile. "So," she asked, her smile deepening, "did you catch the bouquet?"

"No," I answered and then confessed, "I was lined up for a second piece of cake when she threw it."

14

Wednesday night, I again helped Frank set up the video equipment and then nervously withdrew into my office to await a new family I'd be seeing in Helena's time slot. The opening session went extremely well. Frank and I had arranged to meet afterward for a drink, and he was loitering outside of my office when I emerged. We started down the corridor to the rear exit for the back lot, when suddenly we heard a loud noise and a piercing scream. We ran to the front of the building and out into the street, where I could not believe what my eyes took in. Mrs. Hopper was lying on the sidewalk with blood streaming from her chest. Dr. Harley, who was kneeling over her, announced to the onlookers assembling that she was dead. Richard came running out and said that the police and an ambulance were on the way. Mr. Hopper bent down over his wife's body and wept. Mr. Roden stood near by with one arm draped over Harry, the other over Judy. He faced them both into his massive chest. Frank walked over to join them. He stood by, awkwardly, helplessly.

"Christ almighty, Sara. What happened?" asked a familiar voice.

"Mike? What are you doing here? Mrs. Hopper's been shot. I don't know any details."

"I'm meeting Marcy," Mike said. "Jesus, Mrs. Hopper."

I scanned the growing crowd and spotted Marcy. She came over. "I saw the whole thing," she said. "The man leaning over her was walking with Harry and the girl."

"That's Harry's father," I said. "His mother's the one who's been shot."

"Oh. I didn't know who she was," Marcy continued. "Poor

Harry. His mother was walking with that large man over there." She indicated Mr. Roden.

"He's a family friend," I interjected. "What happened?"

"They were heading across the street. I guess they'd parked on the street. Some man ran up and grabbed her purse. The big guy yelled out, 'You son of a bitch,' and started after him. The robber drew a gun and shot back behind him. He hit her and the big man ran back to the woman, Harry's mother. The robber disappeared. I didn't see his face. He had a ski hat and scarf up over his nose. Maybe it was a ski mask. I couldn't see. She probably had five dollars in her purse or something. It's terrible, really terrible."

"I saw that guy," Mike said. "I'll bet it was the same guy. Did he have a beige jacket on?"

"Yes," Marcy replied. "And jeans."

"I did see him. He overtook me and passed me on the way over. Tall, athletic walk. I remember thinking as he passed that I'd have to start running again. He moved gracefully. Do you think we ought to talk to the police?"

"I think so," Marcy said. "What is happening around here? First Helena, now Mrs. Hopper. I can't believe it. I'm going to tell the policeman I witnessed the shooting. Come with me?"

We followed. The policeman asked Mike and Marcy to wait, and I waited with them. The whole staff seemed to be lingering around. Frank loyally remained with the family, although he had a bewildered, helpless look. He must have felt he should stay with them, but he had no idea what do to or how to act. Still, I admired his behavior. Richard came up to me. He stood shaking his head from side to side. "Did you see it happen?" Mike asked him.

"No, not really. I was parked out front so I was here. But I was lost in my own thoughts. I just looked up when I heard someone yell, 'You son of a bitch.' But it happened so quickly, and I was kind of in a fog of my own. I saw this athletic-looking guy run away. That's really all. Someone said the police picked up Mrs. Hopper's purse around the corner. Her wallet was missing. Still, I don't see why he shot her. He had the goddamned purse."

"I saw it, too," Marcy said. "The big guy started after him. That's why he shot."

"Mr. Roden," I said to Richard. "He walked out with Mrs. Hopper ahead of the others. Then he started to chase after the gunman."

"I feel like someone's killing off all our cases, Sara. It's bizarre. Poor Harry. First Helena, now his mother."

"For a lousy wallet," Marcy put in. "It's scary."

"It is scary," Richard agreed. "It's bizarre, too. Two patients within months of each other. And two people from the Caliban Café. Doesn't it seem strange to you?"

We all nodded. "That's where you're taking me for my birthday," I said to Mike. "The Caliban Café. I'm curious."

"The Caliban it is," said Mike.

I finally went home around ten P.M. I hadn't witnessed anything and I was tired. The others stayed pretty late giving statements to the police and theorizing. The prevalent theory, as I heard Thursday, was that the man was an addict. He needed quick money and went out and got it. The police seemed to think he might be a Vietnam veteran, because his one bullet struck her heart. The other possibility was that he fired without aim to scare off Mr. Roden, and by chance, his shot was fatal. Although there were several witnesses, no one had seen his face or hair. Descriptions of his height and body build varied. No one, however, thought he was short or dumpy. The police concluded he was of average to tall height. His build was medium to slight. He moved rapidly. His race was not known. The killing did not fit into a current pattern of street crimes. It appeared to be a random mugging resulting in death.

The clinic was in an uproar. Everyone wanted to talk about the killing. Somehow, gruesome and tragic as the shooting had been, the threat had come from the outside, and that loosened people's tongues. No other topic lasted more than a minute in that atmosphere. Harry was received with outpourings of sympathy and kind words. He appeared shocked and bewildered but not crazy. Mr. Hopper picked him up from the clinic both Thursday

94

and Friday nights and drove him home. Mr. Hopper spent the evenings at home with his children and let Maury temporarily take over the café. His look of fatigue and loss, as he called for his son, was heartrending. I almost couldn't bear to look at him. Frank had offered extra sessions, which were politely turned down. He was, however, welcomed into their home on a condolence call. All he'd been able to say to them was, "I'm so sorry. It's so senseless." I felt for Frank.

I again wheedled my way into Frank's supervision on Friday. I felt there was something ghoulish in my desire to see the tape that had been recorded just prior to Mrs. Hopper's death. Still, I reassured myself, I had been planning on seeing it before she had been killed.

Frank's emotions were raw, and Richard was being very gentle with him. He offered to skip the tape and let Frank talk about almost anything he wanted. He left the direction of the supervision up to Frank. But Frank was as curious as I was. Whatever that need is to try to make sense out of a person's being alive one minute and not alive the next, we both were responding to it. Richard started the tape.

On the TV viewer, we saw the family file in: the children first, Mr. Roden after them, and Mr. and Mrs. Hopper together, bringing up the rear. "Well?" Frank asked. Mr. and Mrs. Hopper smiled. "Not as bad as you thought it would be?" Frank asked.

Mrs. Hopper responded, "I enjoyed myself. Everyone treated me very courteously."

"I like it," said Judy. "I didn't have to clean up my room and put everything away and start on my homework right after school. I think it's a great idea."

"You like having me out of the house, is that it, Judy?"

"Mom, I didn't say that. But it's nice for you to go out sometimes. Not all the time. Mr. Thomas wants to know all about your week at the café, right?" Judy shifted her mother back to Frank.

"Right," Frank rescued her. "Tell me about it."

Mrs. Hopper needed little prompting. "I'd eaten there now

and again, so I'd seen it all fixed up before. But I'd never met the people who work there. The cooks wanted me to sample everything. The waiters are almost all young men." (I nudged Frank with my elbow.) "They couldn't have been more gracious. What's that handsome one's name? Pierre, Emile—no, Marcel. That's right, Marcel. He looks just like Mr. Thomas. At least his face does. What an attractive young man."

"Mom!" Judy yelled. She put her face down in the gesture of a mortified schoolgirl. Then she slowly looked at Frank out of the corner of her eye to observe his reaction. When he looked back at her, she looked down rapidly.

"That was the first time Mrs. Hopper ever said anything at all personal to me, or about me. I was so pleased." Frank said to Richard and me, his voice shaky. "It seems so unfair. I can't believe that after hiding away in her home for years, she gets killed as soon as she reenters the world. It's horrible." Richard and I agreed and waited to see if Frank wanted to say any more. He didn't, so we went on with the tape.

"Marcel's an excellent waiter, as I'm sure Mr. Thomas would be if he gave it a try," Mr. Roden said with twinkling eyes, "It was a pleasure to have Lizzie there. She came with me to see Herb on Wednesday. She even picked out a new wine to try, which we had several orders for. It was a good selection. She acted as hostess during lunch. The customers seemed very pleased at the extra touch. She went around and asked if everything was okay. She relieved the girls at the registers several times, gave them a break. We've been training a new girl since Helena died. It's sad seeing her there. Makes you think about Helena. She was so excited about her work."

Mrs. Hopper spoke again. "I can't help but feel that if I had gotten involved earlier and gotten to know the girl, she might have confided in me and not killed herself. I know that doesn't make sense to say, but I feel it's true. Poor little girl. I remember seeing her here Wednesday nights; she was quite a beauty."

"She was such a skinny, delicate little thing in her light-weight jacket," Maury replied. "What a pity."

Richard stopped the tape and spoke: "Mrs. Hopper was starting to think in terms of physical appearance. She commented on Frank's looks, the waiter's looks, and now Helena's looks. Her hair looks different from last week, too. She really was starting to respond more to others and take more pride in herself. Wasn't it grayer last week? And more tightly drawn back. She looks softer, less severe."

We both agreed with him. Frank remembered noticing that she'd looked younger. He had decided it would be indelicate to ask if she'd colored her hair, but later in the session he complimented her on her appearance. "I'm so glad I did," he told Richard and me. "I was real supportive of all the new things she was trying. Thank God I didn't give her a hard time. Thank God."

"You know," Richard said, "you also helped draw her and her husband closer together before her death. She didn't die a lonely, withdrawn woman. It makes it more tragic, in a sense, for her to die so senselessly just when she was starting to live and become involved with people. On the other hand, I think it's easier to let go of someone when you don't feel so angry or disappointed with them. All that unfinished business. What I'm trying to say, Frank, is you did more than not give her a hard time. I think you helped her and her family, and in the long run it will make her death easier for them."

"That's nice of you to say, Richard. I think it's true in a way. But I still feel like if they hadn't come to the clinic, she'd still be alive. It's irrational, because that kind of crime can happen anywhere. But it wouldn't have happened to her."

"I know what you mean," I said, thinking of Helena. We didn't go any further with the tape but sat talking about death.

15

Mike had made reservations for the two of us to share my birthday dinner at the Caliban Café Friday night at eight. I dressed with care, determined to enjoy my birthday. At least I wasn't in immediate danger of turning thirty. Mike picked me up, for which I was grateful. I had become squeamish about driving places alone after dark. We arrived at the café at eight, opened the outer door and entered.

The decor of the café was unexpected. I'd never heard it described and had not tried to imagine it. But I must have had a conventional restaurant setting in my mind because I was amazed at what I saw. Stepping through the inner door, we entered an enormous, airy room. The ceiling was high and for the most part flat, but against the far wall it sloped gently downward so that it seamlessly connected with the wall. Painted on the downward slope of the ceiling was a blazing sun. The rest of the ceiling was sky blue with cumulus clouds. As you lowered your gaze down the wall the blue became more of a sea green, under which the likeness of a sandy beach seemed, by a trick of shadowing, to come toward you. The effect was startling. It was like suddenly walking onto a sunny beach from a cold, blustery winter's night. A large round light shed its rays from the center of the ceiling, illuminating a magnificent dessert cart. As you drew away from the cart the lighting grew subdued and was dim by the time it reached the furthest alcoves in the room. The effect was one of withdrawing into the shade. The floors were of light, almost white, polished wood. The sea mural surrounded the entire room. The bar was in the room beyond and, as we had noticed coming in, had a separate entrance from the street. The cash register was set up at the entrance way, under a large beach umbrella. Built into another wall, with several tables clustered around it, was a large fireplace with roaring flames. I loved the place. The sensation of being at the beach was compelling. I asked Mike if he'd remembered the suntan oil.

"Yes," he said. "Take your blouse off and I'll rub it in."

"I wouldn't mind *him* rubbing it in." I said. "I wouldn't mind him rubbing anything in." I indicated with my head the direction of an awe-inspiring waiter. He was tall and sleek with short dark hair and beard.

"He looks like Frank," Mike said.

"It must be Pierre," I replied.

"Is that a joke?" asked Mike. "If it looks like Frank, it must be Pierre." Mike turned again to look at the waiter and, for an instant, their eyes locked.

"No, dummy. At their last session, Mrs. Hopper commented on how handsome one of the waiters was. She said he looked like Frank. Her teenage daughter practically went through the ceiling. He does look like Frank. I think she said his name was Pierre."

"We'll have to get Frank in here. It'll be like looking in the water was for Narcissus. I like those outfits they wear. I might get one for work." The waiters all wore stiffly ironed white linen pants with smock overshirts, with large pockets. Peeking out of the pockets, next to the checks, were big, sad dog eyes. I had to look twice before I realized they were white doggy bags with a picture of a dachshund on front. The mood in the café was like that in Renoir's 'Luncheon of the Boating Party.' I looked down, half expecting to see the waiter's feet in sandals. Instead, the illusion of summertime was underscored by light tan sailing shoes. The restaurant was a mixture of a casual style with meticulous attention to detail. I was wondering why I didn't see any waitresses when an ephemeral creature floated in, wearing a white linen skirt, a smock top similar to the men's, and comfortable-looking wedge sandals. The ambiance of the restaurant reflected an active imagination.

Mike and I got down to the serious business of ordering. In keeping with the atmosphere, we both ordered gin and tonics to start. The café specialized in seafood and fish dishes and was also especially known for its baked goods. Mike splurged and ordered lobster, saying, "You only turn twenty-seven once, Sara." I ordered broiled filet of sole, under the acknowledged self-delusion that it would entitle me to sample the bread and the pastry cart. Luckily our dinners arrived before I polished off the entire contents of the bread basket. We were both a little lightheaded and very intent on our food, which was delicious. As I came up for air, my plate wiped clean, Mr. Roden loomed over our table.

He smiled at me with recognition and asked, in maitre d' style, "Is everything all right here?"

"Oh, yes. The food is wonderful," I gushed. "I can't imagine anyone needing one of those," I said, indicating the doggy bag in Mr. Roden's hand.

"Not all our guests eat with the relish that you've shown," he replied genially. "We also get a lot of families in the evenings, and you know children; their eyes are bigger than their stomachs. This way customers go away satisfied and we don't waste food. Have you seen the pastry cart? I recommend the seven-layer rum cake if you can live with yourself in the morning."

Mike and I laughed. Mr. Roden moved on to another table. "Shall we trust him?" I asked Mike. "I can live with the consequences."

"I'm with you. But let's go ogle the cart first. We should also be able to live with the knowledge of the pastries unchosen. You waddle out first. I want to ask our waiter to bring us coffee." Mike caught up with me at a strawberry tart and set a quicker tempo. We circled once and returned to our seats.

"That Pierre character looks so familiar to me," Mike said. "I feel like I've seen him before."

"Well, he does have access to Frank's face. They really look amazingly alike."

"Your spirits seem so improved, Sara. You're like your old self again. It's nice to have you back. I've been meaning to tell you."

"You've helped a lot, Mike. It hurts, but not as much as it did. Still, sometimes I wake up at night feeling like a complete failure. I feel guilty that I can enjoy myself like this when poor Helena lies dead and buried. I miss the way she used to dance around when she talked and the startling things she'd say. I keep conjuring up images of her and telling myself she doesn't exist anymore. It's hard to accept. The worst part is when I think of her family. What they've been going through. And her death was so mysterious. I'm convinced she wanted to talk to me about being pregnant. She was trying so hard to please her family. They were starting to show respect for her rights and she was grateful. She told me that morning that she'd just dropped that mangy winter coat of hers at the cleaners on her way to the clinic, and she was so proud of herself. I think it was symbolic of being an adult. All those maintenance chores that you can take for granted when you're a kid. Maybe she had had a pregnancy test that afternoon. She did race out of the clinic like she had some place to go. I mean, she wasn't due at the Caliban till three and she left at twelve. She didn't hang around to have lunch with anyone. Two months along wouldn't be an unusual time to have a test. If I know Helena, she found out that she was pregnant and immediately did something sexy and foolish. After her immediate, manic response to the news wore off, she probably realized her situation and called me for advice. Or comfort. Everything was going well with her parents, but an illegitimate child would have been more than they could bear. And Helena was nowhere near ready for that kind of responsibility. The thought of an abortion is kind of scary, especially with the type of religious upbringing she had. And she'd been spending all her earnings on new clothes. I'll bet she was panicked, and that was it. She was desperate to talk to me and get some emotional support and figure a way out of her difficulties. She couldn't deal with it on her own and she had no one else to tell."

"One question. Wasn't she working the register while she was here? Wouldn't it be unusual to make a phone call and have you call back? Did the people here say anything to the police about that?"

"I don't think the policeman asked them. Maybe he did. But I didn't discover the phone message until after he'd talked to them. I don't know if he went back again. You know what just occurred to me? She usually went to the clinic Wednesday nights. They had someone fill in for her between six-thirty and nine P.M. I think they had a high school girl who earned some extra money that way—the sister of one of the waiters, that's what Helena said. She'd take over the register that one night a week. If Helena forgot to tell them ahead of time that she wouldn't be going to the clinic that night, this girl would have taken over for her at six-thirty, and Helena would have been free until nine. That makes sense, because she asked me to call her up until nine at the café, at which time she'd have to go back to the register. Then I guess she figured it would be too late by the time she got off duty at eleven. She was pretty considerate. And at that point she might as well wait until the morning. It doesn't seem like she would be so impatient that she would kill herself."

"But you're forgetting that Harry came in, probably around the time she was getting back to the register, since he'd have come from the clinic. He called her a lot of names. Given her upbringing and the fact that she was pregnant, she probably took them to heart. Think of the disappointment, too. She probably loved him when she became pregnant by him. And here she was with his child inside her and the realization that he was not for her. If someone else disappointed her later that night, and she was alone in the bitter cold and fog, and her parents were away and that old woman was the only one waiting for her at home, with her hell-and-damnation view of life—she might have suicided. You did say her grandmother was pretty grim. It might have happened, Sara. I read just the other day about a twenty-seven-year-old successful lawyer, with a lot of friends, who jumped off a building. I'll bet his friends are shocked and can't believe he was actually that desperate. But it happens."

"I know. Sometimes I worry about Mimi."

"Mimi? Are you serious?"

"I think she's under a lot of strain. I mean a *lot* of strain. She certainly thinks about it. If she and Melvin don't work things out."

"A lot of people think about it."

"I know. It's silly of me to worry. Still, she doesn't seem to see many options. She says he's the first really decent man she's been involved with. He's her knight in shining armor. If he leaves her or they can't make a go of it, she'd be pretty despondent, I think. But I think you're right too. A lot of people talk about it, and they come through the bad times. They have more resources at their disposal than they think they have. Helena's death has made me jumpy. I don't want anyone else suddenly disappearing on me."

"Are Mimi and Melvin having troubles?"

"Kind of. It's such a difficult situation with his kids and the separation being so recent. If it were just the two of them, it would be so much simpler."

"But it isn't just the two of them."

"I know. I think they both must wish they'd met years earlier. Life really is not easy. It's just beginning to sink in. You don't get it all."

"What do you think will happen with them? And don't play dumb."

"I don't know, Mike. I'm hoping she'll stand firm about setting boundaries with the kids and he'll hang in there and make some changes. Maybe they'll get married. I doubt if he'll want a new family with her, although you never know. On the other hand, even though Mimi really wants children, most of their quarrels seem centered around parenting issues, and they might do better together without kids. Who knows? He's a pretty difficult man."

"Do I detect a note of criticism slipping into your evaluation of the eminent Dr. Harley? This is a change."

"Well, it's just between you and me, okay? I think he's pretty tough. It seems like Mimi gets stuck doing the drudge work and taking care of his family all the time. He doesn't seem to help her much. I don't know what I'm talking about, Mike. Let's talk about your love life; that's always more interesting."

"You passed up a chance to do more than talk, and now you want to know what you've missed." It was the first reference either of us had made to New Year's Eve. It came out teasing and friendly.

"It was 'take it or leave it'?" I asked. "Like a Columbus Day sale?"

"That's it, Sara. From here on in you'll have to content yourself with hearsay."

"We did come pretty close, Mike. It's better this way, don't you think? I want someone I don't have to beg. Someone who likes the idea of being committed."

"I know, Sara. I guess I brought it up because I wanted to thank you for turning me down. It would have been so awkward. Even though I have this image in my mind of wanting to settle down with one woman, I think the woman is a fantasy object, totally unobtainable. I don't think I'm ready yet for a real person. Not for life. I don't know what it is, but I feel like I'm suffocating if I spend too much time with one woman. I need more privacy and time to myself. I start to anticipate and counter demands even before they're made. If I can control the amount of time we spend together, everything goes well. If I can't, it's a nightmare. I really don't understand it."

"What about Marcy?"

"We see each other now and again. But it's not going anywhere. She knows what the limits are, so relocate your eyebrows. What do I do? Pay at the register?"

"That's right. Thanks for the dinner, Mike." I kissed his cheek as we got up.

16

I was surprised that Mimi was not waiting for me Monday evening, because I was late in leaving. I walked down the hall to her office, and the lights were out and the room empty. My stomach was rising toward my throat as I walked by myself to see if her car was still in the back lot. It was, and as I approached, I could see that Mimi was sitting inside. As I got into the passenger's seat full of questions about why she was waiting in the car, I noticed she was crying silently, her face streaming with tears and contorted in rage. I sat there helplessly. Not knowing what else to do, I offered to drive. Mimi got out soundlessly, and we switched places. I started the car. "What's happened, Mimi?" I asked, my stomach one huge knot.

"Melvin. The bastard. He's speaking in Los Angeles. A big

conference. He's not coming to New Hampshire with me. He won't help me move my mother. We might still go skiing together. *Might.* If nothing more important comes up between now and then. I've got to face mother all alone. I was counting on him. How could he?"

"Oh, Mimi, what a shame. That's awful for you."

"He knows how much his help would mean to me. I would do it for him with no questions asked. He knows that. To think that he said he'd do it and now he's backed out because of some stupid conference. He has all these big plans. What about me? I fit in between six and six-thirty in the morning and eight and eleven at night, when it's convenient. Otherwise, forget it." Mimi began sobbing again, her body convulsing.

"Oh, Mimi," I commiserated. "Was he definite, not just tempted by the offer?"

"He was definite, all right. He'd sent his acceptance in before he even told me, the bastard. How can I ever forgive him?"

But by Tuesday morning, when we again drove into work, Mimi had forgiven him. It turned out that Melvin had offered to hire a packer and mover for her mother and had invited Mimi to come to the conference with him. And he had promised her the ski vacation. He had actually made the plane reservations. She still had to decide whether to face her mother's move alone or hire someone, but either way, the situation had improved.

The community meeting Tuesday morning was tense. Richard and Dr. Harley disagreed as to whether it was appropriate for a staff member to go with a patient to his place of employment. Richard thought the staff member could work with the employer to help the patient over the rough spots and keep him productive. Dr. Harley viewed that as encouraging a debilitating dependency. Mimi got into the act and said that Richard wanted to be everyone's daddy and couldn't confine himself to trying to be effective as a therapist. Richard let the remark go by. I felt sick inside. The issue was left unresolved and the staff divided.

Dr. Harley had an administrative meeting during lunch, so I ran out and got two sandwiches, hoping to surprise Mimi with one. I suppose I was aware of some tension between us, and I wanted to close the gap that was forming. I missed our days of warmth and companionship. Mimi let me in with my offering, but she showed no interest in the sandwich. "Pretty rough meeting this morning," I said, trying to start a conversation. "People left a little bowed and bloodied."

"At least some of us are willing to speak our minds," Mimi responded. "We don't sit there looking superior and judging everyone else."

"Do you mean me? I don't look superior. Sometimes I'm just too confused to know what to say."

"Don't give me that innocent-little-girl routine. You let everyone else do the dirty work and then you're smug and smirking at the finish. Don't think I don't know what goes on in that mind of yours."

"Mimi, I don't know what you're talking about. I don't feel smug."

"No? What's this sandwich for? To help poor Mimi who's in dire distress. I don't need your help. I know how you feel about Melvin. You have no respect for him. I know what you say about him behind my back. You and Richard. You encourage me to be angry with him. I can see your expression when he talks. I'll tell you what I think. I think you're jealous. You can't stand to see me happy with him. You like it when there's a crisis. You'd love to turn me against him. Then you could really worry about me— poor Mimi, disappointed in love. You're what's wrong in my life, not Melvin. And don't think I haven't told him. He knows how you feel about him. He knows you hate him."

"What are you talking about, Mimi! I don't hate him. I'll tell you what I think," I said, tears streaming down my face. "I think I've been under strain with Helena's death and I got kind of withdrawn. I was off in my own world and not very available. But you've been under enormous strain, too, with your mother having to move. It probably affects you more than you realize."

"More than *you* realize. Do you think it's easy to sit and listen to you talk about your home in Connecticut? If you needed to

106

retreat from the world, you'd have a place to go. I don't. You're so insensitive about that. You practically shove it down my throat. And you eat doughnuts and cookies in front of me, with no understanding of what it's like for me. I'm constantly denying myself things and you're totally self-indulgent. And then you sit in judgment."

"But I didn't know. You never told me. You make me sound so cruel, Mimi."

"Maybe you just don't know yourself very well. Even Melvin thinks you're superficial in your work."

"Do you mean to tell me that Melvin discussed my work with you? And that you have the nerve to tell my boss, whatever else he may be to you, that I hate him? You have no right to do that. It's not your place. I'll assume that he doesn't believe the lies you've told him or he would have had the decency to ask me directly."

"You've changed your tune. Don't tell me you didn't love knowing so much about your boss—the way you pumped me for information, only to use it against him. I could kick myself for telling you so much."

"Listen, Mimi. I have not used anything against him. If you're worried that you gave away state secrets, believe me, they're safe. Yes, I liked knowing about him. But I have never used it maliciously, and I don't know how you could think that I would. Mimi, please. We used to have a good friendship. I miss it. I think you're really overwrought. Maybe we should talk again when you're calmer. We're saying things now that'll be hard to erase."

I left and ran to the ladies' room. I must have stayed in there, hiding out, crying on and off, for well over an hour. I missed a team meeting and postsession, which I'd never done before. But I didn't want to face everyone in my condition. Finally I emerged and sneaked into my office. I called Joyce on the intercom to apologize and to explain that something very upsetting had occurred. It wouldn't happen again. I asked her if she could cancel my appointments and let me hole up and do paperwork. She came in almost immediately to make sure for herself that I was all right.

"We were all worried about you," Joyce said in her warm, maternal way. "Do you want to talk about it?"

"I don't know what to say, Joyce. It's embarrassing, but it's also painful. Don't tell anyone. Mimi and I had a fight. We're not friends anymore. I've grown apart from people but never had them yell at me like that and not want to be my friend. She accused me of terrible things. She told Dr. Harley that I hate him. I've never said that I hated him. How could she tell him that?"

"I bitch about him all the time. He knows it. It comes with the territory." Joyce was reassuring. "Don't take this too much to heart. You'll show better judgment in your friendships in the future, that's all." Her comment surprised me.

17

I hid in my office until just after five, so the clinic would be almost empty when I emerged. Then I went to the message board to leave Mimi a message that I'd find my own way home. Instead, I found a message from her saying she'd left without me and expected I could get home myself. I was relieved. I thought of calling Mike and asking if I could come over, but Marcy'd said they had a date that night. I was about to call a cab when an arm encircled my shoulders and I looked around to see Richard. My heart stopped. He'd never touched me before. "Come here," he said and led me into his office. He released me and sat down. I sat down next to him cursing my swollen face and excited by his presence. "What is it, Sara? You look like the Redskins trampled you on their way off the field. Is there anything I can do?"

"I just had a terrible fight with Mimi. I can't believe it. She thinks I've caused all the problems in her life. She told Harley I hated him. He's the first person I've ever worked for on a real job. And he thinks I hate him and that I spread malicious lies about him. And that I've tried to ruin his relationship with Mimi. It's so confusing."

"Let me call Dorothy and I'll take you out for a drink. You definitely look like you could use one. Just a second."

He dialed a number and asked to speak to Dorothy Martins. I listened intently. A drink with Richard—

"Hello, Dorothy. Listen, I want to take Sara out for a drink. What time are you getting home? That late? I was going to make the veal, but it'll keep till tomorrow. If Sara's free, maybe I'll take her to dinner and see you around nine-thirty. You can make the veal Wednesday, and I'll go shopping again Thursday. Who all's going to dinner with you? Sounds impressive. See you later, sweetie."

"Are you free for dinner, Sara?"

I nodded. Could this really be happening? "Do you cook a lot?" I asked Richard.

"I do most of the cooking. It relaxes me. And Dorothy works longer hours than I do. I've turned into a totally domesticated animal. You never know what life holds in store for you. Where shall we go?"

I shrugged.

"How about the Caliban? I'm curious to see it. Especially after your description. Is that okay? We can get drinks and dinner."

"That's fine. Anywhere, really."

"Do you have your car or what?"

"No. Can you drop me off afterward?"

"Goes without saying. Come on."

Richard steered me out to his car, warm and protective. "Now, tell me what's been happening."

"I don't know what to say. You know what good friends Mimi and I have been. All this time she's been angry with me, but she never told me. She has a lot of family responsibility and no support and I get a lot of support and I don't have any family responsibility, at least not yet in my life. I think she resents it. And I haven't been very sensitive about how hard that's been for her.

I'm always telling her about my family. Lots of things. She thinks I'm jealous of her and Dr. Harley. But at the same time she thinks I hate him."

"Are you jealous?"

"I don't know. Maybe a little because he's our boss. But I wouldn't really want him. I don't like him as much as I did before I got to know him, but I don't hate him."

"Maybe Mimi hates him in ways that are frightening to her. I meant, are you jealous of Mimi, not Melvin? Mimi's the one you're close to."

"Oh," I said, surprised. "Maybe I am. I mean, she would be visiting with me and leave within seconds when he called to say he was home. I resented it. But I didn't hate him. I mean, I accepted it. People usually have one really exclusive relationship that takes precedence. I accept that. I don't think my resentment went very deep."

"Do you have an exclusive relationship?"

Our conversation had taken a humiliating turn. "No," I replied. "I don't."

We had gotten to the café, and Richard parked in a lot. We didn't resume our conversation until Richard had reacted to the décor and we'd been seated.

"What brought on her attack?" Richard asked.

"You know what I really think it was? It's a long story and I won't go into details, but Dr. Harley had promised to help her do something for her mother and Mimi didn't want to do it herself, but thought it would be bearable with his help. Then he canceled on her and offered her a way out. Meanwhile, she slaves for his family. He was acting like her family was worthless."

"Want my opinion, Sara? I've known them both longer than you have."

"Yes."

"I think you got triangled into their relationship. There was something in it for you—maybe being a confidante, knowing a lot about your boss, I don't know—but the role was attractive to you for your own reasons. Still, I think they've got a lousy relationship going and they need a heavily involved outsider to stabilize it. Mimi would have felt a lot more neglected if you hadn't been available almost whenever she needed you. When things really started to go wrong between them—I mean the big things that make you wonder if you can ever forgive each other—I think she panicked. I've known her for six years. She's always looked at him with adoration. I think the thought of his not being what she wanted was too threatening for her to face. Instead, she shifted her anger at him to a defense of him against you. She'd already seen you as carrying around her anger toward him. In other words, it was too threatening for her to feel such rage at him. Instead, she projected her feelings of rage onto you and thought that you hated him. Then she could exclude you and protect him. Her conflict with Melvin evaporated. Her future is secure, at least it feels secure for the moment. You're the bad guy. Does that make sense to you?"

"A lot of sense. I am really furious with her. What makes me so mad is that she'd lie to Melvin about me. Then I hate myself for even caring what he thinks. But he is my boss. I have this urge to justify myself to him, but then I think, why should I grovel to someone who can help cause such a mess and who would believe her lies, anyway. I've decided not to say a word to him about it unless he asks. I don't want to vie with Mimi for his favor and have him pronounce us right or wrong. It's a humiliating position and I shouldn't have to justify anything I haven't done. But if he ever criticizes my work or writes me a lousy recommendation—not that I want to leave the clinic, I don't—I'll make damn sure he has professional grounds for it, not something Mimi's been feeding him."

"That's the spirit!" Richard clinked my glass. "I don't think you should take her accusations to heart. The area in which you might learn something is what drew you into their relationship. You are, Sara, very easily seduced," he said with a smile.

"How would you know?" I challenged him. My words shocked me. That hadn't been his meaning, but mine was unmistakable.

Richard's brown eyes turned soft. "Sara. You're the first person I've told, but I'm getting married. Also, I happen to be your supervisor. That means something to me, even though our clinic's becoming a rabbit hutch. Otherwise, by now, I probably would know how seducible you are."

"I shouldn't have said that. I'm sorry, it was stupid."

"Now, don't go beating yourself on the head. Here I am wining and dining you, and you must see how fond I am of you. You looked upset and I like spending time with you. I should have been clearer. Listen, getting married is a big deal for me. I haven't been very good at it. The decision to risk trying again didn't come easy. So don't go tempting me with salacious offers. My life is complicated enough." His tone had lightened.

"This has to be the most embarrassing day of my life." I forced a laugh and was semipleased with the results.

"I can't understand your being embarrassed. There's simply no reason. Can I tell you something, what I think about you?"

I gulped audibly, but nodded yes.

"I think you are one of the warmest people I know and you have a lot to offer. But you don't take risks. Your ambiguous proposition to me was wonderful. You've survived my telling you I'm otherwise engaged. You need to take more chances. You're resilient enough to take a rejection or two—to make some mistakes. You jump into these seemingly safe relationships, like with Mimi. All your energy goes into her life. What's in it for you? It keeps you on the sidelines. What with Mimi and Mike and Frank, it's a wonder you even had time to proposition me." I shot him a warning look. He responded, "Well, I'm taking it as a proposition. It's flattering to a forty-year-old like me. You've made me feel ten years younger. But you ought to do something for yourself. Do you have anyone you're going out with?"

"No. The only men I meet are the ones I work with. I'm really not unhappy. I do get lonely, but it's not like my life is empty. I enjoy spending time with my friends."

"Sara, I know that. I didn't mean to suggest that you lived a dreary, depressing life. Far from it. It's just you're so easy to get close to. I don't understand why you don't have someone—someone whose first priority you are."

"We'd better order," I said. The waiter had just made his third discreet trip over to our table. That taken care of, we continued.

"Don't be offended by what I'm saying," Richard said. "That's the last thing I want. You just have so much to offer, I hate to see you go to waste. I don't mean that you are going to waste. Am I totally off the track? I'll shut up."

"No. You're right. I don't know why it's so hard to admit. I'd like to have one man I could really love and count on. It would be great to be someone's first priority. You couldn't be more right. I'd also love to have children. I guess a family's what I most want in the world. I don't think I shy away from opportunities to meet men. I went out much more when I was in Hartford, but I was in school and it seemed easier to meet men. Here, I guess, I don't really know how. It's hard. Singles' bars frighten me. I like to get to know men first. What should I do? Help!"

As if in answer to my plea, the waiter served us dinner. Our conversation continued at a slower pace.

"If you really want down-to-earth advice," Richard offered, "I'd say force yourself to ask friends to fix you up and force yourself to go. I don't know anyone who enjoys it. But I think you have to do it. It's not like you meet new people at work—it's just us, and it's very closed. If you don't push yourself, you'll sink into a comfortable, but lonely routine. You don't want me to get married knowing that you're out there free and available with a proposition at the ready. I'd be off to a bad start."

"Enough already. I'll talk to my friend Susan tomorrow. Her husband knows a million people."

"I'll ask Dorothy. She works for a law firm that's practically all men. I'll report back to you."

"While we're having true confessions, Richard, can I ask you a personal question?"

"I won't guarantee an answer until I hear the question."

"Did you and Mimi ever have a thing together? Did you ever go out or anything? She seems so emotional about you."

113

"You never asked her? And you were such good friends. Why not?"

"I don't know. I didn't feel like I could ask her. Will you tell me?"

"Oh, Jesus. We went out once or twice years ago, when she first came to work, before I met Dorothy. But it was never anything—one, maybe two dates, nothing really. I don't think she found me very exciting, and I found her unresponsive and self-absorbed. I don't think her emotions about me, or what less delicately could be called animosity toward me, have anything to do with that. We were neither of us scorned lovers. We just didn't click. She doesn't like the fact that I differ with Melvin on a number of issues. That's why she's hostile toward me."

"I always wondered. Want to look at the pastry cart?" I asked, as we had finished eating.

"I'll look, but you get something. I'll just have coffee. Come on."

I headed straight for the seven-layer rum cake. I didn't want to take too many risks at once, and the seven-layer was a sure thing.

"That must be Marcel," Richard said, indicating the waiter who looked like Frank. "He's taller and thinner than Frank, but it's the same face. Strong resemblance."

"Marcel, that's right. I told Mike it was Pierre. He is a smooth-looking creature." Marcel looked up from a table where he'd just exchanged a doggy bag for a tip, and found us both staring at him. He eyed me intently, then turned and walked away.

"Do you need smelling salts?" Richard asked me. "And here I was flattered by your interest. I'd no idea you were so fickle."

I blushed. "He does have rather piercing eyes," I said, clearing my throat. "But you have the mellowing effect of age on your side. Look, there's Mr. Roden."

Mr. Roden headed straight for our table. "Dr. Marks, I'm pleased to see you here again." He nodded at Richard and gave me a wink. "You're bringing us a lot of business. I hope you've enjoyed your meals. Is there anything I can get for you?"

114

"No, thanks," we both protested, and he walked off and disappeared into the other room. "I think he was amused by my being here with Mike one night and then with you. I wonder if he thinks my taste is starting to go downhill?"

"A little barbed wire under that sweet exterior."

"Well, you did turn me down."

"It's the new me who turned you down, but if you keep provoking me I'm in danger of reverting to type. Then we'd both be in trouble. I'm no bargain. Dorothy's the only woman I know who can put up with me for any length of time and who keeps my behavior within the bounds of decency. I'm even at the point where nice comes naturally, but I could crack. It takes vigilance."

"You're not serious. Richard. You're the nicest man I know. And you're loyal to Dorothy, which I admire."

"As I believe I remarked earlier this evening, you're easily seduced. You should have seen me trying to be a married man and, worse yet, you should have seen me plundering the countryside after my marriage fell apart. You wouldn't have liked me much if you'd known me then."

"What were you like?"

"I was a restless husband. Poor Marion, I really put her through the wringer. I was never satisfied with her the way she was. I wanted her to fight with me, to provoke me, to get all steamed up about things. I wanted passionate arguments and lovemaking like there'd be no tomorrow. Everything seemed so important to me. I was a very intense young man. Marion saw everything from my point of view and tried to calm and comfort me. She wanted nothing more than to smooth the way for me. I'd come back from classes or work all fired up about some so-and-so who'd done such-and-such and the moral squalor of it all, the lack of principles, the decadent ethical atmosphere, and Marion would have my dinner ready and offer me a drink and nod in agreement until my venom ran out. I needed something to push against. I was arrogant and willful, and I needed someone to tell me I was full of shit. She was so damn understanding. My behavior became more and more outrageous. After our son was born, she had two demanding infants on her hands. Instead of telling me to grow up, she tried to take care of us both. I don't mean it was her fault for not demanding more of me. I was a jerk. But we were mismatched. I felt so guilty. I knew my behavior was out of bounds. She just kept stretching herself thinner to give me what she thought I wanted and I kept turning the rack to see how far she could stretch. Finally, I left. She didn't want me to go. Then I really got out of hand. I slept with more women in that first week of separation than I had in the rest of my life. I was like an invading army. I raped, sacked, and plundered. I'm exaggerating—I don't mean that I actually raped anyone—but I was so driven, I was out of control. I don't really understand what was compelling me. I got into therapy and was in for several years. But even with it all, I can give you four or five reasonable theories for why I acted as I did, and they all make sense, but I don't really understand myself. There's no question that I was an angry man, but my life hadn't been terrible. I had no cause for such intense anger. And it wasn't just anger—I was searching for something I couldn't seem to get hold of. If I had met you ten years earlier and you had started work at the clinic, I would have checked you out, up and down, your first day there. I would have chatted you up the second day. I would have asked you out the third day and probably, if you'd been willing—and the intense force of my desire and need made women willing—by the fourth day we'd have been in bed together. We'd have passionate repeat performances the fifth and sixth days, and by the seventh day, I'd need a rest, and my interest would have waned. That would have been it. I'd see you at work after that and nod hello. My energy would be spent with someone new. I was a bastard. Mike and I have talked about this together. He reminds me a little of myself, but he truly is much kinder and gentler than I used to be. He's more considerate. I had calmed down quite a bit by the time I met Dorothy, but meeting her really changed my life—which reminds me, it's getting late. We'd better go. My treat. It's a birthday present. Let me just run to the men's room."

Richard returned and he left a tip and paid on the way out.

The cold air slashed our faces and took me by surprise. The café had lulled me into thinking it was balmy outside.

"How did Dorothy change you?" I prompted Richard.

"She took me in stride. She'd shrug me off. She didn't get all excited about every little thing the way I did, but she didn't placate me either. I was on the histrionic side. I'd come back from a racquetball game ecstatic if I'd won, dejected if I'd lost. I was the overly competitive type. I'd come in muttering about that goddamned son-of-a-bitch, he shouldn't have won. I was a real pain in the ass. She'd say, very drily, 'He's a better player than you, Richard. He's also better looking than you.' She might not even know the guy, but she'd say, 'I wasn't going to tell you this, but he's also a better lover than you. He knows things your limited imagination couldn't begin to conceive of. Racquetball's the least of your worries.' Meanwhile, as she'd talk she'd be doing something else, not really even paying much attention to me and my bruised ego. I'd laugh. What could I do? I always knew she loved me. She just didn't encourage my tantrums. Or I'd come home from the clinic all snarled up about someone who had disagreed with me. I'd rant about the stupidity of some clown who didn't know his ass from his elbow. How could such a moron not acknowledge that I had a superior point of view and that his own was shit? And Dorothy, ever the lawyer, would say, 'I'll argue your point of view if you argue his. If I win with yours, it's because I argue better.' I didn't really accept her premise, but I was competitive enough not to want her to outargue me. By the time we finished, I sure as hell saw the other guy's point of view. She broadened and steadied me. I would never do anything to hurt my relationship with her."

"She sounds terrific." I said.

"I think so," Richard replied. "But mostly, we're well suited to each other. Marion is really a lovely woman. I just couldn't appreciate her at that time in my life. Thank God she's remarried and seems happy. They have two children of their own and they're wonderful parents. I don't think I did any lasting damage. My son has a good home and Marion's much better off with her present husband. He loves her just as she is. It shows. She looks younger than when she was married to me."

"You seem pretty content with your life, too."

"I am. It's funny. After Dorothy and I started living together, and she got her first job in a big firm, her salary was higher than mine. I went berserk. I started seeing private patients in the evenings and on Saturdays. I'd start at eight A.M. Saturday morning and work till two—and me a man who loves to sleep in. I drove myself so that I stayed a step ahead of her salary. It was ridiculous. I really liked the clinic work, the sense of community, and I liked working with that patient population, which I think is hard to do on your own—you need the backup, at least I do. I never wanted full-time private practice. I enjoyed the private patients, but doing both, I didn't have time for the other things I enjoyed. Dorothy and I had little time to relax together and I gave up going to the gym, which I love. Finally Dorothy said, 'If I request a salary cut, will you give up this nonsense?' I felt ridiculous. She didn't care. We didn't need the money. It was my male pride or whatever you want to call it. So I cut back my practice and finally stopped taking private patients at all. Now I just work at the clinic, which I enjoy. I go to the gym, cook great dinners, relax on the weekends. I can't complain. I have more flexibility in visiting my son. Part of it is age. I never even try to insult people these days for fear they'll spin around and call me bald." Richard was hardly bald. Just a little thinning in the crown. "I think I really am content, for the first time in my adult life."

We had been sitting, parked in front of my building so we could finish the conversation. I had a vague sense that someone was sitting in the car behind us, but my thoughts were all on Richard. "See how responsive you are, Sara," he was saying. "I don't know when I've talked about myself so much. It was fun. We'll have to talk about me more often. No, I really enjoyed it. Jesus. It's a quarter to ten already. Maybe I should call Dorothy."

"Do you want to come in and use my phone?" I offered.

"No, that's okay. It won't take me long to get home. I'll watch you in. Goodnight, Sara."

"Thanks, Richard. I had a great time." I leaned over and kissed his cheek. I got out of the car and let myself into my building. Safely inside, I turned and waved goodbye. Richard waved back and I walked to the elevator.

I knew I'd be up half the night reviewing every aspect of our evening together. It had been wonderful. And in some way that I didn't understand, it freed me up. I felt ready to start getting out more and taking my own life in hand. As the elevator shot by Mimi's floor, I felt a hurtful reminder that I wouldn't be getting off there anymore. But no more living vicariously through others. I'd take my own chances.

18

I let myself into my apartment and closed the door. I walked into the bathroom and was surprised to see that my eyes were still puffy from crying. It seemed so long ago. Suddenly, the outside buzzer rang, and a muffled man's voice said, "Sara, can I come up for a minute? I need the phone." Richard had changed his mind. I quickly buzzed open the outside door and opened the lock on mine. Then I dashed back into the bathroom and threw a box of Tampax into the cabinet under the sink. I gave my hair a few rapid brushes and rushed out to hang up my coat. No need to appear slovenly. Suddenly, as I was standing at the coat closet, with my back to the door, it occurred to me that I didn't know who was coming in. No name had been given, and the voice had been muffled. It was unlike Richard to change his mind. He was safety-conscious; he would have said, "It's Richard." "Oh, my God," I thought, and turned, ready to step to the door and bolt it. As I turned, a tall, slim man, his face obscured by a scarf and a hat pulled low, stepped into the apartment. He rapidly locked the door behind him and drew a gun.

"One sound, you're dead," he warned in a staccato voice.

"This is it," I thought. My mind seemed to leave my body and look down on the scene. I remember fearing pain and thinking of my parents with an indescribable tenderness. His eyes bore into me, and I had a flicker of recognition. "Why?" I thought. I remained silent, my body frozen with fear. "What does he want from me?" He grabbed a pillow off my couch and held it in front of his gun. He started toward me. "He's going to kill me. He's here to kill me. He doesn't want anything from me." These thoughts were zooming through my mind. Then—we both heard it at the same time—the lock on my door was being opened from the outside. "Who?" I held my breath, waiting, suspended. The noise was real. His eyes wavered from me and began to dart. The door opened. I saw Mimi. She started to scream at the top of her lungs. The man knocked her down and ran out.

"I've called the police," a voice yelled from inside another apartment, but no door opened. I dragged Mimi in and bolted my door.

"Mimi! Are you okay? Say something!" I yelled. She looked dazed. With shaky hands, I poured us both some brandy. Mimi drank hers and a little more color crept into her face. I could barely bring the glass to my mouth, I was shaking so violently; but I got a few sips down.

There was a knock on the door. "Police," a man yelled. I looked through the peephole and saw a man with a badge. I opened the door. A tall, dignified-looking, middle-aged black policeman walked in. "What happened?" he asked.

"A man tried to kill me. Mimi came and saved my life. Just in time. He took a pillow. He was going to shoot me through it. I know who he is," I said.

"You know him?" Mimi asked, speech returning, her eyes widening in surprise. "You know him? Who is he? I've seen him before, too. I know I have. But I don't know where."

"He's a waiter at the Caliban Café. His first name is Marcel. I don't know his last name. Why would he want to kill me?"

"The lady down the hall who called us saw him through her peephole," the policeman said. "She couldn't see his face. It was covered. How did you recognize him?"

"I couldn't see his face either. He had a scarf up over his nose and a woolen ski hat pulled down low. But I know his eyes. He stared at me tonight at the café. He must have followed me home and been sitting in the car behind Richard and me." I felt Mimi's interest quicken at that revelation. I continued, "He rang my buzzer and said he needed to make a phone call. I thought it was the man who had just dropped me off. I let him in. It was stupid. He drew a gun and told me to keep quiet. He got a pillow and was going to shoot me when Mimi came in. Why, Mimi? What made you come? I'll always be grateful, no matter what else has happened."

"You have a key?" the policeman asked, turning to Mimi.

"Yes," Mimi responded. "We each have a spare key to the other's apartment. I just ran up to return her key and to retrieve mine." Mimi handed me my extra key and crossed to the coat closet, which she opened. From a hook inside the door, she removed her own extra key. Then she looked at me. "I called and got your answering machine so I figured you were out. I didn't want to run into you now. I didn't leave a message. I just put my slippers on and walked up."

"Thank God you did. I just got in."

"Why would this waiter follow you home? What's the connection?" The policeman was not interested in Mimi anymore.

"I don't know. I've only been to the café twice. I know he noticed me because I pointed him out each time to the people I was with. He saw me pointing him out."

"Why were you pointing him out?" The policeman looked tired and exasperated.

"He looked just like a friend of mine," I explained.

"You wouldn't mistake him for this friend of yours, would you?"

"No. Frank is shorter and fuller. It was their faces that looked alike."

"Okay. If we find this waiter and put him in a line-up with his face obscured, do you think you could pick him out?"

"I think so. I don't know. It's worth a try."

"Okay," the policeman said.

"The funny thing is," Mimi said, "I've never been to the café, and I know I've seen him before."

"But you didn't see his face," the policeman pointed out.

"It's his body, the way he moves. What he was wearing. The whole look. It's familiar to me." Mimi knit her brows in a look of concentration. "Oh, my God. He shot Mrs. Hopper." Mimi put her hands over her mouth, her eyes opened wide. "If I'd come in five minutes later, you'd have been dead on the floor. Oh, God."

"Who's this Mrs. Hopper?"

I took over and explained, since I knew Mrs. Hopper had been working at the café, and that now seemed to be the link with her death. The policeman was interested. I told him that Marcy and Mike had also witnessed the shooting, and gave him their numbers. As soon as Marcel was apprehended, we'd all go downtown together.

The policeman stood up to leave. "I want this door bolted behind me," he said sternly, "and don't walk unaccompanied. And both of you, not a word to anyone about Marcel. We don't want word getting back to him." Mimi and I nodded and then, without meaning to, I blurted out, "Someone else who worked at the café died recently. One of our patients. She was twenty-two years old. She worked the cash register. She was found drowned beneath Key Bridge one morning after working there. She hadn't gone home that night. The police ruled her death a suicide, but it's hard to believe that she would kill herself. Detective Harrison handled the case. You could check with him. Maybe Marcel didn't get home until late that night."

"Okay. I'll check with Harrison, I know the dude. My name's Larson. Here's my card. We'll be in touch."

He left, and Mimi and I were alone. "What a day," I said. "Have some tea with me, Mimi. We can start not being friends tomorrow. Please. Don't leave me alone just yet."

"All right," Mimi said grudgingly. "What were you doing out with Richard?"

"Here I am practically blown in two and you want to know if

I finally have something exciting going on in my life." I smiled. "He took pity on me. After our discussion, as you must know, I cried my eyes out. He saw me looking like a wreck, and he took me out to eat. It was nothing scandalous; he called Dorothy. He was wonderful to talk to. He told me he took you out a few times, years ago. I asked him. I was curious. You always seemed so hostile toward him. I wondered why." A little of her own medicine. "I can't believe I was almost killed tonight. Something horrible is going on at that café. Until Marcel is picked up, let's carpool together. For safety."

"Okay. Why would he kill Mrs. Hopper?" Mimi asked. "I don't understand."

"I'll bet he was up to something at the café, and she found out about it. Maybe Helena did, too. Helena'd have gone out with him in a minute if he asked her. He's gorgeous. He must have wanted to kill Mrs. Hopper and just stole her pocketbook to make it look like a street robbery and obscure his motive."

"I don't know, Sara. She might have had something in her purse that he wanted. It might have been in her wallet or something else we didn't know about."

"You know what's occurred to me? Wouldn't Mr. Roden recognize him? I mean, he sees him at work every day. Mr. Hopper, too. His form must have looked familiar to them."

"I don't think so. Look at the circumstances. It happened so quickly, and the context was so different. There are a lot of men who look like that. And probably those aren't the normal clothes he wears. Being used to seeing him in one context, dressed in a certain way, probably made them less likely to recognize him in another. Even if they'd have a sense of familiarity, they would probably put it out of their minds because it didn't make sense to them. And it would be an awful accusation to make." My phone rang. It was Melvin asking for Mimi. He was wondering what had happened to her. She told him she'd be down soon.

"I don't know," I said as Mimi headed for the door, an extra set of keys in her hand, my own extra set in mine. "I'll be really interested in where Marcel was the night Helena was killed.

Something very devious is going on. Mimi, thanks again. I'll never forget what you did for me. I mean that sincerely. I'll always be grateful."

"It was luck," Mimi said, and she left.

19

I bolted the door and put on the safety latch, a precaution unusual for me. My main fear was that I'd be unable to sleep and would lie awake, vigilantly straining to identify noises in the night. As it happened, I fell into a deep sleep almost immediately. My alarm could barely rouse me in the morning. When I did manage to unlock my eyelids, I was relieved that it was light and I'd made it through. Mimi was dutifully waiting at my car, but we drove in in virtual silence. All morning I was jumpy. I wanted the detective to call, and I wanted to tell Richard and Mike all that had happened. Finally, about one P.M., the anticipated phone call came. Detective Larson told me they had apprehended Marcel at the Caliban at eleven-thirty that morning, when he reported for work. They were holding him on suspicion of attempting to murder me and of killing Mrs. Hopper; the night she was killed, he had left the café early for a "family emergency" that he refused to be more specific about.

"What about the night Helena died?" I asked. "Does he have an alibi?"

"He claims he went straight from the café to a jazz club. He's pretty much a regular at this club, I gather. We haven't checked it out yet. I want you and anyone else who witnessed Mrs. Hopper's murder to come down for a line-up identification this afternoon between three and four. Can you arrange it?"

"I'm sure they'll let me out. I'll bring as many of the witnesses as I can. Where do we go?" I kept Detective Larson on another five minutes getting explicit directions. When we hung up, I called Dr. Harley, who told me I could come right in. I was uneasy about facing him, but surprisingly, he treated me genially, with no trace of the animosity at which Mimi had hinted. Not surprisingly, he seemed fully briefed on the events of last night. I told him that not only was I wanted at the police station but that Mimi, Marcy, and Richard were also required. In addition, I had to call Mike Sweeney and see if he could come along. Dr. Harley wanted me first to tell Frank what had happened and have him sit down privately with Harry to discuss it. He did not want rumors of the arrest spreading before Harry had a chance to learn all the facts as we understood them. It was the murderer of his mother we were talking about. Then we would call in Mimi, Marcy, and Richard and explain the situation. "We'd also better let Joyce in on it," Dr. Harley decided. "Then the three team leaders will know and they can inform their staffs and patients." When all these meetings were finished, I called Mike and told him everything that had happened, including Mimi's accusations and Richard's dinner, as well as the murder attempt. He was able to cancel his afternoon appointments, and the group of us set out, crowded into one car, for the police station. When we arrived, we asked for Detective Larson and were ushered into a waiting area. He appeared shortly. His manner was courteous and sardonic at the same time. He met with each of us individually for an interview. From subsequently compared notes, it was apparent that he followed the same routine with us all. He took down background material and then asked each of us to recount the events we had witnessed during the nights in question. I went first, and he led me into a small room, one wall of which had a two-way mirror. I could see six men standing in the next room, wearing jeans, beige jackets, and ski hats and scarves. Their faces, except for their eyes, were almost totally obscured. "They're going to each run toward you, then stand and look at you in the mirror. Of course, they'll only see their own reflections, and then they'll turn and run to the back of the room. We've been watching Marcel move and we had him out in the exercise yard, so he's been warned against moving in an uncharacteristic way. We'd spot it. Now try to relax. They're getting ready to bring in the first man."

I took a deep breath and tried to concentrate. The body movements didn't awaken much in my memory, but when the fourth man stared at the mirror, I found my heart starting to beat quickly and fear crept into my stomach. "Him," I said. "There's no mistake. It's him."

"Okay," Larson said. "I want you to stay and watch the last two anyway. Just to be sure." I watched the two others but had no reaction. I think I expected Detective Larson to congratulate me on my perceptiveness. To my disappointment, he simply led me into another room, where I waited by myself until Richard appeared.

"I really wasn't sure," Richard said. "I just wasn't paying attention on the night Mrs. Hopper was killed. I told the detective that I couldn't in good conscience make a positive identification. I can't believe that as I was driving home thinking about what a nice evening I'd had with you, you were facing the barrel of a gun. What a night you must have had, Sara. I talk your ears off, a man tries to kill you, and your archenemy rescues you from danger. Can you take yet another event in your life?"

"What do you mean?"

"I did talk to Dorothy about whether there were any single men in her office. She said they have a new attorney, Joel something, who seems like a nice guy. He's not married, and she had the distinct impression he was looking to meet women. Can she give him your number?"

"Why the hell not, except that I get unhinged just thinking about it? What's the worst that could happen? He could hate me, or I could hate him. I could like him, but he could reject me. He could like me, and I could reject him. Sure, Richard. Give him my number. I really do appreciate it. Really."

Mimi entered and reported that she was certain she had picked out the man who had held me at gunpoint. Our conversation then stopped, and eventually Marcy came through and then Mike. They both were reasonably sure of their identifications as Marcel moved with such unusual grace. Detective Larson came in shortly and informed us that those of us who had been positive in our IDs had all picked out Marcel. He looked very pleased. They would book him and request that bail be set exorbitantly high, given the dangerous nature of the charges and the fact that there were two such charges. "What about Helena's case?" I asked. "Will it be reopened?"

"The first step," Detective Larson replied, "is for Harrison and me to sit down together and discuss it. Let's say, for now, that I'll be unofficially seeing if it links up. I'll keep you informed." He passed out cards to everyone present and thanked us for doing our duty as citizens. He made a comment about our being here at the expense of Virginia's taxpayers, which also seemed to give him pleasure. Then he dismissed us.

We drove back to the clinic exuberantly. It was as if we'd all passed final exams. But my mood evaporated when I saw Frank. He had spent the afternoon with Harry, who had grown more and more morose as he grasped that the alleged murderer of his mother was someone from the café and not a street thug.

Frank could spare no time to talk, but he, Mike, Marcy, and I had plans to have a late dinner together that night, so he promised to fill me in then. We met in front of the clinic at eight-thirty. Frank looked whipped after his session with the Hoppers, but he wanted to go to the Caliban Café for dinner. He couldn't resist his curiosity and felt that there were no longer any therapeutic constraints against his going; Mr. Roden had stopped coming to the meetings and Mr. Hopper was going home with his children and would not be at the café tonight. We all agreed with Frank's suggestion, being primarily anxious to give in to him after what he'd been going through. Frank and I took one car, Mike and Marcy the other.

"I'm almost too tired to talk about it," Frank started out. "What a day."

"You don't have to," I offered. "You look beat."

"No, I'll tell you. But once we go in for dinner I don't want to have to repeat everything for Marcy and Mike. I'll tell them tomorrow or you can tell them tomorrow."

"Fine. What happened when you told Harry about Marcel?"

"First he started muttering about a 'blood feud' and 'the bloodshed must end.' He was so confusing, but finally I figured out what he was talking about. Harry is convinced that Marcel murdered his mother as retribution for Harry having killed Helena.

"Harry killed Helena?" I asked, horrified.

"I don't know. Harry doesn't know. He can't remember anything. He has no memory at all of the night Helena was killed. At least not after he and his father left the clinic and headed for the restaurant. But in his mind, the only explanation is that Helena left him for Marcel and they were lovers. He thinks Marcel must have seen him come in the night that he yelled at Helena, the night that she died. He doesn't even remember yelling at her or calling her names, but there were enough witnesses to convince him it happened. He's sure that Marcel thinks he killed Helena and that's why Marcel murdered his mother. To pay him back. Sara, he was pleading with me to lock him up as a sign to Marcel. As a truce. If they were both locked up, Marcel would see that everything was equal and the killing would stop."

"My God, Frank. What did you do? That's incredible."

"I didn't know what the hell to do. I called Joyce and she called Dr. Harley. We all discussed it. We were getting desperate. Dr. Harley decided to call a colleague of his, Dr. Finestein. He's evidently a big hypnotist. What we finally decided to try, which we're going to do tomorrow, is have Finestein hypnotize Harry. He's going to try to recover the lost events of the night of Helena's death. Actually, he's going to start with the afternoon that Harry disappeared and couldn't remember where he'd been or what he'd done. You remember—the same afternoon Mimi's cup was thrown into Harley's car. Both that afternoon and the night Helena died Harry had been worked up into a rage and was verbally abusive. Then he disappeared and the time was lost to him. Finestein thought we should start with the less emotional incident. Less threatening. He wanted to start with the afternoon and see if Harry could respond and if he seems genuine. Then, on to the scary one."

"This is happening tomorrow?"

128

"Tomorrow afternoon. Harry is dying to have it done. He didn't even want to wait that long. He feels like he just has to know. Who can blame him? Mr. Hopper also asked if he could be there. I don't think Finestein will let him in the room while it's going on, but I think it's good that he'll be there when Harry comes out."

"So do I."

"You'll see on the videotape where we discuss all this. You're coming Friday to my supervision, aren't you?"

"I wouldn't miss it."

"Here we are, Sara. I can't go through talking about all this again tonight. I want to see the famous Caliban and be fed and soothed."

"You got it."

As I anticipated, Frank loved the Caliban. He raved and cooed and looked and examined. He wanted to rent the dining room for a winter beach party, everyone to dine in bathing trunks. He couldn't wait to bring his new honey, Randy. Marcy and Mike arrived, and we were seated in a darkened alcove.

"This was Marcel's station, I think, wasn't it, Sara?" Mike asked. I nodded. "Too bad you didn't get to see him, Frank. He looked just like you."

"I get the creeps thinking he might pop up any second," I said. "Seeing him in the line-up, I thought my heart would stop."

"His replacement doesn't look bad," Frank interrupted, pointing out a blond, blue-eyed man in his early twenties who approached our table to give us menus. "My Lord, pressed white linen plays havoc with my hormones. I'll bet they're running a homosexual vice ring here. Look at these men. It's like waking up in heaven surrounded by heavenly bodies. Was Marcel head-waiter? He must have hired these sweet young things. I'll bet he rents them out by the hour. Think of it—come in and browse, have a nice meal, then pick from what's truly an embarrassment of riches. Slip Marcel an extra tip, who's to notice? And go to the back room or some designated place."

"Are you serious?" Marcy asked. "Do you think that's really going on?"

"Well, why not?" Frank asked. "Something's going on. And it's hard to believe men of this aesthetic caliber are straight. With one notable exception," Frank said, smiling appreciatively at Sweeney. Mike blushed. "What a loss," Frank whispered to me, eyeing Mike.

"Let's order," Mike suggested. I studied the menu and had decided on salmon when I saw an order of coquilles St. Jacques drift by. The scallops threw me into indecision, but I returned to the salmon. We all ordered.

"You know you could be right, Frank," I said. "It's improbable, not impossible. What was that joke of Mr. Roden's on the videotape? You know—he said you'd make a good waiter like Marcel, if you gave it a try. It was a little insinuating. Do you think he meant that you had an easily peddled ass?"

"Let's face it, someone here has a good eye. There's no reason why it shouldn't be Mr. Roden," Frank replied.

"Let's be serious about this," Mike said. "If this really is a vice ring sort of thing, then either Marcel was running it or he was reporting to Mr. Roden or Mr. Hopper. Maybe Helena found out. And Mrs. Hopper. I didn't know either of them. Would they be likely to figure something like that out?"

"But why," Marcy asked, "should those two figure it out within a month of working here and no one else figure it out? It doesn't make sense. What about the other employees? They can't all be involved. And we'd have heard if any other café employees had been murdered recently, don't you think?"

"You're right," I said. "But Helena and Mrs. Hopper were both extremely intrusive in their own ways. Helena was more seductive and provocative. She wasn't very good about boundaries. I can see her trying to seduce someone like Marcel, who was handsome, older than she was. He might have turned her down, and she might have made a nuisance of herself. She could be very indiscreet. Or he might have said he wasn't interested but he could find her some men who were. He might have offered to put her up for sale. That's possible if he was running a prostitution ring. That might have been what she found out, and maybe she was threatening to expose it. Or, knowing Helena, she might have innocently said something like 'Let me check with my therapist.'"

"What about Mrs. Hopper?" Mike asked. "She's really the only one we know was murdered. If the other things did happen to Helena, she might have decided to kill herself."

"She was a meddlesome woman," Frank stated matter of factly. "At least that's how her family viewed her, and it was my impression seeing her with them. She liked to keep track of what was going on, how things were being done—you know the type. She liked details and was very stubborn about finding things out. She also seemed honest and even righteously so. She didn't want anyone sneaking around. She wanted to know what was happening. She was also part owner of the café. She could have insisted on some changes. She had some legal rights. Also, I remember Mr. Roden making a point of the fact that once she made up her mind to do something, there was no way to stop her. It wasn't worth the effort to try."

"Although," I said, in a sinister tone, "her husband did try. Let's make a list of things we'd need to know to see if this is plausible."

"A list, Sara? A list? You should have seen her in graduate school," Mike said to Marcy and Frank. "She'd have these long lists posted all over her apartment with things like, 'File my nails,' 'Take out the garbage,' 'Write chapter one of my dissertation,' all thrown in together."

"Well," I defended myself, "I could always cross off a couple things each day that way. Some people relieve anxiety by eating and others by making lists. I just happen to do both. It's like being ambidextrous. Come on." I took a small pad from my pocketbook and a pen. "Okay. One, who hires the waiters? Obviously the owners have to approve them, but who interviews and selects them? Two, how long did Marcel work at the café? Three, who hired Marcel? Four, did Marcel and Helena spend any time together? Did Helena have a crush on him? Five, has Marcel's alibi for the night of Helena's death been corroborated? Six, who told

Marcel where to find Mrs. Hopper Wednesday night, and was it a setup or inadvertent? Seven, why didn't Mr. Hopper want his wife to work at the café?"

"Why, I would like to know," Marcy interjected, "would Marcel try to kill you? Does he think you know something? That's what really puzzles me."

I had already thought about that, and Larson had seemed to agree with me. "I think he thought I was trying to identify him from the shooting. I mean, he saw me in here on two different occasions very close together, with two other people who had witnessed the shooting and whom he probably noticed the night he shot Mrs. Hopper. He passed Mike on the street and Richard was on his way to his car. Maybe he thought I was an undercover cop or something. I wonder if he's pleaded guilty or not. I've got to call Detective Larson and see if he can answer any of these questions. He might know the answers by now. Especially if Roden or Hopper set up the killing."

"My dear Dr. Marks," Mike said, "you haven't been called in as a consulting detective. He might not like you bugging him. He might also wonder at your relationship with Marcel. You've been acting more suspiciously than you think. Helena calls you with a cryptic message. Marcel tries to bump you off. I'm curious, too, but I'm not sure it's a great idea to call him."

"Oh, come on, Mike," Marcy said. "The worst Larson could do is to tell her to butt out. Give him a call, Sara. We're all as curious as you are. Mike's just a little cautious about getting involved," she said, giving him a rueful look.

"I'll certainly plead guilty to that," Mike said. "Will you excuse me a minute?" As soon as Mike left for the men's room, Frank and Marcy urged me to call.

"Go on," Frank said. "Just let him do the talking. Just ask if there's any news." I got up and asked where I might find a pay phone.

As I approached the phone booth, I realized that I hadn't brought any change. I must have looked disappointed because Mr. Roden walked by and asked if I was all right. "It's nothing. I forgot to bring change for the call. I'll call when I get home. It wasn't important."

"Come, call from my office," he offered graciously. "It's that door over there. Give a knock first and if no one answers, go right in. The phone's on the desk."

"That's very kind of you, Mr. Roden. It's really unnecessary. It wasn't an important call."

"It's my pleasure, Dr. Marks. You keep bringing us a lot of business. I notice you've switched back to your younger boyfriend. Very attractive young man. I also wanted to express my concern over the events with Marcel. We were all shocked. No one who knew him would have believed it. I'm sorry you had such a terrifying experience."

"Well, it's all over and he's in custody, so I'm relieved."

"Were you and Marcel acquainted?"

"No, I really didn't know him at all."

"It is curious. I had formed the theory that he was an old flame of yours and you kept parading these other men in front of him and he blew up. He had always been so responsible in his work here. It's difficult to understand. Although he can be impulsive at times."

"Did you hire him yourself?" I asked boldly.

"I do most of the personnel work. Mr. Hopper likes to leave employee relations to me as much as possible. He's uncomfortable with people. Yes, I hired Marcel. He was a boy when he came here, eighteen or nineteen. He's been here eight or nine years already—the time goes so fast. I'm just stunned. Well, I've got to keep working. I've been taking over some of Mr. Hopper's responsibilities this week. You'll excuse me. Please feel free to use my phone."

I thanked him again, thoroughly charmed by the man's courtesy. I walked to his office and knocked timidly on the door. There was no answer, so I furtively stepped in. On the vague suspicion that Mr. Roden might have tapped his own phone, I called Mike's number and let it ring. Then I hung up. I could always call Detective Larson from home or from the clinic tomorrow. I was surprised to see another door slightly ajar within the office, which on closer examination opened into a bathroom. It made sense for him to have one. Mr. Roden worked long hours and mingled freely with the customers. He could pop in here for a quick shower and shave. Feeling guilty and frightened, I walked in and shut the bathroom door and opened the medicine cabinet. Just curious, I told myself. There was nothing much inside. An electric razor, deodorant. I left. On my way out I made a note of the phone number on Mr. Roden's desk. I wanted to check it with the number Helena had left for me. Had she called me from that room on the night that she died?

When I returned to the table, I was met with a concerned group of faces. "What took you so long?" Mike asked. "We were getting worried. Did you talk to Larson?"

"No, I didn't call him." I explained what had occurred. As I was talking, our waiter passed by with a tray of dirty dishes and signaled us that he'd be right back for ours. I must have given him an intent look, because Mike said that I'd have this waiter also following me home if I didn't return my gaze to the table. The others were excited that I'd infiltrated Maury's office, but we stopped talking when our waiter returned to collect our plates and take our dessert orders. As we finished ordering, Mr. Roden walked by carrying a doggy bag for the table beyond us in the alcove. He nodded in greeting and returned several minutes later to welcome Frank to his restaurant.

"Mr. Thomas, it's a pleasure to see you here. What a loss we've suffered. I hope you're continuing to work with the Hoppers throughout these difficult times. You know I can always make time if you'd like me to come in again."

"You've been very generous with your time," Frank said. "And I know you're assuming much of Mr. Hopper's workload right now. I appreciate the offer. It's such a sad situation."

"Life wasn't meant to be easy," Mr. Roden commented. It was the most serious I'd seen him. "People survive the best they can. That's the main thing." He nodded again, this time to signal his departure.

134

Frank was close to tears. "Why couldn't I repair shoes for a living?" he asked. "Sit down at a bench and take something tangible and make it better." We all grew more serious. Dessert was a minor diversion from our private thoughts, but it didn't work its old magic. I was thinking about the inevitable losses we would all suffer down the road. Timing and circumstance made a death tragic, but the death was inevitable. It was terrifying and reassuring at the same time.

Mike must have snapped out or pulled himself out of his thoughts first, because he addressed me, "You look miles away, Sara. And very sad."

"I don't want anyone I love to die," I said, "myself included. That doesn't seem too much to ask." Everyone sat silently, and I began to feel awkward and uncomfortable. "I have some news," I announced. "A young lawyer, innocent of his destiny, will probably be calling me up for a date soon. His name is Joel."

"Don't hold back," Mike encouraged in a mock therapeutic attitude.

"Richard wants to see me married off. He asked Dorothy if she knew of any eligible men for me. She came up with Joel. She's giving him my phone number. More news to follow, as it occurs. I'm a nervous wreck at the thought."

"Take heart in the fact that Dorothy's living with Richard. She's got good taste," Marcy offered. "Have you met Dorothy? I wonder what she's like."

Back in the soothing cocoon of gossip, I found my dessert became tastier. The warmth of the company muted the ticking of the clock, and I arrived home reassured and at ease.

I checked for messages immediately. Since Helena's death, I'd become a fanatic about it. The red light was on, and I hit the playback button. "Hello, Sara. My name is Joel Fox. Dorothy Martins gave me your number, and I thought maybe we could arrange to meet each other. You can call me at home tonight or at work tomorrow." He'd left his numbers.

It was too late to call tonight, but I put his work number in my purse. As I did so, I noticed the number I had jotted down in

Mr. Roden's office, and I set about replaying Helena's last message to me. It was eerie to hear her voice. "Dr. Marks, this is Helena. I know I shouldn't call you at home, but I found out something and I have to talk to you. I need your help. You can reach me at the Caliban till nine. It's 485-0300. Or else make time for me tomorrow, please." The number was the same as Mr. Roden's office number. What arrested my attention, though, was a noise in the background I hadn't noticed before. As Helena began reciting the phone number, a steady sound began and remained. The closest I could come to identifying it was that it was running water. Someone had been in the bathroom while Helena made her call from Maury's office. Was that someone Marcel? Had he thought that she'd found out something about him? Had that phone call sealed her fate? I told myself that I was letting my imagination run wild. I was probably just nervous about meeting Joel Whatshisname. This was a diversionary tactic to keep my mind off my real anxieties. Nevertheless, I did want to call Detective Larson and tell him about the tape and find out what he'd learned. But that call too could wait till the morning. I didn't want to hound him with late night phone calls.

20

Armed with a cup of coffee and a doughnut, I called Joel back at nine A.M. Thursday morning. A secretary answered, but Joel picked up promptly. "Hello," I said, "Joel? This is Sara Marks. You called me last night."

"Hi, Sara. Yes. I'm glad you called back." His voice was pleasant and deep. "Dorothy Martins gave me your name. I wondered if we could have dinner together sometime?"

"Yes. We could." I laughed a little awkwardly.

"How does Saturday night sound?"

"Sounds good."

"How about if I pick you up at quarter to eight? Unless, of course, if you want to meet me there. That's okay, too. Dorothy said you lived on Connecticut Avenue, and I thought we could go to Chico's. It's a Hungarian restaurant near where you live. But I'm open to any suggestions you may have."

"Chico's is fine and that would be great if you could pick me up." I gave him my address. "It's sort of hard to park, so why don't I wait downstairs?"

"Okay. I'll be the man in a beige Rabbit."

"I'll be the woman looking nervously around for a beige Rabbit. At least you have one of the two or three cars I can identify."

He chuckled. "I'm looking forward to meeting you, Sara. I'll see you Saturday."

"Yup. Goodbye." We hung up and I took a deep breath. So far so good. No pathology jumped out at me over the phone. And I liked the sound of his voice.

I turned my attention to calling Detective Larson. He was in and willing to talk to me. I told him about Helena's tape and that the call was probably made from Mr. Roden's office. I felt shy of mentioning the homosexual vice ring. Somehow, in the light of day it seemed ridiculous. But after I'd asked him a series of questions about who hired the waiters and how long Marcel had worked there, he began to sound impatient and asked what I was getting at. So I told him. To my surprise, he responded to the idea thoughtfully. He said they'd look into it. He also answered some of my questions. Marcel's alibi for the night Helena was killed was corroborated by several regulars at the jazz club Marcel frequented. He didn't leave the club until one or two in the morning. He left alone. Marcel himself had done no more talking since his arrest. He would talk only to the private lawyer he had retained. He seemed to have more money than one would expect for a waiter. The police had searched his apartment and were not a little impressed by his high-quality accommodations. The man lived well. Very well. His tastes were expensive and refined. He had only one pair of jeans and one beige jacket. His other clothes were finely tailored and made of costly fabrics.

When I got off the phone with Detective Larson, I knew I had to change my thinking on several accounts: Marcel probably had had nothing to do with Helena's death, or at least nothing directly causative. And Mrs. Hopper's death might not have been a setup. Mr. Hopper and Mr. Roden might both be innocent. It would have been hard for them to recognize Marcel in jeans when he habitually shunned them. I couldn't let myself get caught in a rigid way of viewing the information. Maybe Helena killed herself for her own reasons. She was pregnant and highly unstable. Maybe Mrs. Hopper picked up something, a scrap of paper with a message on it that would be incriminating to Marcel. Maybe he saw her put it in her purse on Wednesday and he decided on the spur of the moment to get it back. He thought up an excuse to leave the restaurant and took a chance trying to grab it from her under the guise of a street robbery. He was impulsive, Mr. Roden had said. He obviously was involved in something illegal. It didn't have to be at the café. Maybe he really didn't have any intentions of shooting Mrs. Hopper. He might have panicked when Mr. Roden started after him because he feared that Mr. Roden would recognize him. Mr. Roden's reaction, to yell and give chase, seemed in keeping with his character. He was not an easily intimidated man. Certainly, such a series of events made as much sense as the conspiracy theories I'd been thinking up.

The reality of my work pulled me out of my imaginings. I had a new patient to interview before the community meeting. I was determined to give her my full attention and to push my own concerns to the back of my mind. I managed to concentrate and to work hard the rest of the morning. But Harry's hypnotism was scheduled for the afternoon, and I didn't have the discipline to work during that event.

The first hypnotism session took place Thursday right after lunch. Frank and Dr. Harley were present in the room with Harry and Dr. Finestein. Mr. Hopper sat in the waiting area, lost in his own thoughts. Those of us who were not allowed to be present found it almost impossible to settle down. Patients and staff alike buzzed around waiting for the participants to emerge. The wait seemed interminable. At least I knew that Frank would eventually fill me in. Finally, around three, they opened the door and Dr. Harley stepped out. Dr. Finestein also walked out of the office, but closed the door behind him. Frank and Harry remained inside together. Dr. Harley said he would come by to each of the three team meetings, which were just about to convene. He came to our meeting about ten minutes later. He said, in a voice laced with sorrow, that Harry had remembered throwing Mimi's cup at the car window. The implications were clear. Harry had committed and repressed a violent act. But Harry wanted to continue with the hypnotism. The next session would explore what Harry did and thought about on the night Helena died. Dr. Finestein, Frank, and Dr. Harley would keep the information confidential if Harry so desired. "What Harry remembers in no way constitutes proof, one way or the other," Dr. Harley took pains to reassure us. "We are doing this to help Harry gain some understanding of his unconscious and learn to exert conscious control over his actions. Our mandate is to help our patients. Unless our patients pose an immediate danger, any other issues are secondary. Is that clear?" Dr. Harley asked rhetorically, seemingly to convince himself. "If," he continued, "Harry's remembrances lead us to believe that he is potentially dangerous, we will consider recommending hospitalization. We will try to enlist Mr. Hopper's cooperation and do what is best for Harry and the community at large. I'm going to meet with the other two teams now, and then go back in with Harry and Frank and Dr. Finestein and see if Harry can continue now. Please remember, memory is a tricky faculty. We don't know that hypnotism actually gets at the truth. It does seem to give people access to parts of themselves otherwise cut off from their awareness. I'm not going to answer any questions now or discuss it further. If there are any major decisions made this evening, you will all be informed in the community meeting tomorrow morning."

The realization that Harry might have killed Helena kept penetrating and receding from my awareness. I couldn't quite grasp it and hold it in place. He had shattered the car window. Melvin's daughter had been innocent—wrongly accused by Mimi,

I thought with a touch of satisfaction. As soon as the team meeting broke up, I raced to the message board and scribbled a note to Frank: *Call me as soon as you get home tonight. I have to know what happened with Harry. Please!!!! I'll be home all evening. You can call or come by if you want. Dinner, drinks, anything goes with this invitation. Sara.*

Frank rang the buzzer around seven that evening. He'd come straight from the clinic, and he looked depleted. "Well," I said, swallowing several times in succession, "did he remember anything?"

Frank sat down. "You know it's confidential, Sara. I can tell you, but Dr. Harley promised Harry the information would not go outside the clinic without Harry's express authorization."

"Of course," I said. My legs were losing strength and I had to sit down. "Did he kill her, Frank? Did he remember killing her?" I braced myself for the horror, but Frank just shook his head from side to side.

"He had no memory of killing her, thank God. You don't know what it was like in there. I thought I'd have a heart attack, I was so frightened. I kept imagining that Harry would start describing walking with her to the bridge and picking her up off her feet. I kept seeing it in my mind and waiting for him to describe it. God, I've got to drink something, Sara. Water or juice or something. I haven't eaten anything."

"Sit down at the table," I directed. "You can eat while you tell me about the whole thing." I poured a glass of club soda for Frank and set cheese, crackers, and apples on the table.

"Then let me tell you about the first session first. That Finestein did a good job. I'd never seen anyone hypnotized before. Probably the fact that Harry really wanted it helped. He couldn't stand not knowing what he'd done. Anyway, Finestein put him under, but Dr. Harley and I coached Finestein about what Harry would respond to and the things we needed to know. He talked to Harry a lot about loyalty and the importance of loyalty. He talked in a soft, lulling voice about love and what it can mean to people, then he went back to Helena's breaking up with Harry and how that felt. Harry's response was 'Shattered.' He said her love had glued him together and without it he was just unconnected fragments. He talked a while about that and then they went on to Mimi, and Harry's feelings about Mimi. He called her a destroyer. Said she splits people in two. Then he started talking about two children at home, the father at work all the time. It really did seem as if he was identifying Dr. Harley with his father and Harley's wife and kids with his mother and Judy and him. He saw Mimi as the force that kept them apart and wrecked their home life. Although, I don't know if Mr. Hopper ever had any lovers or a particular woman. It's never come up in our sessions. He seems more like a workaholic type. I'm getting sidetracked. Finestein led him around to the community meeting and his yelling at Mimi. Harry got right back into the meeting. 'She's a destroyer,' he said.

"Finestein asked him what happened after the meeting. He told Harry in a slow, melodic voice that people were leaving the meeting and he said stuff like, 'and you, Harry, were sitting there, your body was stiff and as you were sitting there with a stiff body you had thoughts racing through your mind. Your thoughts were racing. What were these thoughts going through your mind as you sat in the yellow chair in the meeting room?' And Harry picked right up with his thoughts. He went on about Mimi being a home wrecker, a bitch.

"'And what did you do?' Finestein asked him.

"Harry told him. It was all there, locked in his memory. He said, 'I watched everyone leave. I got up to leave. I looked down and saw a mug on the floor. I picked it up and it said Mimi. I was thinking, The wicked must be punished, and it said Mimi.' You should have been there, Sara. He went on about Circe and temptation. Women deceive. Anyway, he described leaving the center by the back stairs with Mimi's cup and going out to the back lot chanting 'Smash the destroyer' in his mind. He smashed the cup against the window with all his strength."

"What then?" I asked.

"His thoughts seemed to jump from 'Smash the destroyer' to 'Protect the innocent.' He wandered the neighborhood with the idea of patrolling for Mrs. Harley. Guarding her. He must have known that they lived in that area. But he didn't know where or even know the area very well. It sounded as if he wandered around, getting different phrases caught in his mind that would replay like a broken record for a while and then be replaced with a new phrase. After a while the phrases seemed to focus on love. 'Love destroys' and 'Love heals all'—stuff like that. We didn't go on too long after the car. Finestein did something I liked. Evidently he's used to using hypnosis to teach and suggest expanded ways of doing things. He uses it to help people open themselves to new possibilities. Anyway, at the point when we were ready to stop, he asked if it might be helpful to suggest something to Harry about his interpretation of events. Dr. Harley asked if Finestein could tell Harry that Harley's marriage had ended before he'd gotten to know Mimi. He said that he and his wife had misunderstood each other. It had been destroyed from within. It didn't take any outside force. Finestein explained that to Harry in human terms. He talked about people sometimes hurting others they love. Even while they love, sometimes they cause pain. He told Harry that Dr. Harley and his wife couldn't figure out how to love each other and not cause pain, that Mimi came later. He suggested that Harry would find himself thinking about ways in which he responded to people and misunderstood people. He would find himself wondering, 'What are people really like?'"

"Did he start to wonder?"

"I don't know. It was just this afternoon, Sara. Give me a break."

"I like that suggestion. It makes me want to learn hypnosis."

"I'm exhausted, Sara. I don't know when I've felt so wiped out. The other session is anticlimactic once you know that he had no memory of seeing Helena after he left the café. But there is one interesting thing. Even when Harry was in the café yelling at Helena, the main thing in his mind was his longing to touch her. He wandered around much of the night, thinking, 'Close to Helena,' and 'Connected to Helena,' 'Always with Helena.' It was incredibly sad. He walked around the monuments thinking, 'Pursuit of happiness,' to himself over and over. He remembered being at the Lincoln Memorial reading through the Gettysburg Address. He kept thinking about 'all men are created equal.' It seems that he walked home over the Memorial Bridge. What a relief that it wasn't Key Bridge. That tasted good, Sara. I'm half asleep. I'd better get my carcass home before I fall asleep. Maybe, could I just have a cup of coffee to revive me enough to leave?"

I got Frank the coffee. I could see how tired he was, but I couldn't resist one more question. "What about Mr. Hopper?" I asked. "How did he react?"

"Oh, that's right. I forgot to tell you. He looked terrible. He's losing weight, and he just looks beaten up by the world. You'll see how he looks tomorrow from Wednesday night's tape. Anyway, he was really scared. Not just nervous, but scared. You don't usually see people who look frightened, but he sure as hell was. He was present at the second session. He asked if he could be there, and Harley let him. He didn't say anything throughout the session; just left it to us. And Harry really didn't seem to see or be aware of anyone but Finestein. But I kept an eye on Mr. Hopper, and it was like he let out his breath when Harry said he'd walked home over Memorial Bridge. He must have thought Harry'd killed her, or at least thought he might have done it. He was so relieved. Afterward, Dr. Harley explained about the car. Mr. Hopper was totally apologetic. He insisted on being billed for the damage. When Dr. Harley said his insurance had already paid for it, Mr. Hopper insisted on writing a check to the clinic. Dr. Harley offered no objection to that," Frank commented with a sly grin. "That was about it. Mr. Hopper put his arm around Harry and they left together. And now, while I can still stand up, I'm going to leave."

I gave Frank a hug and thanked him for coming by. It was only nine-thirty, but the worry over Harry had done me in. I was asleep almost before I realized I was in bed.

21

"Well?" Richard asked when I entered his office Friday morning to join Frank and him in viewing Frank's videotape.

"Well, what?" I asked, thinking that either there was something I'd forgotten to do or that Richard hadn't heard the outcome of the hypnotism yet.

"Well, did Joel call you?" Richard asked.

"Well, yes," I said. "Now that you mention it, he did."

"Well, when are you going to see him?" Richard persisted.

"Well, well, well," I said. "He and I are having dinner together tomorrow night. You've turned into quite a yenta. I tell you what—if we get married, you'll get a commission."

"Now, Sara, my interest is not mercenary. It's merely an intrusive, invasive, and meddlesome need to know. Nothing to be disparaged."

"All right," I said. "I'll tell you all about it on Monday."

"That's more like it," Richard said. He turned to Frank, who had been enjoying our interchange. "Shall we look at the tape from Wednesday night? It was just Mr. Hopper and Harry and Judy, right?"

"Yes," Frank said. "I already told Richard about the hypnotism sessions," he said to me. "And do you know what Harry did this morning? Wonders never cease. The child brought a new mug in for Mimi. He showed it to me and told me he wanted to give it to her. I saw her in the hallway, so I asked her to come over, and he gave it to her and apologized. Now, that was heartwarming."

Richard and I agreed, and Richard started the tape. We both reacted immediately to Mr. Hopper's appearance. His face was losing flesh and taking on a gauntness reminiscent of pictures of concentration camp survivors. Either he was physically ill, or stress was eating away at him. Richard directed Frank to ask Mr. Hopper directly whether he'd been to a doctor. If not, he was to urge him to go in for a checkup. "And be forceful about it," Richard said.

"He's wasting away before our eyes. Tell him to start taking care of himself. Talk about what he's eating and how much sleep he's getting. Be concrete. Show him your concern. He has to take better care of himself."

"A yenta and a Jewish mother," I said to Richard. "How my image of you has changed."

Frank opened the session by asking the family if they had heard the news about Marcel being arrested. They all responded that they had. Judy started to cry. She curled herself up in a ball on her chair and started to rock back and forth. Harry stiffened. Mr. Hopper looked pained and helpless. Frank got up and led Mr. Hopper over to Judy's chair, where Mr. Hopper put his arm around her and held her. Frank sat down next to Harry. Mr. Hopper continued to comfort Judy in silence but eventually resumed his seat.

"I know how painful this is for all of you," Frank said. "Losing your mother"—to Harry—"and your wife"—to Mr. Hopper—"and now learning that someone you knew killed her. Can you try to put into words some of how it's affecting you?"

Mr. Hopper spoke immediately. "I blame myself," he said. "I should never have let her come back to the café. I'm not a strong man. I'm not forceful. I don't know how to insist on things. I could have prevented this. I should have told her no and made it stick. I blame myself. I'm weak."

There was a minute's silence during which the children looked down and Frank looked bewildered. "I don't understand," Frank finally said.

Mr. Hopper explained, "I had a premonition something terrible would happen if Lizzie came back to work. I knew she'd be in danger. I tried to prevent it, but I thought if I said no to her she would leave me. She's threatened to leave before. I've failed her. I should have let her leave and live her own life. I'm a selfish man. I've tried to keep everyone I care about. It can't be done." Mr. Hopper lapsed into quiet spasms of grief.

Frank gave Mr. Hopper a little time and then asked him, "What sort of danger would the café pose? What makes it a dangerous place?" It was the question I had been waiting for. But before Mr. Hopper had a chance to respond, Harry jumped out of his seat.

"It was a vengeance killing!" he yelled. "My mother's blood is on my hands." Harry's eyes were wild and he had started to pace. His agitation was growing.

There was a noticeable weariness in Frank's movements as he started to pace with Harry. Frank matched his rhythm to that of Harry's and then, when they were in sync, slowed down the pace. It was a technique Richard had taught us. Harry responded to the extent that his movements became less frantic. Although Harry was still talking, Frank turned to Mr. Hopper and explained Harry's theory about a "blood feud" to him. He also told him about the decision to hypnotize Harry the next day and invited him to attend. Mr. Hopper looked surprised, alarmed, worried; it was hard to read his expression. But he said he'd be there. Frank thanked him and fell silent. Harry's words could again be heard: "Revenge. Marcel thinks I killed Helena. I knew she had someone else. Maybe he loved her? Really loved her like I did. Everyone thinks I killed her. You think so, Dad. You think I killed her."

Mr. Hopper looked down.

"Did you?" Frank asked Harry. "Do you have any memory?"

"No memory. No memory. What have I done? Marcel wanted to hurt me. Why else shoot Mother? It's all my fault. Why doesn't someone lock me up? The killing must stop. Get a message to Marcel: I'm locked up, too. Can't you help me, Mr. Thomas?"

"We'll know more tomorrow when you're hypnotized. In the meantime, Harry, I think the best way to help right now is to spend some time talking about your feelings about Helena and your mother, even the angry, maybe disappointed feelings. All the feelings. I think that's the first step toward coming to accept their deaths."

Richard stopped the videotape. "How does the session continue?" he asked.

"I would say that this was an interlude and it went from bad to worse," Frank admitted. "Maybe I was trying to be too rational with Harry. It seemed like he was listening to me, but then he got agitated again and started back in about blood feuds."

"What about Mr. Hopper and Judy?" Richard asked. "Did they respond at all?"

"Interestingly, Mr. Hopper responded. He started to talk about his feelings toward Lizzie being confused sometimes. But Harry took over again with his talk of killing. It was downhill from there."

Richard looked serious and thoughtful. "Let me tell you what I think. First off, you've done a good job with a bitch of a case. And I appreciate that when you're in there with them you're on the spot and you don't have the benefit of hindsight. But I think if we can detach ourselves from the emotions and focus on the process, then what comes into view is that Harry is maintaining his old role in the family. When they first came in, his role was to protect both parents from separating or from openly airing their conflicts, which would have given them a chance at resolving them. In this session, he's protecting his father. Whenever father begins to blame himself or take on any responsibility, Harry gets crazy and father is pushed into the background. Father says that he tried to keep her from the café. Well, why? What were his real motives? If he did try to keep her away because he suspected danger, then he must blame himself for not being strong. If he actually knew of a danger—I mean, concretely knew—he might be into something illegal or shielding some dangerous undertaking. Either way, he bears some responsibility. If that's all a lot of crap and he didn't want her there because he didn't want her there, for personality reasons, he didn't like having her around much of the time, then he's going to feel guilty anyway just because he harbored such negative feelings toward her and now she's dead. But each time father begins to talk about these thorny and essential issues, Harry acts crazy and the focus is deflected onto him. Nothing is resolved. It's diversionary. I think it would be useful, if and when this occurs again, to comment on it. Say something to the effect that every time Mr. Hopper begins to speak of his own reactions, Harry steals the show. If Harry persists, I would even consider having him leave the session. If he's disruptive, ask him to leave so his father can continue. I think once his father has a chance to do some of his own work on this, Harry will calm down.

I wonder if Harry's afraid that his father had his mother killed. Not consciously, but unconsciously afraid. He's certainly keeping his father from admitting to anything. Imagine if he did have her killed. That would be devastating."

"What a thought," I said. "I don't even want to think about it. You know, I pushed the thought down, but yesterday, when Frank was telling me about how relieved Mr. Hopper was that Harry remembered walking home over Memorial Bridge and not over Key Bridge, I had a flash of Mr. Hopper killing Helena and living with the fear that his son had witnessed it. It gives me the creeps."

Frank looked stunned. "But why would he kill Helena? I can't believe it."

"I don't know," I admitted. "But they did drive to and from the clinic together Wednesday nights, and she was awfully fond of him. And she was so cute. Who knows? I don't know what happened with Helena, but I think if Marcel was paid to kill Mrs. Hopper, which he might have been—I mean Marcel barely knew her—then Mr. Hopper is the likely suspect. Men have been known to want their wives out of the way before."

"No," Frank protested. "She'd threatened to leave him in the past. He didn't want to let her go."

"That's true," I conceded. "But she owned a third of the restaurant, isn't that true? And she might have refused to be bought out. From one of your old sessions, it sounded as if she had equal standing and none of the three could force anyone out. She might have made a lot of trouble. What if something illegal is going on there? With a hit man for a waiter, it wouldn't be surprising. She might have threatened to leave, but the price might have been high. She might have come back to the café and looked into everything or demanded changes or taken them to court. Lord only knows. This way, her interest in the place reverts to Mr. Hopper, doesn't it? I'll have to check with Detective Larson. No one's going to go through the books and demand this and that. It's very different."

"You make me crawl with goosebumps," Frank said. He wrapped his arms tightly around himself. "The man is devastated."

"Maybe by what he's done." I was merciless. "It's just hard to believe Marcel did it on his own. And that leaves Mr. Hopper as the person to gain the most."

"Or lose the most," Frank put in.

Richard broke into our debate. "It sounds as if neither of you give any credence at all to Harry's theory about Helena and Marcel."

"No," I said, and Frank agreed. "Harry's nuts."

"Very sophisticated diagnostic thinking, Sara. Well, we've got to stop. Time's up. I hope this was of some help to you, Frank. We got a bit off the track."

"It was helpful," Frank said. "I'll try to stick with the process more next time."

"You know what I'd like to do?" I said. "If you think its all right, I'd like to go over some of the old tapes. I've been much too involved, even just as a spectator, to really detach enough to view the process. I'm also curious to see if anyone's said anything we overlooked before that might give us a better understanding of what's going on."

"You want to search for clues, Sara. You can come out and say it. I don't see why you can't replay the old tapes."

"The old tape," Frank corrected Richard. "I only have one cassette with two sides, so there's this week's and last week's tapes. Is there any way we can get more cassettes?" he asked Richard. "Because this way I can only have two sessions on file at any time. Then I have to tape over one of them."

"I'll put in a request," Richard said. "But if you're in any hurry to get them, you just ought to go out and buy a few."

"Yeah, that's what I'll do," Frank agreed. "I wouldn't mind rewatching last week's tape either," Frank said, turning to me. "Want to come in tomorrow, Sara? We could do it together. And we wouldn't have to take work time."

"Sure," I said. "Want me to pick you up? We could get some croissants and coffee and bring them here and run the tape."

"It's a date," Frank said. "Ten o'clock, okay?"

"Sure. Do you want to come, Richard?"

"I'm tempted, but I can't. I've been building some cabinets and I've been letting them drag on too long."

"You are a homebody," I said.

"And furthermore," Richard responded, "tell Joel to have you home by twelve and himself home by twelve-thirty."

22

Frank and I arrived at the clinic at ten-thirty Saturday morning with fresh croissants and steaming hot coffee and the delicious feeling of being in our place of work with no work that we had to do. I was pleased to have an engrossing task that made it easier to put my impending date with Joel out of my mind. Since we'd just seen this week's tape, and I thought it might be excruciating to sit through it again, we flipped in last week's. It was taped the night Mrs. Hopper was killed. Only ten days ago, but it already felt like history, like the replay of assassination attempts. By the time you'd watched the tenth runthrough, it no longer felt immediate. The paradox of instant communication: It brought you there immediately and whisked you away again.

Frank hit the Play button. I watched the Hoppers file in, the children first, then Mr. Roden and after him, Mr. and Mrs. Hopper together, smiling in response to Frank's opening pleasantries. I tried to remember Mrs. Hopper as she had been during that first interview Frank and I had done together, the one when the family had walked out. She had been tighter then, with a firm tension maintained in her face. The Mrs. Hopper we were now witnessing, on the last night of her life, was more accessible, more in contact. She spoke of enjoying the café. Judy spoke of enjoying her mother's newfound activity and Mrs. Hopper tensed up again. But the tension dispelled quickly when Frank intervened. I looked over at Frank, viewing the tape, and realized he was crying silently. I figured that he'd have sniffed out loud if he'd wanted a hug, so I turned back to the tape and let Frank cry to himself. A minute later, though, I stopped the tape. "Did you hear that, Frank?" I asked.

He took a moment to compose himself. "What, Sara? What did you notice? My mind wandered."

"Listen," I instructed. I replayed Mrs. Hopper saying, "The waiters are almost all young men. They couldn't have been more gracious. What's that handsome one's name? Pierre, Emile, no, Marcel. That's right, Marcel. He looks just like Mr. Thomas. At least his face does. What an attractive young man."

"What of it, Sara? I don't see what you're getting at."

"Frank. Don't you see? She noticed that the waiters are almost all young men. The vice ring. It was your idea. Remember? Do you want to do this another time when you feel more up to it?"

"No, go on. You think she realized that he was running a gay vice ring. Or didn't realize it, but had noticed some of what was going on without putting it together in her mind. And maybe she started bugging Marcel with questions about himself, especially since he looked like me. She might have asked him if he was related to me and then probed further about his family and social life. She was so withholding when she first came in, but we were working on her asking questions of her husband and drawing him out. She might have gone overboard, like those assertiveness training graduates who ought to be kept on a leash for the first month after training. Then they get more comfortable with it. She might have thought she was using her new social skills and in fact turned Marcel inside out interrogating him."

"I'll make a note of it, then let's go on. But let's err on the side of putting too much down. We can always go back and eliminate."

The tape continued. Judy got embarrassed at her mother's reference to Frank's attractiveness. Then Mr. Roden spoke up. "Marcel's an excellent waiter, as I'm sure Mr. Thomas would be if he gave it a try."

I stopped the tape again, "I'm just going to note it," I said to Frank. "Mr. Roden refers to Frank's showing potential as one of his waiters, with a question mark."

I hit the Start button. Mr. Roden was talking about Mrs. Hopper accompanying him to the liquor wholesaler's. Then he listed some of her activities at the café. When he mentioned her covering the cash registers to give the girls a break, Helena's name came up. Mrs. Hopper had spoken of her compassionately, "I can't help but feel that if I had gotten involved earlier and gotten to know the girl, she might have confided in me and not killed herself. I know that doesn't make sense to say, but I feel it's true. Poor little girl. I remember seeing her here Wednesday nights; she was quite a beauty." Again, I stopped the tape.

"It sounds silly, Frank, but why do you think she thought that she could have prevented Helena's death? Mr. Hopper felt he could have protected his wife from danger and Mrs. Hopper thinks—thought—she could have helped Helena. Do you think they had something specific in their minds when they thought of danger, or it's just their human instinct to think they could have had that much control? Like my thinking that if I'd called Helena back right away, she'd still be alive. I wish I knew which it is."

"I know, Sara, but let's not stop at everything. We'll never get through this, and I'm starting to feel a little shaky, like I might be coming down with something. Tell me if I feel hot to you."

I put my hand on Frank's forehead, but I didn't think I'd be able to tell if he had a fever or not. Surprisingly, I could tell that he was warm. He also looked kind of glassy-eyed.

"I knew it, I knew it," Frank said with venom. "Randy went to all kinds of trouble to get us ballet tickets at the Kennedy Center, second row seats, and we had a whole evening planned. I hope he believes that I'm sick."

"Why wouldn't he believe you? Of course he will. But he'll have to go with someone else. You're getting a sickly green tinge to your skin."

"Jesus, Sara. It's bad enough getting sick, missing the ballet, and sending Randy off with another. The least you could do is to tell me I look like Camille and hold a cup to my lips."

"Okay," I said, letting my sympathy show. "Do you want me to pack this up and drive you home? I really don't mind if you're not up to it."

"Thanks, Sara. I feel awful. It was really sudden. I'm sorry. If it's a twenty-four-hour thing and I'm better tomorrow, we could come back then."

"Don't worry about it. Mike and I are spending the day together tomorrow. Come on. Think about going home and crawling into bed and getting rid of this thing. I probably just wanted to keep my mind off my date with Joel. God, I hate blind dates." I went to hit the Rewind button, but trying to imagine the unknown Joel must have unnerved me, because I hit Play by mistake. Mr. Roden was saying, "She was such a skinny, delicate little thing in her lightweight jacket. What a pity." I hit Stop and stared at Frank.

"Come on, Sara." Frank walked over and pushed Rewind. "If we wait any longer you'll have to carry me. I'm starting to ache all over."

"Frank!" I yelled. My flesh was tingling, and a shudder passed through my body. "Please, Frank. Didn't you hear that? Mr. Roden said Helena was a skinny little thing *in her lightweight jacket.*"

"Sara, I must be stupid, but she was a skinny little thing in that jacket. Actually, I never saw her in a little jacket. She always wore that big grub-ball of a coat. What's the point?"

"That's the point. She only wore that light jacket once. On the day she died. Don't you see? She told me that morning she had taken her other coat to the cleaners, to surprise her parents. She wore the light jacket on Wednesday. She'd never worn it to the Caliban before; she'd only worked there in the winter. Richard saw her leave in it and told her to dress more warmly or something. Anyway, he noticed. She said she wouldn't be out much in the evening, she usually got a ride home. Remember, it wasn't too cold that day, but the forecast was for freezing temperatures and sleet. That night you came over. Helena left the clinic at noon. She didn't stick around; I bet she had a doctor's appointment. But anyway, she was due at the café at three P.M."

"So Mr. Roden saw her at three and he also noticed that she wasn't dressed for the cold. Help me slide back the TV, Sara."

I gave Frank a hand. "But Frank, he wouldn't have seen her come in at three because he spends Wednesday afternoons with Herb."

"Who the hell is Herb?"

"The liquor wholesaler. Don't you remember they had that big discussion the previous week about Mrs. Hopper wanting to go and meet their suppliers and the only one he went to in person was Herb and she could come there, but she wanted to be home when Judy got home from school. They went back and forth on it, and you told her to take a cab because Mr. Roden wouldn't get done with their business till after school was out. I don't remember the exact time, but it must have been three-thirty or four. He said he went there *every* Wednesday. At two-thirty. I'm sure of it. He said he always got there around two-thirty and left around three-thirty or four."

"Wait a minute, Sara. You're saying that Maury could not have seen Helena come in the Wednesday that she died. Because she came at three and he was at Herb's. Is that right?"

"That's right. And he said that he didn't see her leave that night. That was the weird thing. Nobody saw her leave. She was at the cash register one minute and gone the next. No one in the café remembered seeing her go. Mr. Roden must have lied."

"But, Sara, she could have left and come back for something any time. She might have needed something at the drugstore and run out to get it." Frank steered me purposefully toward my car, weak as he was.

"No. Let's think about this. Let's say her replacement took over between six-thirty and nine, as if she'd gone to the clinic. I'd forgotten that. Maybe she did run out during that time. Damn, you're right. When she realized her replacement had come, she might have gone out after Mr. Hopper left for the clinic and done errands or just made herself scarce so as not to hang around. He might have seen her in that jacket during that time and not thought about it one way or the other. I thought we finally had a clue. I don't think Detective Harrison told us one way or another if she went in and out at all during that day. Still, you'd think someone would have mentioned it if she had left, especially Mr. Roden if he'd seen her leave or come in during that time. It would have been important information. So my statement stands. He either withheld information or lied." We stopped at a traffic light. I wrote myself a note to call Detective Larson re the light jacket and Mr. Roden. I felt better.

I dropped off Frank and went out to get some Tylenol for him. I also picked up some juice in case he needed it. When I returned with his goodies, he shambled to the door in his bathrobe and let me in. I told him to get into bed, poured him a glass of apple juice, and brought him two Tylenol. I enjoyed playing mother. Just as I was about to let myself out, I heard Frank's plaintive cry, "Sara, come back. Come here a minute." I thought he was joking and would ask for a hot water bottle or a back rub, but his expression was serious.

"You can't call Detective Larson about this," he said. "Those tapes and everything on those tapes are confidential and not to go out of the clinic. I gave them my word. You can't tell Larson about the jacket. Even if there is something in it. I'm sorry."

I sat down. I'd been so carried away. "Thanks for reminding me. I forgot, Frank. Don't apologize. I'm glad you stopped me in time."

I was grateful, but my disappointment punctured my mood and I returned home to eat ice cream on and off until it was time to get ready for my date with Joel.

23

I could see the hazard lights blinking on the car that had pulled up right in front of the entrance to my apartment building. I raced forward through the lobby: My watch had said eighteen minutes to eight when I left my apartment, but the lobby clock said seven-fifty. As I ran closer, I could see that the car was the beige Rabbit. At least I wouldn't have to stand there anxiously waiting for him. I darted out the building door and headed straight for the passenger seat; but a slender, attractive man with dark curly hair got out from behind the wheel and walked around the car to me.

"You look like a woman nervously in search of a beige Rabbit," he said smiling, his eyes twinkling.

"Yes," I said, relieved and grateful that he was making everything so easy. "I'm Sara. I'm sorry I'm late. My watch is a little slow . . ."

"The timer's off, you're not being billed," he said with a laugh as he opened the door for me. I slid in, trying to keep down my excitement. I was drawn to his looks and his voice and his manner, and I prayed that he would like me and want to see me again. He looked to be around thirty. How could he be unattached? In Washington? The Sweeney syndrome popped into my mind as the most likely explanation.

"Richard said you're new at Dorothy's firm. Do you like it there?" I asked.

"I'm still adjusting. But I like it so far. It's a lot of work; the firm handles general litigation, and the pace is ridiculous. I still feel that I have to prove myself, and the work is different from what I've done in the past. It takes me much longer than it should, or I hope, than it will once I figure out what I'm doing." He shook his head and laughed. "I'm in over my head, but I'm starting to catch on to the way things work. I've only been here three months. In fact, this is the first time I've been out for fun since I moved to Washington."

"Oh," I said, my heart thumping out of control. "You just moved to Washington?" He might not actually know any other women here.

"Yes. I went to law school in New York and worked in the district attorney's office there for four years." Probably twenty-nine, I thought. "Then, when I decided to find work in a firm, I started to think about moving. It was hard because I have a lot of friends in New York. I like living there, although it can wear you down. But it's a hard place to raise a family—" Raise a family! Does he want a family? Or has he already got a family? Visitation rights? "Calm down," I admonished myself. "Pay attention!" "—and I wouldn't really want to move out to the suburbs, because I like living in the city, so I thought as long as I was going to switch jobs I ought to think about where I really wanted to live. I have a close friend in Washington whom I've visited over the years and I've always liked it here. The pace is slower and the city's accessible from residential areas."

"Yes," I agreed. "I really like it, too. I just moved here in August." How could I steer him back to this raising-a-family bit?

"Where are you from?" he asked.

"Hartford," I answered as we got out of the car. Our walk to the restaurant acted as enough of a transition for me: "You mentioned wanting to raise a family," I said, but then, as he looked at me, I didn't know quite how to continue. "I mean," I said stalling for time, "are you divorced, do you already have a family, or are you just thinking about raising one?" "And with whom?" I thought to myself and "How academic a thought is this?" but using my only shred of self-control, I managed to keep the actual words from spilling out.

"No. I'm not divorced. I've never been married," he said straightforwardly. "But I would eventually like to get married and have kids, and I thought it made sense to establish myself professionally in a place I'd want to settle down in."

This was no Sweeney syndrome! I could not believe it. I'd lucked on to someone new in town, before he'd met anyone else—it had happened to others, but never to me. "Too good to be true," I warned myself. But I couldn't keep my expectations from soaring.

The next morning it was still winter, but that Sunday morning the sun shone through the slatted blinds into my kitchen/dining area, teasing me with the promise of spring. Mike was due over momentarily. I could feel the sun's heat through the window, but winter sunshine could be deceptive. Although the *Washington Post* was lying before me in its habitual breakfast spot, I had not done more than set it down. My thoughts kept returning to Joel. Not wanting my delirium to get out of hand, I focused my eyes on the paper and found the weather report: unseasonably warm, with a high in the low to mid sixties. Sunny, 0 percent chance of rain. What a glorious day! I opened all the blinds and remembered Joel saying, "I really had a good time tonight. I'd like to see you next weekend, if that's okay." Okay!

"I'd love to," I had replied demurely. He wasn't too much taller than me. He just inclined his head down and to the side to kiss me good night. When would Mike get here? I couldn't wait to get outside; the air's sweetness was palpable.

The buzzer rang. I buzzed the outside door open and hunted up my light jacket. Impatiently, I paced back and forth. A day like this deserved to be breathed in fully, every minute. Mike knocked at the door, and when I opened it he breezed by me and headed for the bathroom. "I have one question for you; I'm just going to ask one question about last night," he called over his shoulder.

I practiced an arabesque I'd learned as a third grader taking ballet. When Mike reappeared, I grabbed him by the arm and threw him out the door. "It's gorgeous out," I cried in a frenzy.

"One question, Sara," Mike said as we got into the elevator. "Did you score last night?" It was an old routine between us. In fact, we never gave each other any intimate details. But with my elderly neighbor squeezed into a corner of the elevator and the resident manager's ears taking up the rest of the space, I pretended Mike had been clearing his throat and I remained silent. Outside I filled my lungs with the fragrant air, kicked Mike in the rear for good measure, and answered his question. "No. But I'm working on it. I have another crack at him next week."

"You liked him?"

"Let's put it this way," I said. *"I liked him!"*

"You mean you really liked him?"

"I mean I *really* liked him."

"Want to tell me?"

"I'm scared to jinx it by getting too excited, but he's funny, cute, charming, real nice, and he wants to get married and have kids and he laughs at my jokes."

"You don't waste time, Sara. Does he want a large wedding or a small private ceremony?"

"Okay, okay, he didn't propose." I laughed. "I'm trying to keep calm. But he does want a family, as, you might have noticed, do I."

"I thought I noticed that," Mike said, giving me a hug. "He sounds great."

"It's only the first date. I don't want to get too carried away."

"Well, you know my philosophy," Mike said, chuckling. "Go as slowly as you can possibly get away with."

We'd arrived at Mike's car, but I couldn't bring myself to get inside. We decided to walk to the nearest subway stop, at Van Ness and Connecticut, and take the subway downtown. We drifted along, feeling weightless in the warm air. I needed to buy a birthday gift for my mother and Mike wanted to get one for Marcy, so we decided to do our shopping and then stop for lunch. We went underground at Van Ness and had a long wait for the fare-card machine, since only one was operating. We plied the machine with money to save ouselves the same trouble on our return trip. We took the Red Line and got out at Dupont Circle, a circular park surrounded by a rotary of streets. We had both been impressed with the noiseless, graffiti-free, smooth ride. But the most astonishing sensation was emerging from the Dupont Circle station. The escalator was endless. A silver ladder climbing toward the sun, it glided up the steep incline, threatening me with vertigo whenever I dared to look down. We emerged as from a cave, blinking in the sunlight. Mike started off ahead of me, and I gave him another kick in the rear. I was in a feisty, exuberant mood. Either that, or I needed to abuse somebody. But as Frank had often noticed, Mike's ass was well toned, and I'm sure he felt no pain. It was as if the whole city had come out of hiding. People were everywhere. Their movements were fluid, as if the air itself had massaged away the jerky, enclosed, stiff gestures of winter. People loped and sauntered and stretched in the sun. I picked out a pair of small gold earrings for my mother and a larger pair of bronze pierced earrings for myself. Why not indulge? Mike was looking at pottery for Marcy. I had helped him pick out gifts for his lady loves before: exquisite, delicate gifts that they got to keep as a door prize long after the affair had become a memory. From comments Mike had made and others he had neglected to make, I knew, in the way that those things are known, that he and Marcy were not long for each other. I tried to dissuade Mike from an extravagant gift that was sure to confuse her and lead her into endless hours of rumination about his intentions and true feelings. But Mike was Mike, and Mike was a gift giver. I bit my tongue in an effort to let the inevitable run its course. We made our purchases and resumed our stroll, heading back past the Metro entrance on our way to Dupont Circle. From the sidewalk, I looked down into the subway opening to watch the awesome ascent and descent of the escalator stairs. As I did so, I saw a familiar figure gliding downward. Although his legs were supporting him, he looked hunched over in a bundle as if warding off further assaults. "Mr. Hopper!" I cried from above with some urgency. He gave no indication of hearing my cry, but continued his sweeping descent. "Mike," I said, suddenly frantic, "it's Mr. Hopper. Look at him. He looks ill. Please, Mike," I pleaded, as I stepped onto the escalator. At the bottom, there was no sign of Mr. Hopper. I was not even sure that it was he whom I had seen. The sunlight was dazzling and the subway aperture, by contrast, dark. We reversed directions and started back up.

"Why the panic?" Mike asked. "What just happened?"

"I don't know. I'm sorry. I just saw him or thought I saw him and felt alarmed. I can't explain it." I told Mike about what Frank and I had seen on the tapes. He was interested but unconvinced that Mr. Roden had necessarily lied about seeing Helena. We were walking past a pizza shop, and hunger struck with a familiar intensity. "Can we go to the Caliban Café just this one more time?" I asked Mike sheepishly. "You said yourself the food is delicious, and it's open for lunch on Sundays and it's not outrageously priced. It is close by. I'll treat."

"You don't have to justify your compulsions to me, Sara. I can make exceptions for a driven person unable to control her impulses. The café's fine. You think I'm cruel to continue with Marcy when I know she's not the right person for me, don't you?"

"Mike, I wouldn't say cruel. But I think it's unfair to her. She doesn't know where she stands with you even though you say she does. I know she doesn't. It's the old intermittent reinforcement. You could keep her hanging on like this for years. You're involved enough to give her hope that down the road you'll see the light and realize you're in love. I think you give just enough to tantalize her with the illusion that you could change. But it's not like you're really trying to change. You don't try to see her more. You don't push yourself to respond to her. From what you've told me, you keep things as ambiguous as you can and make small concessions when she pushes you. I don't think it's fair. You're twenty-nine, Mike. She'll be thirty next week. She deserves to know if there's any hope that you'll ever be serious with her, and from what you've said, there isn't. At least if she knows you're hopeless, even if she continues to see you one night a week, she'll start pushing herself to go out and meet other men. You asked me, Mike."

"I know you're right, but I hate to think of losing her. But she's not what I'm looking for and I can't convince myself that she is. It's nothing the matter with her. She's just not the right woman. I'll have a talk with her."

24

We entered the café and were seated in an alcove. Mike continued, "I wonder if I really want to get married. Sometimes I think I do, down the road, but I could be fooling myself. Oh, there's your old charmer Roden buzzing about. What a contrast to Mr. Hopper."

"Well, Mr. Hopper's wife did just get killed. Or maybe he just had her killed. How do people get so tangled up? Something seems to be eating away at him from the inside. How could you ever come to disregard someone so much that you could kill them? As if her life was secondary to other considerations."

"I always think it springs more from an intensity of feeling than a disregard."

"Yeah, but maybe in the intensity you become so fused with the other that their life seems a function of yours. You disregard them in that you no longer see them as a separate person whose life exists independent from your needs and wishes. Maybe Mr. Hopper felt so tied to his wife he couldn't let her go and he couldn't get closer to her. Now, without her, he can't go on either."

"Sara, you were just telling me that Mr. Roden had lied about Helena and, you know, Mr. Roden was the one who chased after Marcel and gave him an excuse to turn and shoot Mrs. Hopper. What happened to your theory about the café? Aren't we here to resonate with the café and have its secret revealed to us? Please. I guess I feel like you're trying to draw an analogy between Mr. Hopper and me: He can't live with her, can't live without her. The only solution is murder and then the guilt ravages you. It's gruesome. My sins are venal, not mortal. Come on, Sara. Here comes the waiter, and it's too nice out to spend all afternoon eating. Pick what you want, or I'll order for you. I should have gotten tough with you years ago."

I made up my mind immediately and we ordered. Sweeney was a master at changing the conversation. He'd had a lot of practice. "Does this Joel know what he's letting himself in for?" he asked. "Tell me more about him."

"First off, he's well within normal limits. He spoke warmly of his family. He seems to have a number of close friends. Never been married. No pending paternity suits. He doesn't appear gay."

"Can't ask for more than that."

"If next weekend goes well, maybe I could have you over with him and you could screen him, just to make sure I haven't overlooked anything major."

"You tell me when."

The waiter brought our meals and we set to work on them. I had ordered coquilles St. Jacques this time, having remembered it as the dish that got away last time. It was scrumptious. Mike and I both ate with gusto. We were waiting for our dishes to be cleared when Mike unceremoniously left to use the men's room. He returned intrigued by what he'd just seen. Someone had left a $50 tip at the table next to ours. We were convinced it was a mistake, but we couldn't remember who was sitting there to try to catch them. It turned out not to matter because seconds later a man returned with an embarrassed air. He replaced the $50 bill with a $5 bill and headed back to the register, check in hand. "You know," Mike was saying, "I think it's easier to make that mistake when you pay at the register on your way out. You pick up the check, and throw a tip on the table. I think you're less careless when you pay the waiter at the table. Even if you don't charge it, you give him the cash and you're still sitting there when you figure out your tip. It seems more relaxed to me. Maybe I just prefer to pay the waiter; it's easier."

"That's 'cause you're rarely in a rush. You don't eat out as part of a business day. I'm sure it's more convenient to leave whenever you're ready after the waiter gives you the check. They get a big business crowd on weekdays. And it encourages them to pay the tips in cash instead of using a charge card."

"That's true," Sweeney agreed. "You would have more control over the time. It still seems a little funny to me, though. This is a pretty high-class operation. Even though the setting is casual, it's hardly inexpensive, and there is a formality about it. Think about this," Sweeney said, warming to his subject. "If there was a vice ring here, as Frank suggested, and you decided that you had to have a particular waiter, wouldn't it be easier to sit in that waiter's station and pay him directly for the meal, including in your tip a down payment for his services and a note about where to meet? The way the setup is doesn't exactly seem ideal for a vice ring."

"Now, now. On the other hand, if Marcel was the head organizer, or pimp, or whatever, people who knew of the service might know to sit in his station. Then, with their tip they could leave him a note and their down payment. Get with it, Sweeney. It's a good setup because nobody in any of the neighboring tables would ever suspect that business was being transacted. A man could even bring his family and send them out ahead while he lingers to pay the tip."

"A touch of cynicism about the marital state."

"But, listen. Say I had a yen for a particular waiter."

"A yen, Sara?"

"A fancy, an insatiable lust, and I was a regular customer of his, I mean with him as a prostitute, not as a waiter. Any time I knew that I just had to have him again, I'd write out my little note at home, tape a fifty-dollar bill beneath a five or a one—who knows what they cost—and come here for dinner. After I finish, I get my check and then I keep an eye out for Marcel, and when he's headed in this direction, if he gives me a nod, I leave my tip and go to pay at the register. Marcel swoops down and picks up my tip, and pockets it. Then, when he gets a chance, he darts into Mr. Roden's office, goes into the bathroom, reads the request, maybe keeps some of that money and tells the waiter. There's probably some provision if the waiter can't make it. Probably just a phone call with a message that you're unavailable. It's not totally ridiculous, is it?"

"No, I'm sure that kind of stuff goes on all the time. There goes your friend, Maury. He must think I've beaten out all the competition for you by now. Those doggy bags remind me of when I was a little kid. My mother always said my eyes were bigger than my stomach. I'd order everything in sight and eat a fraction of it. Then I'd have the leftovers the next day."

"Your sex life seems to have taken on the characteristic of your eating habits."

"That was low. That was really low. You're going to pay for that. I reveal a personal childhood memory, stirred by the sight of a doggy bag. What is it Sara, what's the matter?"

I had suddenly frozen in my seat. The doggy bag had jarred something in me. Something wasn't right, didn't make sense. It was like being dimly aware of a false note in a therapy session. It was that sense that someone was running something by you, covering up, faking an emotion. You could sense it before you understood it. And I sensed something and held my breath trying to make it come into focus. In my mind I kept seeing Mr. Roden carrying a doggy bag to the man in the alcove behind us the last time I was there with Mike, Marcy, and Frank. Mr. Roden carrying the doggy bag. I had registered it at the time. I had known something was wrong, but I hadn't concentrated on it. The image had been shoved aside. Suddenly, I knew. The knowledge made me swallow several times. I had an urge to curl up in a little ball.

Mike's voice penetrated my consciousness. "Sara, please, say something. What is it?"

"Jesus, Mike. Remember when we were here on Wednesday. We watched Mr. Roden deliver a doggy bag to the table behind us in the alcove, then he came over to speak to us."

"Vaguely."

"The man he delivered the doggy bag to was the man who ordered the coquilles St. Jacques. I kept an eye on his plate. First, when I saw them, I wanted to order them. Then I decided not to, but I watched him to see if he was enjoying his meal. Then, when the waiter cleared his plate, I watched again. Mike, he ate everything on his plate. You know how I can be obsessed with food. I swear to God, there was no food on his plate when the waiter cleared it away. Nothing. You even impugned my character for staring at the waiter. Remember?"

"Sara, you mean that the doggy bag contained something that Maury wanted to slip to this man secretly. There was no food in it."

"They're running drugs, Mike. They must be. Think of it. What a setup. It's not a vice ring. They're pushing drugs. Mr. Roden must have passed that man a pound of cocaine or heroin in full view of everyone. You know what that means, Mike. This was Marcel's station, where that man sat. Roden and Marcel were in it together. Roden had a hand in killing Mrs. Hopper. He set her up. His best friend's wife. He's a dangerous man." Mike and I were intent on our conversation, oblivious to all other movement.

"You're right about the drugs. You must be. But Mr. Hopper might be in on it, too. He's the secretive one. He's the one who didn't want his wife involved. He and Roden go back a long way together. What a cold, calculating thing to do." We sat silently, then Mike spoke again. "One other possibility, Sara, before we jump to conclusions. Maybe someone gave Roden the bag. He's the obliging type. Just asked him to drop it off at that man's table. Someone who usually went through Marcel."

"That's stretching it. I think Roden's dangerous. We'd better get out of here and call Detective Larson. I'm frightened, really frightened. How did we get mixed up in all this? Where the hell is our waiter?" I looked up for the first time since my discovery. Mr. Roden loomed over our table. I had no idea how long he'd been hovering.

"Dr. Marks, what a pleasure. You're becoming a regular with us. Your friend seems to be a regular with you now. I think it's time we were introduced. I'm Maury Roden." He held out his hand to Mike.

"Mike Sweeney." They shook hands.

"We have a special dessert today, a delicious walnut torte. You must try it, Dr. Marks. I've noticed you do our desserts justice."

"We were just looking for the waiter to get our check," Mike said. His voice sounded natural. I was speechless. I seemed incapable of producing sound.

"What, and skip dessert? I insist. If you want to diet you must start tomorrow. It's on the house. My treat. I'll have John bring a walnut torte for Dr. Marks, and what can we bring you, Mr. Sweeney?"

"I'll just have coffee, thanks."

"Two coffees then?" Roden looked at me and I nodded. "And one torte."

He left.

"Oh, Mike. Why couldn't we get out of here? I can see the headlines: 'Psychologist poisoned by walnut torte. Too polite to refuse dessert.' You made one good try, but we both caved in. Did he hear us? He's dangerous, really dangerous. I'm not going to eat the torte."

"But I'm not having one, Sara. At least I managed to refuse, even if I didn't get us out of here. It wouldn't do him any good to poison you and not me."

"Mike, damn you, this is no joke."

"Quiet, Sara. I'm trying to watch him cut your piece. It's hard. He's on the other side of the cart. I can't really see his hands." I also began to watch and saw Roden handing the waiter a tray with the torte and two coffees.

I eyed my torte suspiciously. There was no question that it looked delectable. It was a dilemma I'd never anticipated. Mike finally picked up his fork. "Okay, Sara. I'll take a bite. I just can't see Roden poisoning you in such an obvious, provable way. He's too clever for that."

I shoved Mike's fork aside. "Okay, I'll eat it. If I die, you bear witness."

The torte was as good as it looked. I cleaned my plate, managing to take the last bite of torte with the last sip of my coffee. Perfect.

"The coffee, Mike," I whispered urgently, as I set my cup back in the saucer. "We both drank the coffee!"

Mike only laughed. "I wondered when you'd notice."

"But, Mike!"

"Sara. Roden frightens the hell out of me. But I just can't see him poisoning us in his restaurant. It's ridiculous. Come on. Let's get out of here." I went to the register to pay the bill while Mike left the tip. Then he caught up with me and we stepped outside.

To be caressed by a gentle warm breeze in the middle of winter is one of life's finer sensations. The air enveloped us and seemed to escort us down the street. I was overcome with a sense of utter well-being. There was a flower vendor on the corner, and I bought a bunch of daffodils. Mike and I put our heads together and sniffed in their fragrance. I took the candy dinner mints I'd picked up on our way out and popped one into Mike's mouth and one into mine. I savored the sensation of the sweet mint flavor slowly dissolving in my mouth. Mike put his arm around me and massaged my shoulder as we strolled along. The slow, sensual kneading of my shoulder and occasionally of my neck made me turn to Mike and kiss him on his neck, just beneath his ear. He moved his hand up to my head and began stroking my hair. We wandered around directionless, soaking in the sun. Mike suggested we ride the escalator down as we again approached the Dupont Circle subway entrance. "Let's just go up and down for fun," he said. I nodded in agreement, feeling receptive to any- and everything. Mike started walking down ahead of me, enjoying his springy steps on the stairs. I felt a pleasant swooning dizziness as I looked down, so I remained stationary, holding on to the rail. I imagined that I was being carried out to sea on a voluptuous wave. Mike bounded back up the stairs to me, as the escalator continued to move us both down. His face looked tense, and I began to smooth his brow with my free hand. "Sara," he said with insistence, "snap out of it. It's Roden. He *did* put something in our coffee. He's in the Metro station with an overnight bag. He's up to something. Come on."

We were close enough to the bottom that I didn't mind moving. Luckily, we had our fare cards and rushed through. Mike spotted Roden waiting for the Red Line, and we followed him there. The station was nearly empty, and we were hardly inconspicuous. We saw him enter the train, and we got on. "He must have slipped a narcotic into our coffee. You were right to be worried, but not about poison. He must have heard us at the table. All he wanted was time to get away. We've got to see where he's going and call the police. I still feel like my head's not attached to my body. Whatever he slipped us, I wouldn't mind trying again at a more opportune time. Damn. Look at the subway map. The next stop's a big changeover point. Please snap out of it. We've got to see where he goes."

I did my best to pull myself together. At Metro Center, I spotted Roden leaving the train, and we ran after him. He turned suddenly, with us at his heels. "Hello again," he said cordially. "What are you two doing underground on such a glorious day?"

I looked to Mike, who said, "Just enjoying the subway."

"Well, believe it or not," Mr. Roden said, "I have a wedding to attend. My niece is getting married. I've got my dress clothes in here. But everything is such a rush these days with our problems at the café. I have to be back tonight in time to close up. No rest for the weary. But a wedding's a wedding and champagne is champagne, so *l'chaim.*" Mr. Roden made the gesture of a toast and walked off quickly in the direction of the Blue Line. We followed rapidly. It was the line that went to the airport. The train was already there and the lights were flashing, indicating it was ready to leave. We raced on board.

"Where the hell did he go?" Mike asked. We were frantic. Mike wanted us to separate and search the cars, but I must have still looked a little dopey, because he dragged me with him. I had less weight to absorb the narcotic, I told myself. We almost walked right by Roden. He had a newspaper in front of his face nd was looking out the window. But Mike noticed his bag and stopped. We seated ourselves behind him and across the aisle. He must have caught our reflections in the window, because he turned and asked if we were also headed for the airport. I was again mute, but Mike said it was a nice day to watch the planes take off. Weak. But who were we kidding anyway? The man's politeness was unnerving. I was starting to think it was all a mistake. Mr. Roden chatted on about his niece's wedding and the young man she was marrying. Roden was taking the Eastern shuttle to New York, he said, and would return on it tonight. The wonders of modern transportation. I had visions of restraining him from boarding the plane by the miraculous intervention of the police and then finding a wedding gift in his bag. The favorite uncle detained. Everyone worried sick. My name synonymous with stupidity. I was getting very nervous, and not for my safety anymore. I was starting to worry about my reputation and was not at all convinced that we should call the police. There was no way to discuss it with Mike.

"Why don't we accompany you to your plane?" Mike suggested casually. "We're just whiling away the day anyway." Where did Mike get his cool? We kept pace with Mr. Roden, walking toward the Eastern terminal.

"I'll pay on board," he said, and waved us a goodbye. "Enjoy the day, kids," he called out.

"Stay here and make sure he doesn't back off the plane. I'll call the detective. No, you call the detective. He knows you better. I'll stay here. Go, Sara." Mike was so authoritative, I did what he said automatically. I simply pushed the doubts from my mind and followed directions. There were phone booths everywhere. I fumbled through my purse and pulled out Detective Larson's number. I called. He was out but would get back to me. "It's an emergency," I shrieked. "Get me Detective Harrison. He might understand." I was told to hold the line. I was sure Harrison would think me nuts, but my faculties were returning and there was no question I'd been drugged. Roden was running away. Otherwise, why the drugs? Harrison was out, too. Off duty. "Can I leave Larson a message?" I pleaded. "Will you get it to him as soon as possible? There's a murderer headed for New York. He has to stop him." The voice on the line was trying to calm me down, and I realized I was not being coherent. Why hadn't Mike done the calling? One step at a time, the voice instructed me. "Tell

Larson," I resumed, more in control, "Maury Roden is headed for New York on the Eastern shuttle. He's carrying an overnight bag. The Caliban Café is a drug transfer center. He was probably in on Mrs. Hopper's murder and the attempt on me. This is Sara Marks. My name. He drugged Mike and me so he could make his escape. Can't you pick him up in New York?" The voice repeated my message. She thanked me and hung up. I raced back to Mike. He was still standing there. Mr. Roden had not reemerged.

"I guess that's all we can do," Mike said. "Let's just wait till the plane takes off, to be on the safe side." The plane lifted off in five minutes' time, and we headed back to the subway. We were whipped. The narcotic probably had a depressing aftereffect. We took the subway back to Van Ness and began the trek to my apartment. We could barely pull our weight. The walk took us about forty mintues, most of which we walked in silence. Mike was coming in for an unadulterated cup of coffee, but we agreed we'd go our separate ways after that so we could both sleep off our sluggishness. My apartment seemed dark, coming in out of the sunlight. The red light was on my machine, and, with some nervousness, I played back the message. "Dr. Marks. Detective Larson here. We had Roden picked up as he left the plane in New York. New York's finest said his overnight bag was stuffed full of cocaine and money. I'm talking a lot of big money. Thanks for the tip."

Mike and I stared at each other. It had all been real. Even the danger. The entire day had felt like a kaleidoscoped dream. It took some time for Larson's confirmation to sink in. "Good work, Sara," Mike gave me a hug. "Your excessive pursuit of food made it all possible. I can't really believe it."

"I think something clicked inside me when I heard Roden talking about Helena's lightweight jacket. I knew he wouldn't have had any reason to see her in it unless he left with her. She was probably acting out her fantasy of Mimi and Harley. You know, secret meetings with the boss. That made me suspicious of him. But I still don't see why he'd want to hurt Helena. Could she really have figured out the whole thing?"

"Maybe Roden will confess and we'll find out. At least, the police will search the café and that might reveal something. I can't believe it. You are so obsessed with food. You really watched whether or not that guy finished his scallops?"

"Mike, I could probably tell you everything you've ordered the last few times we've had dinner out together. That's the sort of thing I notice. You could probably describe the attributes of every waitress. I have to say you were great, too. I'd still be going up and down the escalator, pretending I was floating out to sea, if you hadn't realized what was going on."

Mike decided to hang around for the rest of the afternoon, and at six, Larson called. He reported that the New York police had charged Roden with being a fugitive from justice, which gave them the right to hold him until he either waved extradition or had an extradition hearing within 30 days. Either way, they had him, and Larson didn't anticipate any problems on his returning to D.C. In addition to cocaine and money, Roden was carrying a false passport and had made reservations under a phony name to fly out of Kennedy Airport to Switzerland. Roden himself remained courteously silent when the New York police questioned him. He had spoken only to one person, his lawyer.

Larson had talked to Mr. Hopper, but he was equally unenlightening. He was evasive under questioning and appeared ill, so Larson left him with his card and a warning that he'd be subpoenaed before the grand jury and asked questions under oath. That gave him something to think about. Meanwhile, Larson was going to get a warrant to search the Caliban. I was impatient to have all the pieces fit together nicely, but there was no more information to be had.

25

Monday, the entire clinic was astir with the story. Mike and I were celebrities for a day. Although I'd made Larson promise he'd call me if he had any news, no calls came. There was, however, one disturbing note. Harry did not show up in the morning. Frank called his home several times, and there was no answer. By noon, Frank was sick with worry, and we were all getting anxious. Harley was away on two weeks' leave: first his conference, to which Mimi, having decided to leave her mother to her own resources, had accompanied him; and then their ski vacation. Richard was in charge. Frank got Richard and Joyce together and told them he wanted to go on a home visit. They agreed and saw no problem with my accompanying him, which I had volunteered to do. I think we all had visions of Mr. Hopper having hanged himself. I really didn't want to come upon a dead body, but I felt involved with the entire affair. Frank, who had been terrified of going alone, was grateful.

The Hopper home was a fifteen-minute drive from the clinic and not difficult to locate. In a gracious residential section, the house stood out as larger and more elegant than the others. The front yard was terraced in slate, with gardens set at different levels just waiting for spring to blossom into beauty. The house was a large, two-story structure made of grayish blue stones. It had a side porch opening onto an expansive terrace that was shaded by a second-story balcony. The café had provided for an abundant lifestyle. The shades were all drawn in the house, and there did not appear to be any lights on behind them. Frank and I approached the door, both of us breathing audibly. I rang the bell, and we waited. No answer. Frank lifted the large brass knocker and let it fall. Still no response. We headed for the garage to see if the cars were there. They were. We both had the same thought about carbon monoxide poisoning and wanted to open the garage door, but it was locked in place. Peering in through the windows did not provide enough light to see inside the cars. The entire family might have been there dead. We could not tell. Unable to leave and unable to think of anything to do, we spent several minutes aimlessly wandering around the front yard. Frank suddenly bolted back up the yard to the front door and rang the bell repeatedly. I could see him furiously pushing it in, over and over. Then, with one hand on the bell, he pounded on the door with his other hand. I was thinking of how I could calm him down when the door opened. Frank moved inside, and I raced up to be admitted too. It was dark inside and cold. Mr. Hopper, in his bathrobe, unshaven, his face a mask of agony and his body little more than a skeleton, led us into the living room and sat down. Frank took a minute to compose himself. Mr. Hopper and I sat silently and stared.

"I didn't mean to disturb you," Frank apologized. "But I tried calling all morning. There was no answer. We were worried about Harry. He's not at the clinic." As Frank was talking we heard a toilet flush, and Harry, resembling his father in his unkempt appearance, entered the room. He sat next to his father and eyed him protectively. I was at a loss. Father and son sat shoulder to sagging shoulder. Frank addressed Harry, "Is there some reason why you didn't come in today?" Harry shrugged. I felt the same way I'd felt when Frank and I had first interviewed the Hoppers. The minutes dragged by.

"Can I open the blinds?" I finally asked, but neither father nor son replied, so I remained in my seat.

"Is Judy here, too?" asked Frank.

"She's at school," Mr. Hopper said.

I thought the tension would push me under for the last time, and I fought it, finally saying, "Mr. Roden's arrest must have been a great shock to you. You look very ill, Mr. Hopper. Have you seen a doctor?"

"I'm not sick," he said. "Just tired."

"Have you been unable to sleep?" I asked.

"I toss and turn for hours. That's why I disconnected the phones and took a sedative. I can't go on like this."

"You too, Harry?" Frank asked.

"The son is the father of the man."

Frank and I both let that one go by. "What's keeping you up, Mr. Hopper? Can you try to talk about it?" I implored. "You really can't go on like this, and your children need you."

"I don't seem to come through in the clinch, do I? Maury used to. Always. In the clinch. If you were sick, if you were tired, he'd carry you to safety. My God. What have I done?" Tears ran down his furrowed face, and mucus escaped freely from his nostrils. His control was shattered. Harry rocked his father slowly back and forth. What had he done? Frank took out a handkerchief and offered it to Mr. Hopper. He took it and blew his nose. Harry stopped rocking him.

"What have you done?" I asked. "What you say here is confidential. It's still a therapeutic relationship. You can't keep it inside to eat away at you like this."

"I loved Maury. Not like these young kids who brag about being homosexual. I don't mean that. I loved him. I had to know he was okay. I trusted him. We were partners. I knew he played rough. 'Survival first' he always said, 'ethics second.' In the Pacific, he was right. Here, at the café, we were surviving. He didn't have to play rough. I knew he was up to something. I closed my eyes. You don't rat on your best friend. I kept to myself, stayed in my office. I kept my family away. I didn't want them involved. I shut myself up. I shut them out. But I owed him that. He was the only one. We'd come through together. I sacrificed my family. I should have died in the Pacific. I've done nothing good since then." Mr. Hopper buried his face in his hands.

"Did you know he was using the café to deal drugs?" I asked. I had to know. Frank looked on the verge of tears.

Mr. Hopper responded. "Maybe I knew. I knew he insisted on buying liquor from Herb when Herb's selection was poor and his prices were high. He said they were friends. But I knew Maury. Business is business. He wasn't giving something for nothing. I knew he had something going with Herb. The liquor was a cover. But I shrugged. I don't have to notice everything that goes on. Maury depended on me. Some things weren't my business. It's funny, I would have done it, paid high prices for poor quality if someone I cared about needed it. But not Maury—never. 'You're soft,' he'd tell me. 'You're in business. You're swimming with the sharks. Be a little ruthless. You've paid your dues.' Nope, I knew something was up with Herb. There were other things. This doggy bag business. It was undignified. It kept our waiters rushing around, the kitchen extra busy, and for what? We didn't need it. 'Give a little extra,' Maury would say. 'It keeps them coming back for more.' But they got plenty. They didn't need extra. I never trusted it. But Maury wanted it, what the hell."

"What about Marcel?" I asked, relentless.

"Killer. Murderer!" Harry shouted. He fell to the floor and made stabbing motions into the carpet. Frank started to respond to Harry, but I stopped him, remembering what Richard had said.

"Marcel was a bum. He dressed fancy, he talked slick, but he was a bum. He was a hustler. At first when he came, he was really just a kid, around Harry's age. He did his job okay. He worked hard. He was polite to me. I was so pleased, a son for Maury who would bring him joy. His two boys, they're into cults, they go on fasts. They went their own ways. Marcel seemed like a true son. Hardworking, ambitious. He wanted to learn from Maury. Humble, when he first started. Absorbed everything he could. But he turned arrogant. Oh, was he arrogant. He used Maury's office like his own, feet up on the desk, showers whenever he felt like it. What hurt, though, was the way he'd talk about Maury. I'd hear him. That boy had big plans for himself. He thought Maury was washed up. 'Things are happening and Maury's blind,' he'd say. 'You used to be tough, used to keep your back covered. Now you're lucky if you can see what's in front of you. You've lost the scent.' He didn't trust anybody. You'd mention someone in conversation, he'd say, 'I know about him. I've got his number.' He had something on everyone. Everyone was out to get him. No one was above suspicion. How did Maury get involved with him? A son in his own image. That's what he wanted." Mr. Hopper shook his head from side to side. He began to cough.

"Let me get you some water," I offered and got up without waiting for a reply. I had to keep some momentum. He drank the water and cleared his throat. Harry, lying on the floor, had been listening. He kept looking toward his father and then away.

"Do you have something you want to ask your father?" Frank asked Harry.

He blurted it out. "Why'd you let Mom go back there? Why?"

"A mistake. I misunderstood. Ruthless in business. Never with me, my family. I tried to stop it. Maury said to let her. He encouraged her. I thought he was telling me it was okay. I thought he'd stopped what he was doing or that he thought she couldn't find out. I thought he was signaling me that it was safe. We never discussed his activities in the open. Just hints. He was my friend. Survival meant for us both and both our families. I thought he meant to reassure me that my marriage was important. He could work around her. That's the worst part. She didn't know anything. She couldn't have kept it to herself. When he told her to come back, he knew she'd have to be killed. Like in the army. You launch an attack and you anticipate a certain number of casualties. I should have known. He wrote her off as a casualty. She was a stubborn woman. He knew it. It's true. Once she'd decided, you couldn't have dissuaded her. I should have sold out with her. Moved away. I can't even blame Maury. I was always in the middle, pulled by them both. He was desperate. Otherwise, he couldn't have done it. Not to me. He sold out to me Sunday morning. Gave me the business. Said he had to leave the country. Gave me an address in Switzerland to send money to. Said he hated to desert me now that Lizzie was gone. I think he meant it. But he had to go. All he said . . . he said things were closing in on him. He'd had some illegal dealings. That's how he put it. 'Tell Herb,' he said, 'nobody else. Give Herb the address.' It was a post office box. He told me that, and I knew he'd had Lizzie killed. I couldn't look at him. But I can't hate him. Poor Lizzie. Can you forgive me, Harry? Can you ever forgive me? I thought she was safe. We should have both sold out and moved."

Harry had been motionless on the floor, listening to his father's answer. Slowly, he crawled over to his father's feet and grasped his hands around his father's ankles. He rested his head on his father's feet, and curled the rest of his body into a ball. He started to sob. "Blood money," he exclaimed between sobs. "He killed her for money. Uncle Maury, Uncle Maury. A smiling face, an evil heart." Harry's sobs convulsed his body. His father sat still. Frank met my eyes, and we both got teary. I could think of no consolation. Again I thought of Richard's last supervision as I tried to find some direction.

"Is there any food here?" I asked Mr. Hopper. He nodded. "I'm going to get lunch for you and Harry. You must eat something." I went into the kitchen and made them peanut butter and jelly sandwiches and poured them each a glass of apple juice. The scene was unchanged when I returned. Frank sat down on the floor with Harry, to soothe his sobbing and encourage him to eat. I sat next to Mr. Hopper and offered him the food. He ate it. His movements were slow and listless, but he got it all down. "Will you talk to the police?" I asked Mr. Hopper. "They'll want to know who Maury bought from and distributed drugs to. Will you tell them?"

Mr. Hopper shrugged again. "Testify against Maury? My best friend. He carried me on his back. Maury, Maury." Mr. Hopper stopped short and gave a cry of pain. Harry had bitten into his ankle.

"He killed Mother! Mom. He had her killed!" Harry was screaming, but his thoughts were coherent. "I'll never forgive you. Not if you don't make him pay. Didn't you love her? Isn't she anything to you? I'll never forgive you!"

Mr. Hopper reached down and touched his son. "I'll tell them. He'll pay. I loved your mother. You and Judy are all I have left. You must forgive me. I'll tell them everything I know."

"Let me call a doctor for you," Frank offered. "That bite should be looked at and you need some help getting your strength back right now. What's your doctor's name?"

Mr. Hopper told him the name and got out his address book. He seemed to have come to a decision. He let Frank call the doctor and make an appointment, and then he called Detective Larson. Larson said he was on his way over. Frank and I called in to the clinic and canceled the rest of our appointments. We insisted on driving Mr. Hopper to his doctor later that afternoon. When Larson came, Mr. Hopper told him what he'd told us: He had always thought Maury's dealings with Herb were suspect. He gave him Herb's full name and address. He also gave him the names of some of Marcel's regular customers. But he didn't know which ones were receiving drugs. We all witnessed Mr. Hopper's statement, and by the time Detective Larson left, Mr. Hopper looked relieved. He'd carried that weight a long time. Harry, too, was calm. We drove them to the doctor and back home afterward. Judy arrived shortly after we did, and with some money from her father, she and I headed back out again to buy groceries. Judy offered to prepare dinner that night, and Harry and his father gave Frank and me their word that they would eat. Before Frank and I left, Harry promised he'd be at the clinic in the morning and Mr. Hopper promised to call an employment agency and hire a house-keeper, at least temporarily, to put things back in order. Frank and I left feeling sad, yet satisfied.

26

After the day spent with Harry and his father, I was not quite as impatient for news as I had been. Yet I had enormous quantities of energy at my disposal, springing from some unknown internal source.

I approached Frank Tuesday evening as we were leaving the clinic to see if I could entice him to accompany me to a movie. I had hardly gotten the invitation out of my mouth when Frank took a step back from me and gave me appraising look. As his scrutiny made me increasingly uncomfortable, I asked what was passing through his seedy little mind.

"There's no way to put this politely," he said, heaving a sigh. "You can no longer afford to spend your leisure time sitting on your butt. You're already starting to lose control of it." I opened my eyes in amazement, but Frank continued. "I've had the aes-thetic shudders over you for some time now, but you were so upset with Helena and we've had so much going on that I've forced myself to overlook and ignore what leaps to the eye. Let me finish. You're starting to date again. Also, spring can't be too far away, and that means fewer and more revealing clothes. Personally, it's been a strain for me to hold my critical faculties in check. You need to lose a little weight, nothing drastic, maybe five pounds. But we simply must tone those muscles of yours, and I insist that you allow me to come the next time you go shopping, which, Sara dear, you can't afford to postpone any longer. You need clothes with flair, with pizazz. Something to make people want to stop and look."

"You've never heard of dressing inconspicuously?" I asked, trying to salvage a little pride. But I didn't really mind, and I realized that Frank also must be feeling a sense of relief and closure regarding Harry. The upshot was that Frank would see a movie with me, but I also agreed to go with him to his gym on a guest pass after work on Thursday. We would work out first and then have a dietetic dinner together. Friday night he would take me to Bloomingdale's to shop. Joel and I had a date for Saturday night, and I liked the idea of having a new outfit to wear.

I prayed to die as I worked out with Frank on Thursday night. By Friday I almost thought my prayer had come true. I could barely move, and I hurt in places I'd never known I owned. Nevertheless, I persisted with the program and dragged my aching muscles through a full workday, a spartan dinner, and a controversial shopping trip. Frank and I could scarcely agree on negotiating terms for a start. Comfortable to me meant encircling, familiar, long-lasting. Comfortable to Frank meant flimsy, silky, unconstrained by clothes. Frank thought my taste matronly, old and dowdy. I thought Frank's taste stylized slut. In order to effect concessions on his part, I reminded him of my efforts in the dietary area, not to mention the fact that I had practically exercised myself into oblivion. I ended up buying a slinky red blouse, and we compromised on how many buttons I would wear undone. I agreed to two, so as not to be rigid, and he relented from demanding three. I bought a basic black woolen skirt to wear with it, and we both decided to call it a night. We had not heard from Detective Larson all week. Harry had been attending the clinic regularly and looking well. His last family session had also been a good one, with Mr. Hopper back in the world of the living. Frank had been following Richard's advice about monitoring Mr. Hopper's health and eating and sleeping habits. Mr. Hopper was taking better care of himself; the only side effect seemed to be that I was getting the spillover from Frank's methods.

Saturday morning, again feeling restless, and a little nervous about my date with Joel, I gave Mike a call. Although I waited until what I thought was a reasonable hour to call, when he answered I got the sense that he was still in bed with a woman to whom he'd been recently introduced. At any rate, he was in no condition to make impromptu plans for the day. Rather than wait around trying to reach someone else, I grabbed my coat and headed for the subway. I was tempted to get off at Dupont Circle, but knew it would serve no purpose to wander aimlessly around the Caliban. I restrained myself and got off at Gallery Place. A legacy from my shortlived friendship with Mimi: I enjoyed wandering around art museums.

Footsore and hungry, I lumbered home around two-thirty and practically crawled to the refrigerator. Nibbling a piece of cheese to gain time as I prepared a sandwich, I answered the phone with a wad of food in my mouth. When I heard Detective Larson's voice, I almost choked. "Things are cracking here!" he informed me with exuberance. "We surprised Herb with a search warrant and found enough cocaine on the premises to keep all the white folks in Northwest floating ten feet high from now until Easter. We made a *haul!* And we got two of Marcel's contacts who dealt street business. Am I keeping you from something?"

"It's thrilling. What else?"

"We backed Marcel into a corner. He was pleading innocent and singing the blues. He figured he had a chance of beating the charge in a trial because our evidence was all eyewitness, and he's an expert on discrediting people. He thinks everyone has something to hide, even your respectable self. He thought you could be broken on the stand. He figured he could at least raise doubts about the identification, since all his accusers knew each other. Discussed it among themselves, that sort of thing. Talked each other into it, played on each other's memories. What we didn't have was motive. Or hard evidence like his gun. We never recovered that. And no motive. His lawyer would ask the jury why a gainfully employed waiter would shoot his boss's wife, when he had no quarrel with his boss and no reason for wanting her dead. But we backed him in so tight, he couldn't wriggle out. We told him Maury had cracked open and spilled his insides out. Told us everything. He hadn't. He hadn't said a word. But when we told Marcel that we'd booked Herb and Marcel's two prize customers—which we did, thanks to Mr. Hopper—he thought Maury had turned on him to save his own neck. Once we had the drug ring, Marcel had a motive. He was cooked and he knew it, and he also thought Maury was fingering him for the shooting of Mrs. Hopper. He let out his venom. He wanted to deal. All we promised was to recommend leniency, and he turned state's evidence. The man has a mouth on him. I'll censor what he said for a well-brought up lady like you.

"First off, this drug ring's been operating in the black for nine years. Steady, dependable trafficking. Marcel blames all their troubles on Helena. He had it in his head that she was an undercover narcotics agent. It all made sense to him. I think he still believes it. Marcel thought Roden was getting careless, and Marcel was getting jumpy that the narcotics division would get wise to them. When this foxy young girl gets hired with no warning, he thought it was a plant. Particularly when she started playing up to him and Roden. I think he's used to having women flirt with him, but he became suspicious when this young fox started sidling up to Maury and making suggestive overtures. He thinks Maury is over the hill and down again. He thought Helena was forcing herself to seduce Roden for her job. He was suspicious of her to begin with, flitting around the place and insinuating herself. The Wednesday she died, he overheard her propositioning Maury for a 'secret meeting' where they could become lovers and he could 'teach her all the unimaginable things that a man of his experience would know.' Marcel said at that point he knew she was an agent. Also, he had a steady coke customer who came every Wednesday night; and that same night, when he darted into the bathroom in Maury's office to put the cocaine in a bag for delivery, he couldn't get into the bathroom. The door was locked from the inside and the shower tap was running. He was beside himself with rage and fear. Everything had to be carefully orchestrated, and he had to get back to his other tables. He went back to the dining room frantic. He waited on a few tables and signaled his contact there was a delay. He was barely in control. He went back to the bathroom door and finally heard the shower stop. He knocked, and she said she'd be out in a minute. Then she asked who it was. When he gave his name and said he needed to use the bathroom, she opened the door to him. Stark naked. He was scared. Told her to put her clothes on and get out. At that point he was convinced she had found their cocaine and records. She was just trying to distract him. She put her clothes on and emerged. He went into the bathroom, locked the door, and put the water on as a cover. There was a safe built into the wall behind the medicine cabinet. If you knew where to press, you could lift the cabinet out of the wall. Then there was a combination safe. He didn't think she'd actually gotten into the safe, but he jumped to the conclusion that she'd discovered its whereabouts. Just as he got the safe opened, he realized that she was dialing the phone in the outer office. He put his ear to the door and heard her leave a message for you saying, as he remembered it, that she had discovered what was going on and had to talk to you. By her urgency, he realized that she now knew enough to call in reinforcements. He knew that she'd have to be killed before she could make her report."

"She *was* murdered. Oh, my God."

"Marcel told Roden that he had positive proof that she was an agent. Told him about overhearing her call in her report and that she was asking for immediate instructions. He told Maury she had to be killed before she talked to anyone. Maury wasn't completely convinced, but he agreed it was a chance they couldn't take. He told Marcel he'd take care of it. He said he could monitor all calls coming in. He and Helena had arranged for a 'secret and sexy' meeting later that night. She was to slip into his office, unseen by anyone, at ten-forty-five so they could leave together after everyone else had gone and no one would know. Maury would take care to disconnect his phone before that time so she would have no opportunity to use it while waiting for him. They would leave together after the café was closed up, and he would take care of her in his own way. That's what they'd agreed upon. It was fortuitous that Mr. Hopper didn't come back that night. They wouldn't have to worry about him snooping around."

"Maury killed her," I said dully. "He threw her over the bridge."

"More likely than not," Larson replied. "But it looks as if he loaded her with alcohol first, and she might not even have been aware of what was happening to her."

"She really did want to seduce him," I said. "She was all juiced up about an affair at the clinic. One of the staff members had started seeing our boss. It had been kept secret from the patients. Helena learned about it that morning and was turned on by the idea. She really wanted him."

"Look, that's what I figured. No one in our department has any record of her. So I knew she must have been for real. But I didn't try to convince Marcel of that. I want him to think that Maury was careless and not that his paranoia sunk the ship. Which it did. We didn't have a clue that there was anything illegal going on there. He blew the whole thing. But I want to keep him mad at Roden."

"Her call to me did seal her fate. Are you going to tell her parents she was killed?"

"I think we'll have to revise the probable cause of death, which means we'll tell them. But you realize, Dr. Marks, we have no proof that Roden killed her. We don't have one piece of tangible evidence. We might not be able to bring him to trial for it. But Marcel linked him up with Mrs. Hopper's shooting. Said Maury and he planned the shooting from start to finish. Maury agreed to steer her out ahead of the others, and they rehearsed their moves together. Marcel will testify that Roden told him exactly where to be and when, and that he delivered Mrs. Hopper up on a platter. We'll get him for that one. Any questions?"

"Why did they keep the stuff in the bathroom? Why was everything so open?"

"You're the shrink. My guess is they figured it as a great cover. Open, above board. Anyone could come in. But the bathroom did lock, and you would have never discovered the safe if you didn't know where and how to look for it. We searched that place and didn't have a clue. If Marcel hadn't told us, it would still hold its secrets. If there's nothing else, I'd better get back to work. You're part of my public relations time."

"One more thing. Did Maury open up when you told him all this new stuff?"

"Not a word. 'Talk to my lawyer, gentlemen.' But we'll get him." We hung up.

Would it have been different if I hadn't been in the shower that night that Helena called? What if I had answered the phone and Marcel had thought Helena'd already made her report? Or what if I'd answered and Marcel had overheard Helena telling me that she was pregnant and didn't know what to do? Would he have rethought the entire thing and spared Helena's life? And what of Mrs. Hopper's life? Had Marcel and Maury not already felt vulnerable to discovery, might they have tried to work around Mrs. Hopper? They didn't even try. The questions kept coming. There were no answers.

27

I was still preoccupied thinking about Helena when Joel arrived to pick me up. He remarked on my pensiveness, to which I responded by telling him about Helena and the events that surrounded her death. Joel listened intently, and by the time I thought to glance at the clock, we had missed our dinner reservations at the restaurant. Neither of us minded. I scrambled up eggs and salami, Joel toasted bread and poured us drinks, and we stayed in and feasted.

The following week I saw Joel Wednesday and Friday nights and also Saturday morning. I was still anxious for Mike to meet and approve of him, but by that point, I couldn't imagine anyone not thinking that Joel was wonderful. Mike, who loved to cook, had invited us and a woman he'd been seeing named Andrea over for dinner Saturday night. Joel and I arrived at Mike's apartment at eight with a bottle of wine and were let in by Andrea. As soon as we entered, we heard the angry squeal of the smoke detector. The squeal was joined almost immediately by the heavy drone of a fan, as Mike, smiling sheepishly, emerged from the fuming kitchen.

"Hello," he said buoyantly, ignoring the clamor and vapors billowing around him. "I'm very pleased to meet you, Joel," he said, extending a potholder in Joel's direction. I grabbed the pot-holder, and they shook hands. "Good to see you, Sara," he said, giving me a hug and kissing my cheek. "Andrea, you know Sara, this is Joel Fox. Andrea McCoy." We all greeted each other.

"What are you barbecuing in here?" I asked, entering the kitchen to see what was causing all the commotion. My gaze fell on a platter of charred pork chops. Mike followed me into the kitchen and Joel stayed behind in the living room with Andrea.

Under cover provided by the squealing and the whirring, I whispered to Mike, "Well, what do you think?"

"About what?"

"Mike! Joel. Do you like him?"

"Sara, for Christ's sake. I haven't even talked to him."

"Well, what are you doing in here?" I asked. "Let's go join them."

"Sara, calm yourself. You can see what I'm doing. I'm burning our dinner. It takes concentration."

"Can I help?"

"Yes. You can offer Joel a drink and assure him and Andrea that I always offer up one dish as a sacrifice to the gods at every meal. When the smoke detector stops squealing, that will be our sign that the gods are appeased. Luckily," he continued, opening the freezer, "there's a frozen pizza! It should go well with zucchini au gratin and buttered noodles." We both started to giggle.

185

"Go on," Mike said, getting a grip on himself. "Ask Joel what he wants to drink. I'm going to make an omelette and we'll be ready to eat in ten or fifteen minutes. Everything's under control. I don't want him sitting out there alone with Andrea all this time. He's nice-looking."

"Do you really think so?" I asked, eager for a more detailed analysis of Joel's looks.

"Sara, would you get out there or do I have to pick you up and dump you on the living room floor?"

"I'm going. I'm going." Andrea and Joel were chatting away amiably. Joel had evidently remarked on a desk that Mike had refinished, and I could tell that Andrea was trying to act as if she knew Mike better than she did. She already had a drink, so I got Joel's order and headed back into the kitchen. I poured beers for Joel and Mike, and uncharacteristically, I poured myself a beer, too. With my first sip I remembered that I hated the taste, so I set it aside for Mike to finish and concocted myself a white russian. I'm not a heavy drinker.

I returned to Joel and Andrea, and we all sipped our drinks and chitchatted about the news headlines of the day. In no time at all, Mike had our dinner on the table and we sat down to eat. After filling all our glasses with wine, Mike held his glass up, saying, "Here's to old friends and new." We clinked and drank.

"Sara tells me you do general litigation, Joel. Sounds exciting. And demanding," Mike added as we passed the food around.

"Yeah. It's interesting work. The hours are crushing." Joel chuckled. "So are some of the clients. You can't believe the schemes people get involved in. But I enjoy it. And I get a kick out of going to court."

"How bad are the hours?" Mike asked.

"It varies. But I work late at the office—till about nine or ten at night—a good three nights a week. And I usually have to work the better part of a Saturday or Sunday."

Mike whistled. "Those law firms can eat you alive. Although it suits a lot of people to work that hard. I guess the problem is, it doesn't leave much time for anything else." It was a statement,

186

but it was also a question. With a flash of clarity, I realized that Mike was determined to learn from Joel just exactly what his intentions were toward me. My ears started to feel hot as I saw Mike pour himself another glass of wine. The ruined pork chops took on a new meaning: Mike was not in firm control. What would Joel think? We'd only been dating for three weeks.

"You're right," Joel responded to Mike. "It doesn't leave me with a whole lot of extra time. My hope is that the work will ease up a bit when I become more adept at what I'm doing. I'm still learning the ropes."

"So, what do you like to do in your spare time, when you have spare time?" Mike asked, his tone friendly. Had I not turned to look at Mike, his tone alone would have reassured me. But I did look up at him and he sent me a look the meaning of which was clear: "Let's see how he answers this one."

Joel looked a little surprised by Mike's persistent questioning, but he answered, "I used to have a weekly tennis game in New York, which I miss, and I'd very much like to start up again. It's hard to think how I used to spend my spare time. It seems so long ago. Mostly hanging around. Seeing friends. I used to live with a woman in New York and we'd go out weekends to explore the city. Walk around different neighborhoods. I don't have any real hobbies. Like refinishing furniture. It's great that you can do that. I was admiring your desk while you were in cooking." Joel had alluded to his old girlfriend once before, but he'd never really talked about her.

Mike honed right in, no longer masking his interest with a semblance of subtlety. "Thank you," he said, in response to the compliment, as he refilled all our wine glasses. And then, "So, does this woman still live in New York?" I held my breath waiting for Joel's answer.

"As far as I know," Joel said. "It's been almost a year since we were together." I let out my breath and noticed Mike swallow down a sip of wine. Even Andrea, who was listening with a look of fascination on her face, appeared relieved.

"How well do you play tennis?" Mike asked. Mike was an excellent player, always in search of partners.

"Not bad, not great. I'm probably more of an enthusiastic player than a good one. Do you play?"

"When I get a chance." Mike was not in the market for an enthusiastic player. He wanted a good one. "It's easier to get racquetball courts around here than tennis courts. I just recently joined a gym. It's no trouble for me to make a reservation. Would you like to play sometime?"

"Sounds great. I'd appreciate it. I'll get your number from Sara and call you from work so we can set it up."

Mike seemed to ease up after that. I guess he figured he'd have the chance to nail Joel in the locker room if he needed more information. I finished my second glass of wine and turned to Andrea to draw her into the conversation. Although I was slurring my words a little, the conversation moved fluidly and Mike released it to flow in a more general direction.

When it was clear that everyone had finished with the main course, Andrea got up to use the bathroom and I stood up to help clear the dishes. By now my balance was a little off, and I tipped a plate, spilling the leftover contents down the front of my pants and sweater. Not quite realizing what I had done, I still held the plate in one hand and a serving dish in the other. Mike and Joel jumped up to help me at the same time. Joel, quite sweetly I thought, took a napkin and bent down to clean me off, while I leaned over him to put the dishes back on the table. It was perhaps too intimate a cleanup job for Joel to do at someone else's house. I didn't actually think about it one way or another until Mike put his hands under my arms and pulled me back away from Joel. Joel's mouth opened in surprise, and I was completely astounded. Mike literally dragged me into the kitchen and sat me down in a chair. Then he wet a paper towel and bent over me, prepared to start scrubbing away until, as his hand approached my thigh, I said, "Mike!"

"Here," he said, throwing the towel in my lap. "You do it." I was too embarrassed to do anything but clean up the mess as Mike silently busied himself making coffee and clearing the table.

"Can I take anything in?" I asked as I stood up to go back into the dining area. Mike handed me the cream and sugar.

Joel was talking to Andrea when I returned, but he turned to me immediately with a bewildered look on his face. I walked over and kissed him, and he looked more at ease. Then Mike came in carrying dessert, a frozen chocolate mousse, and we all reassembled around the table. The tension was unhinging me, but I didn't know what to say to break it.

"Did I miss something?" Andrea asked, looking at each of us in turn.

Joel answered instantly. "Yes, you did. But I'm not exactly sure what it was." He turned to Mike. He wanted an explanation.

Mike's features relaxed into a smile. "Joel," he said, "I apologize. There's no excuse. Sorry, Sara. I will never again physically move you from room to room at my will. It's a tacky way to treat guests." Mike looked at Andrea's baffled face and grinned. "But you, my dear, are a different case." He sniggered devilishly and lunged for her.

All the tension disappeared as Andrea ran to escape Mike. Joel smiled at me, and I grinned back, joining in his appreciation of Mike's antics. Joel moved closer to me, but Mike had other plans: Andrea had made her retreat behind us, and Mike cut neatly between Joel and me to get to her, deftly separating us.

"Quite a chaperon you have there," Joel said helplessly. But Mike had forgotten us—he'd caught Andrea, and for once he was still interested after the chase was over.

28

As the cherry blossoms bloomed, and spring came and went, Joel and I spent more and more time together. By August, not only were we seeing each other exclusively, but we were talking about getting married. To my extreme relief and pleasure, Mike adjusted to my involvement with Joel, and the two of them became racquetball partners and friends.

Mike had had simultaneous love affairs with two different women throughout the spring but moved into summer on his own. He went away on vacation and returned deeply in love with a woman who lived in Arizona and had no intention of moving. Mike spoke of her with passion and longing and wrote to her regularly, but they knew it was hopeless. He resolved to enjoy the rest of the summer without worrying about women. I lost control of my eyebrows on hearing that resolve.

Frank and his honey Randy had evolved into a couple, each of whom, on occasion, went his wayward way but was welcomed back with forgiveness. Richard seemed the same married as he had unmarried.

Dr. Harley and Mimi also continued as a couple. Not that I knew much of what went on between them outside of the clinic. At the clinic, where their relationship was finally acknowledged, they stuck together. It still caused some problems among the staff, as in any organization where the boss has a special relationship with one subordinate. But their teaming up had become established and, therefore, generally accepted. If you didn't like it, it was your problem. I tried to stay out of their way and was pretty successful at it.

I never heard from Helena's parents, Dr. and Mrs. Morgan, again. I sent them a note in the spring to let them know I was thinking of them and would be available should they ever want to see me, but I received no reply. Although through Marcel's testimony Helena was believed to have been murdered, it was by "person or persons unknown." There was no hard evidence to bring Maury Roden to trial. But he was charged with conspiring to kill Mrs. Elizabeth Hopper and buying and selling narcotics and evading income tax. I was a witness in the narcotics trial and exulted in the guilty verdict after only thirty minutes of deliberation. I was also pleased to read that he was found guilty in Mrs. Hopper's death.

Marcel pleaded guilty to all counts and testified against Roden. He was rewarded with a relatively lenient sentence, but would be behind bars for years. Mr. Hopper spent much of the year in court as a witness, continuing to come in with Harry and Judy to meet with Frank Wednesday nights. They made steady two steps forward, one step backward, progress. Harry was making plans to reenter college in the fall, and the restaurant flourished. Frank's training year at the clinic was coming to an end, and he planned to return to North Carolina in the fall to work on his dissertation. Although Frank had stopped meeting with most of his patients, he saw the Hoppers his last week of work. Richard and I viewed the videotape with Frank, the following day during his last supervision with Richard. Frank brought the images into focus.

Mr. Hopper walked in first. He had regained some of the weight he had lost and looked fuller and healthier than during the winter. His bearing was somehow less tentative, and he seemed to move with greater authority. His first words to Frank were, "I hate to see you leave. You've helped my family very much. We'll all miss you." Then Harry and Judy walked in together. They sat down together, across from Frank and their father. Judy started to giggle and fuss around in her purse for a piece of gum. She found a piece, unwrapped it, put the stick in her mouth and wadded the wrappers into a ball that she tried to shoot into the wastebasket. She missed and got up to retrieve it, then handed the wrappers to Harry to give him a turn. Frank indulgently watched them carry on, but as their activities started to escalate, he stepped in.

"It's hard to say goodbye," he said, looking at the two of them. They sobered up immediately. Judy looked down, and Harry looked away.

"There's something Judy wants to ask you," Mr. Hopper said.

Judy turned crimson. "What is it, Judy?" Frank asked.

"Do you have a picture of yourself I could have, to remember you by?" she almost whispered.

"Certainly," Frank responded. "Not with me. I'll send it to you."

"You know," Frank continued, "we've been working together about a year now. Not quite a year, although it's been so eventful it seems like five years, at least to me. Of course, when we started

191

Mrs. Hopper was here too. I know what a loss her death has been for you all. But in spite of your grief and the devastating discoveries about Mr. Roden, you've all grown so much. Have you given much thought to some of the ways you've all changed as individuals as well as a family?"

"I don't know how to describe it," Mr. Hopper said, "but we all seem more together and more separate at the same time. I guess we know each other better and treat each other more as individuals. If that makes sense. I personally feel more accepting of myself, less conflicted all the time. I think Maury always pulled me away from Lizzie. I shouldn't blame it on him. Something in me pulled toward him and away from her. But I don't think he ever liked her. It was subtle because he was always pleasant with her, but I think when he looked me up after all those years, she was a disappointment to him. He spent a lot of his time at the café and didn't see much of his own wife and kids, and he tried pulling me in the same direction."

"He succeeded," Harry said, somewhat ruefully. "You were rarely around. It always seemed like you wanted us there, I mean, wanted us to exist as an idea, the wife and kids, but that you didn't really want us around. I can remember as a kid praying that the café would burn down and you'd come home. I even thought about burning it down. Then I'd feel guilty and try to be good. But it always seemed like Uncle Maury wanted us there and you didn't. Like he loved us more than our own father did. I always thought Mom left the café after I was born, and it was my fault you and she never said much to each other. Things are so confused. The Maury who killed Mom doesn't seem like the Maury who used to bring us seven-layer cake. Did he hate her, Dad? Do you think he really wanted her dead or just out of the way for his scheme?"

"The truth is I don't know. I don't think he ever really warmed up to her. It felt like he separated us, although I can't tell you how, kind of like he separated me. He was gregarious and I was quiet. He'd say, 'I'll take care of the people business; we're partners; you don't have to do what's uncomfortable for you.' I

192

never knew if it was comfortable or not. I don't mind talking to people. He'd always tell me, 'Lizzie's a wonder with the kids. She'll take care of them. Let's close up and have a drink.' Who knows? What do you think, little quiet one?" Mr. Hopper asked Judy.

Judy shrugged. "I don't know." Her eyes were filled with tears. "When you finish your dissertation, will you come back here to work?" she asked Frank.

"I wish I could answer that. I don't know. I don't know how long it will take or what I'll be doing. It's sad to leave. I'll miss you all."

Judy broke into tears. The session seemed to be heading into farewells. But Harry brought it back with a bang. His eyes glistened with excitement, and he shot out of his seat. Pacing as he talked, his words came out feverish and fast. "I want to yell out that if you cared you'd stay. If this was more than just a job, if I was more than just a patient, you wouldn't leave us. I want to say that you led us on, and now—abandonment. Abandoned. But I know it's not true. You have your life. I want to be crazy so you'll stay. Something that won't let you leave. That's what I'd do with Mom. It all makes sense to me now. I could feel it. The danger. If Mom and Dad got along, if Mom wanted to meet Dad at the café—the danger. I couldn't let it happen. If Mom and Dad fought, if Mom wanted to leave Dad and take us with her—the danger. I couldn't stand it. I kept them together. I know I did. I never really realized it before." Harry's words were coming almost too fast to follow. Several times we stopped the tape, rewound and played back. "Maury hated her. He wanted my father all to himself. He wanted the café separate. The tension was unbearable, whenever Mom and Dad started to get along. I couldn't let them. It was too tense. I knew I had to keep them apart to keep them together. But not too far apart. I was the juggler. The magician. Keep two balls in the air at all times. Never let them drop. I wore myself out. Not too close and not too far. And I did it. Kept the balls revolving for years. As long as I can remember. Always. But I couldn't leave home. How could I go? Everyone needed me. Judy couldn't do it. Someone needed to keep them together and apart. I was the only one. I couldn't leave." Harry sat back down suddenly. He seemed surprised at what he'd said.

"Did it always work?" Frank asked. "Could you always keep them that same distance apart when you went nuts?"

"Always. I am the master. I was the master. Until we came in here. I couldn't control them anymore. They kept getting closer. It seemed dangerous, but not as much as before. No matter what I did, they got closer. All those years. I was Uncle Maury's secret agent, and I didn't even know it myself. I didn't know. Don't you see? He didn't want them too close: She'd interfere in the café. He didn't want them to divorce: She'd get all legal about her share of the café and move in. I used to think Maury was my real father. I could sense his moods. When he got nervous I went through the roof. I was his agent. I infiltrated my own family. I didn't mean to. I just couldn't stand feeling so nervous all the time. It was easier to be crazy. Everyone relaxed. I just couldn't stand it. I was Maury's puppet: He worked the strings. I never controlled myself. I never knew. It's just making sense to me. So much confusion. I always felt as if I'd stretch so far I'd rip in two. I wanted everyone to stay together and be happy. I was the only one who could do it." Harry's speech had slowed down. He continued haltingly. "When I started college last year I knew I'd never last. I knew it inside."

"What about this fall?" Frank asked. "Can you leave? Do you think your father is capable of living his own life? Do you think Judy can manage?"

"It's all different now. Mother and Maury are gone; they don't need me anymore. I'm free now. I'm ready for college. But maybe after I graduate I'll come back and work in the café. There's nothing wrong with that, is there?"

"No," Frank said. "Not if that's what you'd like to do and your father has a place for you there."

"There's always a place for him. I always hoped he'd take over the business. I think I was scared of involving him because of Maury's activities. It's true what he said. You're very perceptive, son. I used to feel the tension, too. I never knew quite where it came from. If Lizzie and I were doing well together, and I'd ask her to join me at the café for dinner, there was always tension. Maury's tension. But he'd get nervous if I told him she was going to leave me. He'd want to know what she planned in terms of a settlement. Would she insist on her right to the café? We all three had veto power over café policy. Lizzie could have changed a lot of things if she'd wanted to make trouble. She could have refused to let us buy her out. She could have become active and poked into everything. Maury wouldn't allow us to get a divorce. He simply wouldn't allow it."

"The anxiety was contagious," Frank said.

"It's funny," Harry said. "I could have held them together for years. If nothing had changed, I could have stayed home and kept Mom home with me. If we hadn't met you. I'm glad we've changed. But Mom wouldn't have had to die, if we hadn't changed."

"I don't know that your control was ever that great," Frank said. "Judy is growing up, too. She might have changed the balance. Your parents might have changed."

"That's true, Harry. Your mother and I. We wanted something different in our lives. It's hard to say. But I think Mr. Thomas has helped us through very bad times. And he helped us to change. I just wish to God your mother was here with us to start anew. I miss you, Lizzie."

The family sat in silence. Frank interrupted, "We only have five minutes left. I just want you to know that I've learned so much from knowing you all, and I'll miss you very much." He got up to shake Harry's hand, and they embraced. Mr. Hopper also embraced Frank and shook his hand. Judy sat very still. Frank bent down and kissed her cheek. She sprang up and hugged him, tears streaming down her face. Then she ran out the door. Frank hit the Off button. I was crying. Richard offered me a box of tissues.

"A gift," I said. "What a good last session."

"It felt just right to me," Frank said.

Richard nodded in agreement. Then we sat silently, avoiding our own goodbyes to Frank. Finally, I broke the silence. "What can we do for you before you go?" I asked Frank. "Would you like a goodbye party or would you rather a few of us take you out for dinner?"

Frank grinned. "Give me one night alone with Mike Sweeney and I'll never ask for another thing again. Cross my heart."

Richard and I laughed. "Okay, okay," I said. "We'll take you out for dinner. That'd be more fun than a big party."

"Sounds great, Sara."

"And we'll invite Mike Sweeney."

"Sounds even greater, Sara."

I took out my pen to write myself a note about who to call for the dinner and to plan with Frank and Richard when and where. I found comfort in small organizational tasks. The dinner wouldn't stop Frank going and it wouldn't stop my missing him, but I think science still has a lot to learn about the remarkable healing qualities of seven-layer rum cake.